The yellowbacks... classics of popular fiction

The yellowjackets or yellowbacks were a great series of bestselling adventure and crime thrillers that had its origins in the mid to late 19th century following on from the 'penny dreadfuls'. They virtually began the mass market revolution of the early 20th century with a clear standard format and imprint/series livery (what would today be called branding). Hodder & Stoughton published the yellowjackets in two main series with series run dates of: 1923-1939 and later 1949-1957.

As the tagline ('where thrillers really began') on the back cover implies, the imprint and series focused on thrillers that were the bestsellers of their time. This current reissue or retro revival if you will, brings back many of these masterpieces, now classics in their own way and extends it further by including key titles from that period that were either great crime or thriller or even general commercial fiction (including sub-genres of noir, horror, gothic, romance, westerns, etc.) influences of their time. There are some perennial favourites and many rarities either lost or not easily available being revived in the current series. Writers and characters ranged from adventure heroes like Bulldog Drummond, Allan Quatermain, Richard Hannay or the Saint through thriller grandmasters Edgar Wallace and E. Phillips Oppenheim, crime and mystery maestros like Patricia Wentworth, GK Chesterton, Agatha Christie and the Detection club, to western and swashbucklers like Zane Grey, Max Brand, Captain Blood and even romance or general fiction classics like Hermina Black, Denise Robins, Marie Corelli or Stella Morton. These were books that had storytelling at their heart and always entertained.

The yellowbacks had both hardback (with varying design elements) and paperback (which built the series look) versions with the latter still carrying the imprint 'yellowjacket'. The current reissues pay tribute to both and use an amalgam of elements from both editions while retaining the complete yellow (or 'mustard-plaster') livery with the author's name in blue beveled type with a 'simulated emboss' effect and a white outer 'outline', and the book title in black. These reissues retain the distinctive size of the original mass market paperback and follow the three main category variations—the thrillers (crime, westerns, mystery, adventure) had blue lettering for the author's name, while Romance and softer general fiction had red; and other categories like humour had green.

For more detail and a full list of titles visit https://www.hachetteindia.com/home/yellowbacks

THE W PLAN

THE W PLAN

Lieutenant-Colonel Graham Seton Hutchison was a First World War British army officer, military theorist, author of both adventure novels and non-fiction works and fascist activist. Seton Hutchison became a celebrated figure in military circles for his tactical innovations during the First World War but would later be criticized for being associated with a series of fringe fascist movements which failed to capture much support even by the standards of the far right in Britain in the interbellum period. He made a contribution to First World War fiction with his espionage novel, *The W Plan*. Seton Hutchison also published a *History of the Machine Gun Corps* although this non-fiction work was characterized by its vivid accounts of battle that almost read like a novel.

THE W PLAN

Graham Seton

HODDER AND STOUGHTON
YELLOW JACKET

hachette

The W Plan
First published by Thornton Butterworth, London in 1929.

1

The texts in these editions in most cases have been reprinted as is, with minimal editorial changes and by and large no bowdlerizing for political correctness; though in some editions, a few words and phrases considered archaic, or those considered offensive now, along with archaic punctuation may have been modified in places to make the text more accessible to today's readers. The narratives, language, beliefs, social mores and/or cultural depictions, in these volumes are a reflection of their times and must be viewed as such. They may also contain certain cultural, racial and gender prejudices and stereotypes that may be outdated or clearly wrong then and wrong today; but their removal would be tantamount to claiming these prejudices never existed. The Publisher does not endorse or support those depictions or stereotypes; and these books have been made available for a discerning audience that will read it for entertainment value and a chronicle/record of popular fiction of past times.

Cover design by Priya Singh adapted from the original classic yellowjacket by Hodder & Stoughton.

Cover illustration by Ishan Trivedi.

Series note: Some of the books in the series (unless otherwise credited) may have cover or inside illustrations from the original yellowbacks or early editions, and while full restoration has been attempted, some images may be grainy or faded due to the condition of the original material. The end notes or bonus material or blurb details may have been sourced from the public domain or free use publications such as Wikipedia and attribution is hereby made also allowing similar free use reproduction from here. Sources requiring further specific attribution may write in and further detailing and/or corrections shall be made in subsequent printings/editions.

Reprint specifications may be subject to change including but not limited to finishes, paper, colour sections.

ISBN: 978-93-5731-141-0

Hachette Book Publishing India Pvt. Ltd.
4th & 5th Floors, Corporate Centre,
Plot No. 94, Sector 44, Gurugram - 122 003, India

Typeset in Electra LT STD 10/12.5 pt by Manipal Technologies Limited, Manipal

Printed and bound in India by Manipal Technologies Limited, Manipal

MIX
Paper from responsible sources
FSC™ C043100

CONTENTS

1

OBSESSION

The Commander-in-chief, as was his habit when a decision of importance had to be taken, was alone. The walls of the large salon in the Norman château overlooking the English Channel were hung with maps and messages, the table piled with documents and reports. The general paced up and down the wooden floor, from time to time pausing before a great map dotted with coloured flags. It was now after three in the afternoon. In the morning the general had conferred with his army commanders, the chiefs of artillery and of the air, engineers and other technical experts. Later, over lunch, he had discussed the question of man power, reinforcement, transport, the various theatres of war and supply of munitions with officials from London.

Now he was left to make momentous decisions, the result of which might affect the whole course of the war, certainly its higher strategy, for many months to come. The general was satisfied that unless the improbable occurred, his dispositions and supplies were adequate, and when the large reserves from home were fully trained he would be able to take that initiative in offensive action for which he had so long waited.

But in war, it is the improbable, even the preposterous, which so often has reduced plans to pulp and armies to annihilation, rout and defeat.

The enemy had been singularly quiet of late, yet there was no evidence of exhaustion. Prisoners taken in raids were well conditioned and equipped: enemy air-reconnaissance and night raids were consistent, irritating, sometimes almost dominating. The artillery up and down the line was effective with ample ammunition; yet was the enemy inactive. The Foreign Office, through its network of espionage, gave no hint as to the moves the enemy would or could make, what strategy the Commander-in-chief should adopt to force his hand.

Information tested in the light of reality had proved misleading. Officers taken prisoner in those raids, which were becoming increasingly costly, were arrogant, and very silent; the soldiers, mostly unreliable and influenced chiefly to provide witness calculated to give them the quickest comfort in an enemy's hands, gave no clue as to what might be the designs of the enemy one month, possibly three or four months ahead. There was no sure indication whether the enemy commander was nervous as to the loyalty and fighting spirit of an army, now nearly three years in the field.

No one knew, or would tell where and when the enemy would strike, with what force and with what new instrument of warfare as the first shock with which to spread dismay and to break the morale of the British army. These were the problems which confronted the general staff.

But there was a vague uneasiness in the mind of the Commander-in-chief. The quietness of the front disturbed him. It was now over five months since there had been any trial of strength. Many weeks had elapsed since the great offensive in Italy through which Germany had sought to break the blockade and open a way out through the Mediterranean.

The general felt that something momentous was about to happen, but when? where? His uneasiness had been increased within the last two days by a note in a report from the Intelligence Branch. It is one of those odd things, so far inexplicable in psychic research or in the realm of psychology, that the mind pre-occupied with major problems will become obsessed with a trivial detail. No one had paid any special attention to this paragraph, nor had the staff made reference to it.

It was inserted among a collection of miscellaneous information, mostly of the character of rumour or hearsay.

A major of engineers, unattached to any particular enemy division, had been captured in one of our periodical raids, severely wounded. In delirium he had raved incessantly, and the medical officer in charge of the casualty clearing station had thought fit to send for the divisional intelligence officer, a young man apparently thoroughly conversant with the language, but probably unskilled in military affairs.

The report stated that the major had referred repeatedly to "the inverted M breach." He had died of wounds the following day. The bare statement of fact was there, but no comment. The general sat down at his desk and glanced quickly through the latest reports. Pencil in hand he marked those paragraphs the significance of which he did not understand, or which appeared important. Whilst he was reading, his hand, led to action by some unconscious thought, traced upon the wide blotting-pad a series of inverted M's—the letter W. He pushed his chair back and rose, thrusting his papers back upon the desk. Dismissing the thought with irritation from his mind, he again strode up and down the wooden floor.

The conferences had declared nothing new. The Intelligence Service, espionage, aerial reconnaissance, raids, had provided nothing definite, no facts which correlated.

The general opened his door, and walked down the white-washed corridor to the room of Colonel Jervois, his military secretary.

"Jervois, do you remember a hot-headed young fellow commanding a battalion of the Inverness Highlanders at a dugout we visited near Arras in May last year? He was feeding a brace of Boches on port, and lecturing like a university professor. He pushed out his guests with his foot, and then said if 1 had nothing specially important to do he could give me some first-hand information, there and then, saving the necessity of writing a long report and delaying the information."

Jervois paused a moment. "Yes, sir, I recall the incident well. You remember, sir, how having passed over his information he outlined a plan whereby we could obtain definite information about the enemy's plans."

"It was just that plan," said the general, "which made me ask you if you recollected the lad. Is he still alive?" Jervois walked across to his disposition chart. "The 2nd Inverness Regiment is now with the 7th Division, 3rd Corps, 1st Army. I will get the operator to put me right through to the battalion.

"Hullo, orderly, have my line cleared—urgent—through to the 2nd Inverness Regiment, 1st Army."

The general was thinking aloud . . . "Yes, a lad typical of his breed . . . A shock of fair hair, bright blue eyes, strong; independent, too: spoke German like a native . . . told us he had been discussing Marx and Nietzsche with his night club . . . had a great idea of being flown behind the lines, left to his own devices, and then being picked up again, and bringing information, seen through the eyes of a soldier trained to appreciate a situation on the model of Hamley, Henderson and Clausewitz in place of what he described as the clumsy, indefinite methods pursued, forsooth, by General Headquarters."

"2nd Inverness Regiment coming through, sir."

"Hullo, Inverness . . . General Staff speaking here. Is your commanding officer there?"

"Yes, sir, I'll get him to come on the line."

"I've turned up the Order of Battle. I see Duncan Grant is commanding, appointed November, 1916. Should be the same officer," intervened Jervois.

"Commanding officer, 2nd Battalion Inverness Regiment, speaking."

"I am Colonel Jervois, the Military Secretary. You are to report to me personally forthwith. I am informing your brigadier and division, who will send a car with instructions as to destination to meet you at Brigade Headquarters. I shall expect you here within two hours."

Duncan Grant arrived at G.H.Q. shortly after 6.30 p.m. An orderly showed him straight into the office of Colonel Jervois.

"Good evening, Grant, the Commander-in-chief expects you to dinner with him. The orderly will show you where to get a wash. Look sharp and then ask for the Commander-in-chief. I will join you with him."

Grant's mixed feelings were adjusted to those of pleasure and excitement. Dinner with the Commander-in-chief was one thing : a reprimand from an irate staff officer, for any one of a regimental officer's sins of commission or omission, was quite another. He quickly washed away the dust of the journey, followed by a vigorous brush from the orderly, and presented himself in the room of the Commander-in-chief.

The general was standing before the great fireplace, a fine figure of a man, broad-shouldered, tall, dark hair tinged with grey, ruddy complexion, a close-clipped moustache, dark piercing eyes, now a little heavy. His tunic was unbuttoned, and his hands thrust deep into the thigh pockets of his riding breeches—an active, strong man.

The general came forward, his hand outstretched.

"I remember meeting you, Grant, up at Hargicourt. You were entertaining two German professors and . . . then told me how to conduct my Intelligence Service."

"I beg your pardon, sir, nothing was ever . . ."

"No need to apologize. Quite enlightening. I wish I could get a few more hints from young men of your type. Too many commanders agree with me. An army commander needs ideas and we have no monopoly of brains or imagination at headquarters," he looked up, "have we, Jervois? In fact your lecture has brought about this little dinner party. So, after dinner—and that will be short—we will resume." The general rang a bell.

"Sergeant Case, have dinner served at once."

"Very good, sir."

Both the general and Colonel Jervois were very genial during dinner, the general searching in his inquiry—the stamina of young recruits, training of specialists, effectiveness and co-operation of the newly-formed machine-gun battalions, quality of the rations . . . and here Duncan told him that it was a little difficult to induce Jock's belief that pork and beans, with very little discernible pork, were more nutritious than beef steak, despite the medicinal legend imprinted on each tin as to protein and vitamin values. Duncan felt at ease and happy. Dinner, soup, and a meat dish followed by fruit, was pleasantly spiced with easy conversation.

Dinner lasted less than half an hour. The orderly placed the port decanter on the table, but it was a formality: it was not proffered.

"Close the door, orderly. See I am disturbed by nobody." The general rose, and, calling Jervois and Grant, passed through a side door which communicated with his office. He turned on the lights and crossed to the telephone.

"Orderly, put all calls for me through to the General Staff. Colonel Jervois is with me : any calls for him will also be put through to the Staff. We are not to be disturbed." Then turning to Grant he waved him to a chair.

"You will remember outlining to me a plan—it was when I visited your headquarters at Hargicourt—whereby information could be quickly and readily obtained. You stated that you yourself were prepared to give effect to this scheme: and that you were convinced of its success."

"Yes, sir."

"There is information which I require, possibly of supreme importance. It is essential that it be obtained in the minimum of time and its accuracy must be unqualified. You will put your plan into operation, and anything which you may require for the purpose is completely at your disposal. I shall inform you exactly as to the situation, and what is the information in particular which I require. Thereafter you will inform me, please, as to your requirements and proposals. You are prepared, I am assuming, to undertake the task of which you told me some months ago."

"Yes, sir."

"Very well, then, I will outline the position in general. Any further details will be explained and amplified to you by Colonel Jervois, who will also give you such information which we have as to the disposition of the enemy, his plans and the reports which we have secured through the Secret and Intelligence Services.

"You can appreciate the fact that our front has been unusually quiet. We have no information which indicates for certain how, when or where the enemy will move. In some respects, as you will probably have noted, namely in the air and in heavy artillery, we are dominated, at least equalled. Our Foreign Office informs us that there is a grave shortage of foodstuffs causing disaffection among the civil population in the larger towns—but that, of course, in measure we, too, are experiencing at home.

"To me it is clear that an enemy, acting on interior lines, cannot indefinitely remain quiescent. Moreover, the enemy will be well informed as to our own position, and will know that within the space of a few weeks—it was confirmed to me this morning— we shall have available considerable reinforcements both of men and ammunition. We can assume that the enemy is as familiar with this fact as is our own government. The simple deduction is, therefore, that he will strike. Where? How? His quiescence also leads me to suppose that there is a new element of surprise which is now being prepared. I will tell you quite frankly that our Intelligence Service has so far been unable to answer the questions—where will he strike, how will he strike, what is the element of surprise which is being prepared? As, frankly, also I will tell you that the situation, calm as it is reported in our home press, and in fact, as it is, causes me grave anxiety.

"I shall require you to answer those three questions. You will have opportunity to read through our Intelligence reports, both in *prêcis* and in full, and to examine any prisoners or officers of my own staff; but so far as I can judge there is no information yet available which serves even as a clue to the answer of any of these three questions."

The general had been pacing up and down the salon, and now sat down at his desk. The reports which he had been examining prior to dinner were still lying on the table; he shook these together and passed them to his Chief of Staff. The removal of the papers disclosed what he had earlier pencilled on the blotting-pad—the inverted M. A look of irritation crossed the general's face, and this did not escape the eyes of Duncan Grant. The general, old in diplomacy, quickly realized that the change in the even tenor of his recitation had been detected and he looked up, smiling, he would have confessed to himself, a little guiltily.

"I expect, Colonel Grant, you smoke," and he offered him a cigar.

"Thank you, sir; and how soon should I start to obtain your information? At dawn, I presume, or just before? Perhaps you never noticed, sir, how the smell of Havana smoke clings to the hair. There are few Havanas in Germany, nor do active soldiers often keep their company."

The general was about to light his own cigar and Grant swiftly plucked the lighted match from his hand.

"Pardon me, sir, I want to start on my journey without any incriminating evidence."

The general looked intently at Grant. The glance was not one of severity, but partly of surprise and partly interest. Colonel Grant, possessed, also, a fine sense of discipline, and realizing the unintentional insult of his action to his Commander-in-chief let his eyes fall before those of his general. They rested on the blotting-pad. They saw the repetitions of W, . . . W, . . . W pencilled thereon. Quickly the eye, communicating with the brain, informed Grant that since the blotting-pad was otherwise blank, the cause of the chief's change of countenance and of subject, was connected with these hieroglyphics. He raised his eyes and met those of the general, who was smiling. Jervois was standing at his side a little perplexed.

Colonel Grant picked up a pencil from the table and without removing his eyes from those of the general, wrote on the blotting-pad a single capital letter W. He then laid the pencil down, lowering his gaze at the same time. Looking up quickly he saw that the general too was staring at the pad.

There is a curious bond of sympathy which can often be awakened between persons in any walk of life, when one discovers the other's guilty secret. No man or woman can endure keeping a secret exclusively with himself. If it is one which augurs happiness, its retention is a rising crescendo of pleasure, until, emotion overriding reason, the pleasure must be shared with another. Secrets of guilt gnaw steadily into the very vitals of sanity. Murder will out.

Every policeman knows that, sooner or later, there will be a confessor of an accomplice in crime; and often the master-detective to whom the secret of crime is revealed has saved his prisoner from insanity, though he may bring him to the gallows: so with the Commander-in-chief. He had a guilty secret, something which although apparently absurd, perpetually deranged every logical thought. He had found a friend, someone confident, self-assured, and so much his junior that he could afford to be absurd, in order to rid himself of his obsession.

"Jervois, just hand me back those reports. There is a note in one of them, I do not remember which, but it is of quite recent date, concerning the interrogation of a prisoner, a major of engineers at a casualty clearing station. The Intelligence Branch did not appear to consider it of any significance, and I suppose you will not have it in mind."

"No, General, I can't say that I have."

"Just so. I happened to be reading through these reports, and there was something about this note which struck me as odd. Here it is. You will see that this poor devil in a delirium repeatedly referred to the 'inverted M breach.' Well, people in delirium talk abominable nonsense, but there is something curious about an inverted M, I don't say of any military significance, but of course an inverted M is a double U, and I tried it out on my blotting-pad. Some ribald jest probably accounts for the inversion of the M; and, when you think of it, the officer, although in delirium, held high rank, and was not of the infantry occupying that sector, but of the engineers. It is true, of course, that he was raving and there is probably nothing in it; but as you know, Jervois . . . I am looking for a clue. Perhaps you will say the agitation of an over-wrought, over-anxious man, but I discovered myself pencilling this wretched inverted M, unwittingly, I suppose subconsciously, on my blotting-pad. I am going to ask Colonel Grant, who says that he is ready to start at dawn—how and whither as yet I do not know—whether, now that I have made what amounts to a confession of which I might be a little ashamed, he wants to know anything more about the major of engineers. Now Grant——"

"Yes, sir, the report says he's dead. If any papers were taken off him I want them sent here to me at once. I presume he has been buried. I want the body, complete as it is, and I want also the whole of the effects. The report is dated two days ago. I want everything that belonged to the major, including the body, sent to me."

The general unhooked his telephone receiver.

"Hallo, put me through to Major Gaynor . . . is that you, Gaynor? This is the Commander-in-chief speaking. Come straight to my room immediately."

After a few minutes there was a knock at the door and Major Gaynor came in.

"Gaynor, since I telephoned to you, we have seen, from the Order or Battle, that the 27th Division is in the Bailleul area. The casualty clearing station is at Neuve Eglise. We assume that there is a cemetery beside the C.C.S. Two days ago a German officer, Major Ulrich Muller, died at the C.C.S. Neuve Eglise is about an hour and a half by car from here. I want you to go straight to Neuve Eglise and bring back to this office the body of Major Muller and any articles of clothing, equipment, or uniform, books, papers, or other effects. Jervois will telephone to the division to expedite matters. It is now twenty past seven, and I shall expect you back here at the latest by ten-thirty p.m. Jervois has a written instruction here for your authority. That's all, and be quick."

Colonel Jervois communicated with the division; and having instructed the Intelligence Officer to report at the casualty clearing station with all the effects and papers of Major Muller, he asked to speak with its officer in charge.

"I want to speak with the senior officer in charge."

"He is doing an operation, sir; told me he wasn't to be bothered on the telephone."

"Tell him the General Staff requests his presence on the telephone immediately," he said irritably.

After a few minutes a voice exclaimed: "This is impossible, preposterous . . . one of the most interesting operations I have ever performed . . . trepanning . . . and, apart from that, the fellow will die."

"Listen to me, doctor. Colonel Jervois, G.H.Q. speaking . . . Major Gaynor of my staff is on his way now to your C.C.S.

Whatever else may occupy you, these orders are to be carried out implicitly and quickly. A German, Major Ulrich Muller, is reported to have died of wounds at your C.C.S."

"That's true, he did."

"Very well, where is he buried?"

"In the cemetery beside the C.C.S."

"Was the body clothed when it was buried or not?"

"I really don't know . . . yes, I expect so. I was very busy here with cases from the last raid. No time to do anything . . . but, yes, I remember he died of shock . . . I saw him after he was dead. Sure to be buried in his uniform."

"Had he any papers or matter in his pocket?"

"I really don't know—not my business. I sent for the Intelligence Officer as he was raving . . . I don't understand the lingo, anyway. They will know all about it at divisional headquarters. I'm busy. There's a man dying..."

"One of my staff officers will be with you shortly. You are to have the body disinterred at once . . . at once, you understand. Gaynor can bring it back in the car. See that Major Muller's effects are complete so far as you are concerned."

"But we cannot put the body in a car. There wouldn't be room for a stretcher, sir. Shall I have it sent in an ambulance tomorrow?"

"No, do what I say. There will be Gaynor, the chauffeur and the Intelligence Officer in the car, and there is room for one more. Sit Major Muller upright in the car. Gaynor must bring the body back. You understand me? This is to be done forthwith, and see to it yourself. You can get on with your operation afterwards; or, if it isn't necessary, Major Muller's hole will be vacant. Good-bye, and look sharp."

The general rose and sat on the edge of his desk, regarding Colonel Grant.

"Grant, your wishes, you see, are being executed. Jervois, you were a little hard on the doctor, weren't you? Now, Grant, you must consider what you are going to do, and what is the plan. You may be able to make something of Major Muller. I have my own theory as to his possible importance at the present situation.

"We have first of all to determine whether Muller was an officer of the German division occupying the sector, or whether he had been sent there on some special duty.

"As he was not attached to this German division, it is clear that Muller was there upon some special mission. We shall see from his badges if he belonged to any special unit. Jervois, you can tell me if the division was about to be relieved. That, of course, might account for Muller's presence . . . just having a look round."

"No, this division had only been in the line for five days prior to the raid, which was carried out for identification purposes. Muller might have been taking up a new appointment in the division."

"That is quite possible," said the general, "we must not allow ourselves to imagine improbables, though you are right to expect it. Have you got the Order of Battle, Jervois?"

"Yes, general."

"Well, is Muller's name on it ?"

"Not mentioned: he held no staff appointment, nor was he in command of any of the engineer formations."

"Well, we must have a look at him when he arrives," said Grant, "and, until then, general, with your permission, I would be glad to be given all the information available as to the strategic position, and as to any evidence from the Intelligence reports which you consider important, and which require investigation or verification. I will trust to my memory to retain the essentials. And, sir, before you explain the situation to me will you send for a highly competent air pilot, and place at my disposal an aeroplane, capable of a long flight."

"Of course, that was the essence of your plan. Hullo, orderly, give General Lister my compliments, and ask him to come to my room at once."

In a moment General Lister, who had been in the staff mess-room across the passage, entered—"Lister, this is Colonel Grant of the Inverness Regiment. He is an expert German linguist. I am sending him tonight to a point to be chosen by himself, a considerable distance behind the German lines. I want your best available machine and pilot for the task."

"Mayne's the lad for this job, general."

"Where is he now?"

"XY bombing squadron. He led the Tourcoing raid last week."

"All right, phone for him to come here at once. Grant wants a word with him. And, give orders for his machine to be put ready, maximum load petrol, no bombs."

"General," interposed Grant, "I want one of your draughtsmen from the map section. He must be a man whom we can trust. I believe you've still got a friend of mine down here—John Collett— camouflage officer or something of that kind."

"That's true," said the general.

"Well, sir," said Grant with a broad smile, "I've been waiting for an opportunity to give him orders and see how he likes it. He's under the impression, or was, that he's a great artist. I've got a job after his own heart," he said, now laughing. "He must make at once two crosses painted on strong canvas. These will be pasted over our own aircraft signs on the under wing of the machine. Sorry, sir, we must fly under German colours. For the return trip, I will detach the crosses. It's just to cover my landing."

General Lister looked questioningly at the general.

"That's all right, Lister. I have given Grant *carte blanche.*"

"I'll stick 'em on, myself," said Grant, "just before we start. Mayne and we three will be in the know. No one else. You will let me have the dimension of the wing, general, please, and I'll get the artist busy right away."

"That's all, Lister," said the general. "As soon as Mayne has fixed up his machine and is ready, send him here."

The Commander-in-chief then outlined the strategic position. "Frankly, I'm mystified by the present apparent inactivity," he concluded. "So far as we can judge, the enemy has ample men for an offensive, munitions, everything. He must strike. But where? We have a front one hundred and eighty miles long. He must know that I shall not be ready for three months. He must anticipate me, but where and with what?" The general had been speaking for some forty minutes, explaining with the aid of maps the position and disposition of his own forces, and what he believed were those of the enemy. He showed the strategic points of our lines, their strength and weakness; he detailed the probable moves of the enemy, the advantages of one against another. Grant followed him with close attention and understanding.

A knock came at the door. It was now ten-twenty. Without pausing for a reply, Gaynor came in.

"I've brought the Intelligence Officer, 27th Division, and—er— Major Muller."

"Bring them in."

"Muller's in the car, sir."

"Well, go and fetch him. Tell your chauffeur to hold his tongue. Grant, give Gaynor a hand with Major Muller."

The dead German was tightly wrapped in a blanket, still damp and muddy from the grave. The three officers carried in their burden and laid him on the floor.

"This is your business," said the Commander-in-chief as he turned his back and walked over to the fireplace. Grant and Gaynor had already commenced unwrapping the blanket from the body. It was soon completely exposed to view. A man not yet of middle age, with fair hair and complexion, dressed in green-grey uniform. Its badges revealed nothing other than that he belonged to the Corps of Engineers. Grant folded back one of his eyes to ascertain its colour and opened the mouth and examined the teeth. The eyes were of a very dark brown colour, in sharp contrast to the general Nordic colouring. The second and third fingers of the right hand were missing. Grant examined them closely. It was clear that this feature was no new occurrence, no recent wound. The body was completely clothed with the exception of field boots and socks, which had been removed from the shattered legs, from which the right foot was wholly missing. Duncan then turned to the Intelligence Officer and said : "Help me strip the body. I shall require all these clothes."

In silence the gruesome task of removing the clothes, tunic and riding-breeches, linen shirt and undervest, was accomplished. Grant carefully examined the body to see if there were any marks upon it other than those of wounds. The figure was that of a well-developed and muscular man; and in size, colouring and general structure that of any average soldier of the Teuton type. After a careful scrutiny, the body was wrapped up again in the blanket; and speaking to the general, Grant said that it could be returned to the cemetery or otherwise disposed of; while requesting that the clothing be placed in an oven to be dried and cleansed of the grave. The general rang for his orderly and instructed him to take the uniform and clothing and have it thoroughly dried in the kitchen within the next hour. Grant then asked the Intelligence Officer for any effects taken from the body. The young officer produced a military chronometer of first-class workmanship, a compass, barometer, both of them in leather cases. A cigar case, which on examination proved to contain four cigars, two of which Grant removed and laid on the general's desk. There was also a small map of the whole front, one in common use among senior officers, some dividers and a notebook. The Intelligence Officer stated that he had been right through the notebook, but that it contained nothing other than a miscellaneous number of addresses, many of them of women in a variety of towns in the Essen district, and, underneath, Ulrich Muller's own name and address in the village of Hatzberg, which the map showed to be some six miles north-west of Barmen.

"It would appear that Major Muller is a native of Hatzberg; and it is clear from his appointments that he was not a regular officer but of the reserve. The instruments in his possession are of the finest procurable, and I do not recollect," said he, "having seen any quite as good hitherto."

"Was there anything else?" asked Duncan Grant.

"Yes, there was a small piece of paper which I found in the barometer case. Here it is."

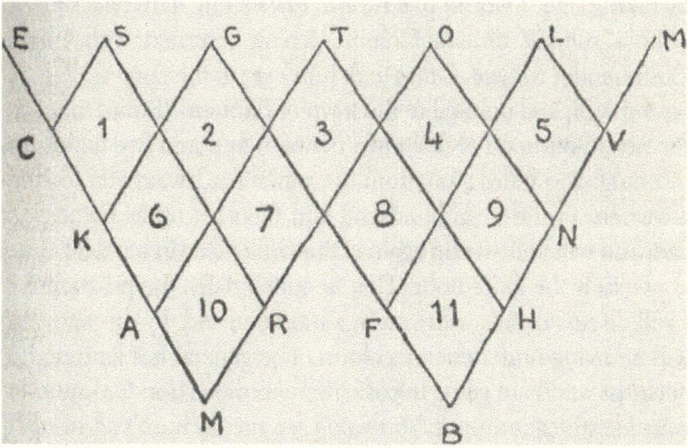

"I didn't attach any importance to the paper, but connected it, of course, with my interrogation of Muller because it is marked with a W, 'the inverted M,' to which he referred. It crossed my mind that probably Muller was proud of his instruments, and in delirium was worried about something technically wrong, or by some alteration in the barometer which he was planning, and that is why this paper was in the case."

"Well, Grant," said the general, "time's getting on, you know. It is already ten minutes to eleven, and I don't think that Major Muller takes us anywhere, so perhaps we can dismiss the question of the inverted M once and for all. I take it you have got your plan pretty well cut and dried now, in fact, you have had it so for many months and the sooner you make your arrangements with Mayne to get away the better. Jervois has just told me that Mayne is all ready and waiting for you outside."

"Yes, general, but I am not going to dismiss Muller. I am adopting him. Just so soon as those clothes are dried, I shall put them on; and by the way, general, I should like to offer you a smoke. I have put two very excellent cigars on your desk. I am sorry my supply is limited; I will be glad if you will honour me by taking one. I would like now to have a talk with Mayne."

In a minute or two Colonel Jervois returned with Flight Commander Mayne. Grant took him over to the large scale map on the wall, and pointed to the town of Barmen. "I want to reach the neighbourhood of that town between four and five tomorrow morning. It is miles away from the war zone. I want you to land anywhere in the neighbourhood and then get off as fast as you can. You will pick me up again at the same place in ten days' time at precisely the same hour. That is, quite briefly, the programme. I will discuss details with you in a moment; and, by the way, you will be flying under enemy colours. The general has lent me his pet artist, and I am going to paste two enormous Iron Crosses over your identification signs. You won't see me do it, so you needn't worry. Before you return I will pull them off all right, so if you are unlucky on the home trip you will get quite a decent funeral.

"And now, general, I think that is just about all. I have just a note to write."

Duncan Grant sat down at the table, took a pen, some foolscap and wrote rapidly. He chose an envelope, folded the half sheet of foolscap, inserted the paper and fastened it. He addressed it to the Commander-in-chief. "Should any . . . accident happen to me, sir, as soon as you hear of it, will you kindly read this message. It is of great importance." He had handed the note to the general.

"Of course, Grant," said the latter genially—probably a note to his nearest relative, but the general would not inquire. Grant repeated : "The note is of great importance." The general placed it in his breast pocket.

"I will report back to your headquarters in this room about dinner time on June 16, today being June 5. I would rather, sir, you didn't see me in the guise of Major Muller, so unless you have any further orders to give me,"—and he pulled himself up to attention— "I should like to say good-bye, sir. I will do my best."

The Commander-in-chief came across from the fireplace. He was visibly touched. It was obvious at least to his chief of staff that a load had been taken from his mind, even though, as Colonel Jervois reflected, the Commander-in-chief appeared to be clutching at a straw. The general laid both hands on Grant's shoulders and said : "Even should you fail, Colonel Grant, your country and I are grateful. Good luck! I will send my orderly to you."

The general left the room. Grant instructed Gaynor and the Intelligence Officer to remove the blanketed body, and, with murmured expressions of good luck, Jervois and the two staff officers passed out into the whitewashed passage. Mayne and Grant were left alone, but only for a moment, for the general's orderly came in.

"Have you dried that uniform yet?"

"Yes, sir."

"Well, bring it right in to me, and find me a safety razor, tooth brush, soap, the latter French, by the way. And, orderly, clear off and go to bed. We don't want anything else. I am leaving a parcel here. Keep it in the general's room until I return. I will call for it in ten days' time."

The orderly returned with the uniform and articles of toilet, laid them on the chair and withdrew. Colonel Grant quickly undressed and then arrayed himself in the uniform of a German major of engineers, tunic, breeches, underclothing, everything complete except the socks and boots. His own black field boots satisfactorily completed the figure, with the field service cap in which the Intelligence Officer had gathered the major's papers and effects.

"And now, Mayne, if you are ready, we'll be off. It's now eleven-fifteen." Grant parcelled up his own uniform in some paper from a shelf in the office, marked it with his name, put on his overcoat and, following Mayne, left the farmhouse unobserved. They walked down the road about a mile to the aerodrome; and there found Flight Commander Mayne's machine in readiness. One of the mechanics came forward and said : "There is an officer from the topographical section here who wants to speak with a Colonel Grant." Grant stepped forward and took two large sheets of canvas and a glue-pot from John Collett.

"Well done, John," he said. "You're a better painter than I thought." He laughed.

"Oh, by the way, Mayne, send your mechanics over to that hangar. I want a private word with you," and while the six mechanics were moving across the grass to the hangar Grant swiftly knelt down under first one wing, then the other, and firmly pasted the two newly-painted crosses over the British identification marks.

"That's all right, Mayne. You can tell your lads to come back again." Mayne blew his whistle and within a few minutes pilot and passenger were seated in the aeroplane ready to move off. The mechanics swung the propeller; and in a flood of light from the flares in the aerodrome, the aeroplane swept into the skies.

"Crikey! Did you see that, Sid? That machine was marked with Iron Crosses. Saw it with me own eyes, I did."

"Och, awa'," jeered a Scotch mechanic as they moved off back to bed, "ye've been up in t' canteen."

"They was Iron Crosses. I see'd 'em with me own eyes," and the aircraftman stood gazing after the machine, now fast disappearing into the night.

2

AT THE WIDOW'S HOUSE

The aeroplane rose swiftly from the ground, and soon was climbing far into the starlit night. Altitude was the first essential. Neither Mayne nor Grant had any desire to come within the range of either friendly or enemy searchlights, or to become the object of scrutiny or suspicion from "night hawks."

The machine climbed steadily until an altitude of fifteen thousand feet had been reached. Then, setting a course due east, Mayne headed his machine to span the two hundred and forty miles from G.H.Q. to Barmen, crossing Belgium, during the remaining hours of darkness.

Time was the essence of the contract. The flight had begun shortly before midnight. Barmen must be reached by four at the latest. By that time the stars would be paling before the coming dawn, the dark skies melting into the neutral grey-blue tints which herald the first approach of the sun below the horizon. All would be still, very still. A few twinkling lights from the larger towns, the belching smoke of a hard pressed factory, its night furnaces being stoked for the coming working day, making a black smear across the landscape; forest silhouetted black against the undefined pasture lands, and rivers pale and iridescent would be distinguished.

Then before the light strode through the gloom, Mayne must select a landing spot, far removed from any town, village or dwelling, so that no one too curious should observe the slipping of the passenger. That was the first essential. But the problem of landing was in itself hazardous. The fields stood high in corn, maize and barley. It was mid-June. Neither the crops, nor the hay would yet have been cut. A forest clearing would have been attractive but the probable stumps of the felled trees would render this impracticable. Mayne and Grant had discussed this problem.

A parachute landing was suggested. There were, however, two outstanding objections which finally ruled out such a mode of landing. It was essential to find a landing ground because the aeroplane must return to the same spot for Grant after ten days. Moreover, landings by parachute were not always entirely successful; even a sprained ankle would destroy the possibility of subsequent success. It might, too, be difficult, quickly at any rate, to dispose of the parachute itself, at least, without arousing suspicion.

Mayne considered the problem anew. The season had been exceptionally dry. A study of the maps had revealed a narrow area shown as swamp some two miles long and half a mile wide, flanked on the one side by the River Wupper, and on the other by the forest. This region was some ten miles south-east of Barmen. No buildings were shown within two or three miles of this place, and then the forest intervened. On the farther side the contours showed that the land rose almost abruptly some eighty feet to form a plateau of pasture or arable lands, with farm buildings dotted here and there.

As he piloted his machine, Mayne reflected carefully upon the problem of landing. Much seemed to depend upon the height of the river. Although there had been little rain to render life more unpleasant for those in the Western trenches, or alternatively to please an avaricious peasantry in swelling the ears of corn, Mayne felt a momentary annoyance that he had not inquired at G.H.Q. what had been the extent of recent rains in the Ebbe Gebirge where the Wupper rises.

A pilot engaged in a long flight has much time for self-recrimination . . . The machine gave a lurch . . . That is always the pilot's reminder that introspection is a dangerous habit, physically as well as psychologically. "Wait and see," mused the pilot . . . Surely, the most English thing ever said by an Englishman about English policy and English habit, albeit to an audience of Scots. Mayne wondered what Grant would see, if he waited, if only for ten days, and incidentally, if Flight Commander Mayne waited, whether he would ever see Colonel Grant, the Scot, again.

So time passed : the machine sped on, aided by a light following wind. The sky remained clear. No word was interchanged between the two passengers, except the almost automatic checking of the half-hours and compass bearings, by Grant, who acted as observer. So far no lights had been observed: the towns were plunged in fearful darkness. War-time curfew and the dread of the unknown horror from the skies extinguished every light. After the passing of the fifth half-hour, however, the blurred lights of a city were visible.

"Passed the scare zone—the River Maas —"shouted Grant.

"One hundred and ninety-five miles. That's seventy-one miles an hour. We should reach Barmen about ten minutes to four."

Duncan Grant, too, had been facing his own problems. His original plan had been a simple one, in conception, if not in execution . . . It was this . . . that he should be flown to some spot in a remote part of Germany, assuming for the purpose the uniform, papers, field book and other effects taken from the dead body of a soldier in No Man's Land. Such a soldier would be reported missing. It would not be known for certain, at least for several months, perhaps never, whether he had been taken prisoner or had been killed.

So long as Grant did not visit the immediate district in which the man lived his domestic and working life, he would be able to move about fairly freely, mingling with other soldiers in the taverns, visiting the towns and villages, and, using his intelligence and military knowledge, acquire information of a very varied character which, after analysis, would prove of high value. Grant possessed a keen appreciation of the dangers involved, of the possibility of detection, but he felt quite confident that an imaginative mind, a capacity for improvisation and some inventive genius, would be his defence in any untoward situation, or should a too awkward curiosity arouse suspicion. His surest weapon of defence was a perfect mastery of the German language.

The plan had not been materially altered by the general's Muller obsession. Grant chuckled to himself—he was Major Muller of the Corps of Engineers, but not quite a perfect replica, blue eyes against brown, five fingers in place of two. Perhaps he might be obliged to wear coloured glasses and remain gloved as an additional camouflage.

He wondered what the Inverness Regiment was doing, who had taken command: "Probably that stiff MacNair" . . . "Two-thirty, fifteen thousand, four hundred feet, compass bearing correct". . . and his mind reverted to the problem in hand.

"After all, even if there was nothing in the Muller complex, at least he was a peg upon which to hang the plan. There were certain advantages in making his first bow as a field officer of engineers. He would not be required to produce a field service book to inquisitive military policemen : he was independent of money and . . . oh . . . Hell!" Grant realized that he had no money, not a mark to bless himself with. That was a tragic error. An ordinary soldier, if he happened in peace time to be a burglar, and why not? could steal with impunity. A major of engineers, a thief? . . . Easier, perhaps. The mind travelled this line or thought for a while.

Grant was discovering it difficult to appreciate the reality of the position now that definitely he had assumed the role of Major Ulrich Muller, whose clothes had been disinterred from the cemetery of Neuve Eglise. Would a colonel of the historic Inverness Regiment masquerading as a major of the almost equally historic corps of German engineers stoop to steal? Damn funny!

Anyway, he would soon be walking the countryside near, but not too near, to Muller's home. He must find out all about Muller : that was certain : and quickly. What was his job prior to the war? What was his job now? To what section of engineers was he attached? When last at home? Whither had he gone? After all, too, one officer's uniform was much like another. Perhaps Muller's tailor—he probably owed him a bit—or his girl, or his wife or both, could recognize Muller's uniform; but for the rest, well, if Muller was unattached, Grant could be unattached too—just a major of engineers, on leave. Such a role would perhaps bring him nearer to Muller's history and home—and to his special duties—than a Muller masquerade presented conveniently some distance from the Muller home. Wilhelm, that was patriotic enough, and, Schaeffer, not too common and not too distinguished—Wilhelm Schaeffer, Major, of the Corps of Engineers. "Good old Muller . . . old pal, met him up the line . . . must visit the family." He might be reported missing by now. Schaeffer could hand out the sympathy to the family. That might be troublesome; details as to how poor Muller died or went missing . . . too trying . . . and the tailor might come round—probably some whiskered Polish Jew—a vulture coming for the pickings. No, Grant had no time to waste. The Muller mare's-nest must first be exploded—inverted M's, fiddlesticks! The mother or sister would put the M back in its right place—the alphabet—for appropriate selection when needed. Delirium, yes, inverted brain-box. Anyhow, the uniform was useful, a safe passport. He could begin that way. Events after that could look after themselves.

He was taking his life in his hands, but, after all, this adventure was no more dangerous than going over the top, or dodging "flying pigs" and other missiles which relieved the stagnation of life in the trenches. But he would be alone, no cheerful, selfless batman beside him, no one to see him fall or to share his fate. If he died he would die alone.

Well, that wouldn't matter much to anyone else. His mother would care, but she had been warned so often both by intuition and by the scraps of news which Duncan imparted, while there was the ever growing casualty list with names of family and of friends to steel her against the shock of loss. And there was no one else; no one who would refuse comfort in her loss . . . He had cut all that out years ago; after she had written *finis* to his dream . . . He wondered what had become of Rosa . . . Memory refashioned the picture . . . there was his uncle's house at Ardersier. It stood upon a little promontory with a background of firs overlooking the Moray Firth, and was built of grey stone. Long windows opened upon close-cut grass, broken by rosebeds and fringed with herbaceous borders and shrubs which sloped away to the water's edge. Beyond lay the narrow sea, backed by yellowing fields and the low hills of the Black Isle. What days he had spent with Rosa there! Rosa von Gleiwitz, the daughter of a German squire, and now he was at war with Germany. Well, thank God, she had terminated that affair. . . .

But how exquisite she had been, a mass of deep golden hair woven in trim plaits, clear violet blue eyes from under heavy lashes sparkled brightly from a face of perfect loveliness . . . How cool her brow, her lips like rose petals. How quickly the weeks had passed, fishing, tramping . . . laughter like a peal of bells, music divine. And then she had disappeared, quietly, firmly, irrevocably from his life. His pulse quickened with the thought, the old desire was stirred. And when Rosa had faded, he had thrown himself fiercely into the study of his profession. And now, superbly equipped, technically proficient, he was being winged to Rosa's country . . . the country of his enemies . . . Enemies? Grant reflected . . . why were the British, Nordic and Teutons, allied with Latins and Slavs? How well could Britons and Germans pull together. The Germans brave and ingenious, the British stolid, liberal-minded, an innate sense of justice . . . playing the game . . . some indefinable quality . . . the British the colonizers, Germans the colonials . . . and Rosa . . . typical of her race . . . what an ally . . . a wife.

"Hullo, old man, are you asleep?" Mayne shouted through the speaking-tube. "It's gone three and I can spot lights, front, right."

Grant's reflections and planning had carried him away from the automatic duty of the observer. His mind returned in a flash to his maps, compass and bearings.

"We're just crossing the River Maas—town of Limburg on our left. There is no raid scare here. Look ahead a bit and you can just see a red glow. Those will be the blast furnaces of Crefeld and Dusseldorf. We shall be well over Dusseldorf in the next half-hour, and in a further ten minutes should reach Elberfeld and Barmen. I hope I shall be able to spot the town. At Barmen I want to turn south-east on a bearing of 125 degrees, and we shall then have to come down and choose our landing ground."

Within a short while a mosaic of lights could be discerned below. The machine was travelling over the vast arsenals, steel and iron works, mines and closely settled area of the Rhineland industrial belt. Huge blast furnaces, flickering like candles below, belched forth their black smoke into the night, making its atmosphere even darker. As the aeroplane passed immediately above the towns of Elberfeld and Barmen, a thick pall of smoke hanging over the towns completely hid them from view.

The smoke had the appearance of a great black sea, the light wind gently rocking its sullen surface into a swell, and occasionally tossing its edges into billows and waves flecked with fleeting spray. This cloud of smoke, by its very density, would dull the sound of the aeroplane to the ears of the inquisitive in the town below, but it rendered Grant's maps momentarily useless. He was able to judge, however, from the speed record and chronometer the moment at which the direction should be changed for landing. A few minutes after the course had been altered the lights of the landscape could again be distinguished. Looking back and across to his right, Grant could pick out the towns in series . . . of Dusseldorf, Elberfeld and Barmen, the latter being almost directly behind the course of the machine.

It was now nearly four o'clock, and as yet too dark to effect a landing. In the east, however, from this altitude the faintest suggestion of the coming dawn could be discerned. The stars were paling and the deep blue-black of night changing to that almost green tint which heralds the coming variations of a new day. It takes but little time from this phase for light to break upon the world. Mayne decided that he would utilize the time in hand by reducing his elevation gradually and continuing the flight in the direction of the Ebbe Gebirge mountains flanking the Sauerland, a territory thinly populated and well wooded.

When the light permitted a landing—the least possible light for the purpose—he decided to turn the machine, flying from west to east. A flight in this direction would certainly occasion no alarm or suspicion, and probably at this stage of air development and war activity would arouse scarcely any curiosity, even from those few peasants and workers who, sleepily enough no doubt, would be going forth to the fields and other daily tasks. In ten minutes the altitude had been decreased to some eight thousand feet, and the landscape was becoming distinguishable. Dark patches indicated the forests, interwoven with little silver threads, the rivers and streams of the Ebbe Oberland. Mayne made a wide turn and began to dip the machine more steeply to earth. He called to Grant through the speaking-tube: "Look out for a landing place. If we can spot something better than the map reference, all the conditions are ideal for a landing here."

He shut off his engine and glided swiftly to within a few hundred feet of the ground. Light had rapidly established its domination over the passing night. It was now nearly half-past four, and the sun was stretching its yellow fingers over the hills while, with the exception of a few fairy lamps still hanging high in the skies, the stars had been wiped away by the gleam of a new day.

Mayne did not dare to traverse the ground more than once for fear of arousing suspicion. The area appeared too rugged in formation and densely covered with forests, while wherever a clearing indicated a village, every yard seemed to be covered with yellowing crops. The rivers, however, shown as being of some size on the map, were very low, as could be observed from the bridges which now stood high over the water, their piles, for many feet above water level, green with lichen moss; while the stream itself flowed now only through one or two spans, where the bridges were designed to cover a far wider flow of water. Grant passed this comment across the speaking-tube, remarking also that the indication was to try first the previous plan of landing on the swamp by Viersberg. Time was now the essence of procedure. Decisions must be made and carried out. The hazard had now to be taken. Closely following the map with the landscape below, Grant directed Mayne, who had again opened up his engine, to the Wupper River line, on which was situated the chosen place.

"Here we are!" shouted Grant.

Mayne dipped the nose of the machine, shut off his engine and sped the approach to the swamp. The landscape was noted in a flash. The right bank of the river, a sluggish deep stream some fifty yards across, rose steeply for thirty feet. There was a gradual bend in the river, almost at right angles, about a mile and a half long. That would account for the steep bank against the hillside which above it rolled in a broad down, tufted with tangled scrub, bracken, and broom, to a high plateau of waving corn. The left bank of the river stretched back to the edge of a thick pine forest. The bed of the stream showed boulder and shingle, then mud flat; then tree stumps and logs piled in confusion by the river in winter torrent; then a belt of reeds and finally a stretch of ground, light brown in colour, flat in texture, some sixty yards in depth beyond the reeds leading up to the forest edge and a bare mile in length.

The landing looked good. Mayne skimmed over the surface of the approach. The wind from the west, caught in the bend between the forest and the high bank as the river bent to the south, caused the machine to lilt from side to side. Two dangers only presented themselves: bog-land which would grip the landing-wheels, or a hidden tuft which might overturn the machine as it sped in a taxi to rest.

Grant called through the tube : "Make over the river. I'll take the water; don't land."

"Damn it all!" shouted Mayne, "we're both in this," and the machine grounded.

The light brown mass proved to be long, dried grass. The ground was hard underneath. The machine bumpedl heavily with a tendency to pitch forward, as the forward wheels sank into the grass, but the rear skid dragged more heavily and the machine came to rest.

Grant climbed out, and threw his overcoat and flying cap back into the cockpit. There was no time to lose. He dipped under the wings and ripped off the sticky black enemy crosses.

"You're flying under our colours now. Go like blazes, kid." He reached his hand up to Mayne in the pilot's seat. "So long, old man, give my love to the Commander-in-chief, don't forget that—my love. Tell Jervois I'll send him a postcard; and, by the way, especially, ask Jervois to wire my regiment as soon as you get back . . . say I've gone on ten days' special leave. Bring breakfast for two with you on the fifteenth, and make the landing a bit farther upstream. You haven't much room on this heavy stuff to clear the trees and bank in front.

"*Auf wiedersehen!*" shouted Grant. They gripped hands. "Good luck, Scottie . . . my God, you've got some guts," and Mayne, guilty of unsoldierly emotion, pulled his hand away quickly. "Give the prop a spin."

The machine bumped like a camel rising, then began to plough heavily forward. It gained speed, then seemed to hang, another spurt forward and the wheels lifted, but the tail still dragged reluctantly in the stubby grass. Then as the machine moved towards the river bend the wind, coming strongly off the cliff face, lifted it, as if by the tug of a string on a kite. It flopped heavily again, and then rose high over the steep bank, Mayne skilfully taking the turn of the river and meeting the breeze full in the face. A perfect start . . . Mayne glanced over his left shoulder. There was Grant waving . . . then the tree tops blotted him from view. The machine climbed steeply up, up, up, higher and higher, five, eight, fifteen thousand feet towards Barmen. Then due west. Keep the compass west and nothing else mattered. Mayne could pick up his bearings later on. Four, possibly four and a half hours' flying in a headwind and he would be safe from the danger of "dog-fights" or scouts dropping out of the blue. Anyhow, he had the altitude. Grant moved into the trees, and watched the aeroplane until it was a tiny speck . . . now only a dot . . . going . . . gone. No one had observed the landing. That was the probability.

Just on five o'clock on a fine morning. Majors of engineers do not prowl about lone pine forests in back war areas at five in the morning; so Grant decided to wait, and for the reason, too, that if his individual landing had been observed curiosity would bring the observer to the spot within a short space of time. He looked through Muller's kit again . . . and there was a parcel of shaving gear . . . a bit bulky, surely. He unwrapped it . . . God bless the orderly! . . . two ham sandwiches and a hard-boiled egg—a wonderful fellow the British batman, probably a waiter from a club in St. James's, and all the restaurants packed with greasy, grasping dagoes! No one came. The sun rose and topped the river bank. Suppose the landing, as such, had been observed from a farmhouse or village. Perhaps some curious person would visit the river bank. Grant must examine the ground. Perhaps there were wheel tracks, and their measurement, not coinciding with the measurement of a German machine, aroused suspicion. Grant walked the distance of the rolled out grass. The ground showed no indentations: the grass had been laid out flat, and the marks might have been those of any machine. Good! And now for plans. He would walk upstream to where the forest and scrub touched the water's edge. There, under cover, he would walk slowly, following the river in the direction of Barmen. He had twelve miles to go, but would strike the road about four miles outside the town.

A major of engineers on ten days' leave . . . Wilhelm Schaeffer, pal of poor old Muller, giving up a day of his leave to visit the relatives, and tell them what a fine fellow Muller was—that would pass as a tale in a credulous world. In wartime those not engaged in the battle area will believe anything.

Grant reflected upon the yarns being spun in drawing-rooms and hotel lounges by elderly officers with dim memories of a South African picnic, and by young staff officers whose chief military qualification was kinship to a bold politician or to a manufacturer selling mock marmalade at immense prices to an over-worked and too often not very scrupulous government department. None of these gentlemen had ever heard a shell in flight, far less a bullet. But, ye gods! the tales! and what a mental intoxication for those at home. Duncan had some tales too . . . but he would keep them.

So, having shaved and washed himself, Grant strolled leisurely along the river bank. He passed two lads operating a saw mill beside the river. First blood! and simple. He would test his disguise. He must play the actor to perfection. Here was a not too critical provincial audience. As he entered the shed the lads looked up and stopped work.

"Guten morgen, Herr Major!"

Grant glowed with pleasure—a slight swagger, a condescension, and seated himself upon a pile of logs. "Pit props?" he queried.

"Ja, Herr Major," answered the boys in unison. He asked the lads about their brothers and fathers. They had nothing to tell, a brother killed, an uncle prisoner, nothing known about the course of the war: and the miners were weary of long hours of work. Some strike agitators had been shot in the square at Elberfeld. But Germany was winning the war . . . the master stroke was being prepared . . . Everyone said so. Food, a little short in the towns; but not for the peasants, however, said one of the boys shyly, as the major became more expansive and appreciative. Grant decided to move on.

He was really enjoying himself, experiencing the emotions of the actor. He bade the boys a friendly good-bye and tramped on towards Barmen. The lack of money worried him and he was growing hungry. He came to a bridge at Beyenburg carrying the high road, and leaving the course of the stream he swung down the road to the town, whose chimneys, church tower and buildings were now clearly visible four miles distant. He passed some peasants' carts, a few heavy lorries, but the way was mainly deserted. A road mender saluted him as he approached the outskirts of the town.

A line of new villas led up to the railway crossing at Langerfeld. Children were playing in the road. They saw him coming, and drawing themselves into line gravely saluted. He patted the diminutive sergeant-major on the head: "Now charge the dirty English," he cried, and with fierce yells the children scrambled in mock attack down the street.

There's war spirit right enough, he mused. The kids may be a bit anaemic as the result of the blockade, but the rot hasn't yet set in. Strikes at Elberfeld, Dusseldorf and Essen? Perhaps? That was natural enough. There was plenty of money . . . behind the lines. The patriotic middle class were pouring their savings into the national coffers, and being taxed out of existence. They had sacrificed a generation of their children to the fatherland. Money? Why, God bless my soul! the *schiebers* are raking it in . . . Profiteers having a wonderful time and the workers mean to have their bit while the going's good . . . a strike's not against the immorality of war, but to secure a bit more of the boodle . . . the profiteers couldn't have it all . . . and, what the hell did it matter anyway? . . . higher wages, higher prices . . . The *schiebers* could pass the buck to the taxpayer . . . no, there was nothing in these strikes other than human selfishness . . . no moral issue involved, no weakening of national spirit. Look at the kiddies!

He entered into the spirit of the game.

"*Ich bin Englander*," he cried. "Fix bayonets! charge!"

The children, who had now come to a standstill at the end of the row of cottages, bore down upon him with renewed fury. He picked up the leader, a thick-set little boy blue-bottle, lightly spanked him and set him on his feet...

Major Schaeffer passed over the level crossing and had entered the town of Barmen. He had decided to seek the best hotel. That would provide both shelter and food with certainly a week's credit. As he had not the remotest intention to remain long so far removed from the battle area, the plan suited admirably. He inquired for the main square of the town, which, from its shop fronts, appeared to be prosperous, with its streets now just before the luncheon hour filled with comfortable citizens; and after a few minutes' walk stood at one corner of the Neumarkt. It was surrounded by pretentious stone buildings, the Rathaus with its fine pillared façade, municipal library and usual local government offices. In the centre was an equestrian statue of the Emperor Frederick the Great; electric trams rattled over the cross points; flower and newspaper sellers occupied kiosks, upon which were posted patriotic posters urging the populace to contribute to the victory loan and to work for the fatherland; motor cars, some few bearing official signs pasted upon the wind screen, but mostly private cars, were closely packed one side of the square.

The restaurants were busy, tables set in the open, some men lunching, others drinking lager from deep glass mugs, gossiping and smoking. Grant looked at the signs and advertisements, searching for an hotel . . . Hotel Imperial. He strolled across the square, a soldier saluted; a lieutenant of infantry sprang to attention.

He crossed the threshold of the hotel, went to the reception office, and asked for a room, one of the best bedrooms. "A double room?" inquired the clerk, familiar with the habits of officers on leave.

Grant, fulfilling the rôle of Schaeffer, decided that he must conform to plan. It might, too, be useful. "*Naturlich,*" he replied.

"And your baggage?"

"It has been mislaid," said Grant.

"Will the *Herr Major* give instructions to the valet to procure anything he requires? . . . They will be entered on his account . . . Will the major sign the register?"

Grant took up the pen. Good God! . . . He must replay that part of Muller . . . Schaeffer was not in the Army list . . . He would be under suspicion within an hour . . . He must take that risk and make a short stay . . . Jekyll and Hyde, not in one person but as two . . . he signed the register—Ulrich Muller. Grant then followed the page to the lift and was shown to a large double-bedded room. He rang for the valet, ordered fresh underclothes—those from the grave would not look so inviting upon a new morning— pyjamas and some miscellaneous toilet requisites.

He washed, and descended again to the great lounge, now filled with an animated group of men and women. There were several uniforms among the crowd; a slim, fair boy on crutches dragged himself painfully to the restaurant; several women, obviously those butterflies who flit through every prosperous town, were sipping wine. Major Schaeffer strolled into lunch. He was shown to a table laid for two. He sat down alone and carefully selected a substantial and attractive lunch, a bottle of Rudesheimer and called for a newspaper. Several women passed slowly beside his table, obviously inviting themselves to be the guest. He continued to read his paper, without looking up, but he took stock of them.

He might require a *confidante* . . . one of these women, probably a harpy, hard-bitten, callous, her attractions brightly-painted to hide the imperfections of age and the ravages of a vicious life, rather than a younger woman with a readier market and too many lovers . . . yes, she might be useful.

But he was hungry : he would first do ample justice to the menu and fortify the inner man. After that there was work to do. He studied the newspaper carefully; then, having finished his lunch, he called for a cigar and ordered a box to be sent to his room and signed the bill, Muller, room 23. He went straight up to his apartment. He must now be quick. He would walk to Hatzberg, just five miles distance. Even as Muller he would doubtless be known in Barmen, though as a major of the reserve he might be far less prominent in a war involving comet promotions than his rank would signify in a regular officer. That was comforting.

As Wilhelm Schaeffer, therefore, he left the hotel and inquired the road to Hatzberg. He walked rapidly. The road left the town and ran through an ugly, blackened countryside decorated with slag heaps, winding apparatus and the tall, smoking chimneys of textile factories. Every yard between the factories was cultivated. After walking for over an hour, after which the countryside became more picturesque, undulating and wooded, Schaeffer overtook an elderly priest. He passed him good day and inquired his destination.

The priest was glad of someone with whom to converse. He had taken over duty in Hatzberg only recently to replace a younger zealot who had gone to the front . . . yes, he knew the Mullers . . . he had been summoned the evening previously, and had heard the terrible news, another son of the village gone—killed, a prisoner, who knew? . . . Ah! Schaeffer had known him . . . he was dead . . . Gentle God have pity! . . . his poor mother. Muller was so clever . . . a mining engineer. Schaeffer agreed, and added : "Selected for special duty, a great loss."

"Yes, ability turned to such waste and destruction. It was he who planned and sunk the new shafts in the Bismarkhôtte, by Kattowitz in Silesia." He had not been much with his mother, a widow, during recent years . . . he had only returned home shortly before his summons to the front . . . he was to have taken an appointment as chief engineeer in Elberfeld . . . dead, ah, dear God! . . . That will kill his mother, so proud, so good a servant of the Church . . . Devoted to each other . . . her only son . . . dear God! . . .

Grant was inclined to feel sympathetic. Then he almost chuckled aloud; a fleeting smile crossed his face. Muller would not be known in Barmen except perhaps by reputation. Grant would, therefore, be safe from recognition for a short while. Meanwhile, the devoted, proud mother with whom, doubtless, the equally devoted son shared his secrets, would have much to tell. He would discover what was Muller's mission. The general was right . . . there was something worth while discovering in the Muller affair. He enjoined the priest to silence. No one must know that Muller was dead. He, the comrade in arms, would break the news gently, then summon the priest, for his ministrations.

They were approaching the village, its little white church centring the cluster of buildings. The priest pointed to a low, double-fronted house standing back from the road. Behind a holly hedge a neat grass lawn stretched up to its walls. Between the trimmed edges of the grass and banked by standard roses and a profusion of old-fashioned flowers, a red brick path led up to the creeper-clad porch. The lawn was intersected by gnarled apple trees, and through the squat windows Grant could observe the sheen of brass and clear glaze of china ornaments.

He lifted the latch of the gate. He must risk the discerning mother-eye upon his uniform. His footsteps rung alarmingly on the path, his heart beat in his throat. The tragic reality of the situation was contributing that stage fright which unawares will assail even the most skilful and experienced actor. His powers of deception would be highly tried. He was to act alone before the most gifted critic, the mother who had borne and known her son from the cradle up. Her questions would be searching. He would bide his time. He must obtain his facts first. Then he would break the dread news and leave the lone widow to her grief, her priest, and, he could not help hoping, her death...

Women . . . mothers . . . had intuitions . . . If his story should in one single respect raise suspicion, a mother's faith and hope would discredit the whole tale. She would cling to hope. She would disbelieve his story of Muller's death. Hope eternal . . . Grant would be discredited. Schaeffer would not save him from discovery. These thoughts flitted through his brain. He knocked upon the low green door. A servant girl, bare-footed, opened it to him: "*Ja wohl!* Frau Muller will be in the garden behind the house."

Grant declared that he would announce himself, and the maid showed the way across the house and out through the casement windows. He saw a little lady, some sixty to seventy years of age, frail like some porcelain figure from the Dresden potteries, silvered hair, delicate features, fine hands albeit strong with toil, clad in dark blue satin, her delicate throat graced with old lace. She was bending to the pea-sticks, but at the sound of voices she turned and started.

"Ah, good afternoon, little mother. Your son prayed me if ever I were in this neighbourhood to be sure to call upon you.

We are close friends, comrades in battle. I know him well. He speaks so often of you. I have some days' leave in Dusseldorf... I felt I already knew you. I have come, you see..."

"Ah! *mein Herr*, you have news." The little woman came across, both hands outstretched in welcome. "My son's friend is my friend. But you have news..." A sob caught her throat, it shook her frail body, "Good news."

"Oh, yes, yes," rejoined Grant. "It is a long story. I will tell it to you. Your son is safe."

"I have received a telegram last night," said the widow. "He is reported missing, but that cannot be true; he is so strong, so clever, so brave and . . . God is good . . . I did not credit it," Frau Muller was regaining courage. Hope buoyed her. She was satisfied. Yes, she would hear the story . . . but yes, later would do . . . she was happy now . . . "Major..." "Wilhelm Schaeffer," repeated Grant, ". . . will take wine, fruit and cakes. We will go to the salon, and I will tell the *madchen* to serve refreshments. You are thrice welcome, Wilhelm, my son's friend."

They entered the low salon. Frau Muller seated herself in a deep upright chair : Grant selected an armchair removed from the light, in shadow. He wanted to avoid the watery, blue eyes. Muller's mother disturbed him. Curse these blasted clothes; even Muller's vest, the initials probably worked by those deft, delicate fingers. But he must give Frau Muller her head. Now that anxiety was removed she would be willing to sing her pæan of praises. Ulrich would be whitewashed in a verbal shroud . . . What a horrible idea! He must pull himself together. This was a bad start. The actor would break down and forget his lines. Then what would the master critic say?

Well, he had some war stories—truth . . . stranger than the fiction of West End drawing-rooms. He would whet her appetite, arouse her pride and then hear some of Muller's experiences. That was the line. Grant had a storehouse of tales, some of which had never been told, secrets in the recesses of his mind. He must tear the widow's heart, capture her pride, enslave her spirituality. No matter if his story were told of the other side. She would not know the difference. In this warfare the experience of British or Germans, Italians, Russians, was all much alike—shells, fear, mud, corpses, lice, blood, panic, drunkenness, sweat, dust, harlots, marching—a kaleidoscope of bestiality, broken by acts of matchless self-sacrifice. Grant would create the atmosphere in which the old lady would unburden her secrets—Muller's secrets.

"I will try to give you a picture of life . . . up at the front. In it you will be able to visualize better the life of your son . . . I remember being appointed to my command. It was a new formation. The officers too fond of alcohol, the older soldiers good material but gone to seed, because they could not get the stimulant which the officers imbibed, and . . . the officers themselves provided no other . . . for the rest . . . a host of untried youngsters, kids of eighteen and nineteen. I am always very grateful for these kids and curse myself eternally for what I had to teach them. My job was, and is, to win the war. I remember that I had to deny myself the stimulant of appearing to be heroic before my men—and I can imagine this must be a glorious intoxication—and go about my job organizing little groups into a sense of sanity, infusing courage by appealing to the manhood in men turned curs, threatening, cajoling, even shooting as a salutary lesson. And I had also to refuse myself the fun of shooting back at the enemy—and it is fun under war conditions— because the brains of my life were wanted to organize a front which was rapidly decomposing. We were hard pressed..."

The widow was leaning forward in her chair, her eyes wide with eagerness, following every word of the story with fixed attention. She was like one hypnotized. Grant had forgotten the widow, all else but his story—untold. He was living again the mental agony of years of war. His acting before the most critical audience in the world was supreme.

"I had formed a little body of scouts. Not one of them was over twenty years of age. They were fresh, clean, bright-eyed, just little adventurers. They had no vices, no fears. They lived with me, where I went, they went. It was like a school treat with this difference, that it was my job to harden their hearts to shocks, and to spoil their minds to the sight and sound of death and bestiality—a face half shot off, turned up to the sky isn't pleasant; a man with his bowels torn out by high explosive can make a strong man physically sick; an old corpse, bloated and black, is terrifying."

Frau Muller covered her face with her hands. "Go on," she said.

"I had to make them coarse to stand the racket of things which I loathed personally, and which I feared too, lest they should weaken when I needed most their confidence, the power and inexperience of their youth and their manhood. I have lived pretty hard, and had seen by that time more than three years of war; but sometimes alone, in danger, I reflect upon how I have deliberately coarsened the minds of these lads by profanity and jibe—anything beastly so long as it neither hurt the brain like drink, nor the body, like women, I utilized to steel these lads for the task which must be theirs.

"I trained them diligently as scouts, and demanded their confidence and love with every artifice of which a commander can make use, in order that on any part of the battlefield, they should be my eyes, telling me accurately what I must know without embroidery, but telling me also without an eye to the main chance— safety or glory—and I knew each one individually for what he was worth. I tested them—a walk here, ten minutes and a cigarette there, sometimes sharing a blanket, a lad by himself as himself, not in the artificiality of the presence of a corporal, or their comrades—I needed them to do my will: I required their confidence, my external and internal spies, my intelligence corps, my scouts. I have degraded these lads, debauched my soul to win a battle; my personal honour has been seduced by the habit of war, my brains prostituted by its necessities."

Grant checked himself. He had confessed to this stranger, this little waxen figure, the mother of his enemy, now dead and naked in a damp blanket, the innermost secrets of his soul, the hellish agony of his mind. He stopped and sipped his wine, reflecting that now again would war's grave necessity make a supreme call upon his finer instincts. He must excuse himself. The situation was horrible.

He continued: "History will provide evidence of the practical effect of such training, but it will tell nothing of what it cost me personally, in giving it. I am ashamed of war's necessity—that it has compelled me deliberately so to debase the souls of men. It is not as though I lack culture or like so many others am submerged in an orgy of drink. I love beauty in nature, in art, literature, in little children, in the minds of philosophers and . . ." he hesitated, "in women such as you, little mother."

Frau Muller bowed her head. Grant's story, his final thrust, had struck home. His very sincerity loosened the widow's tongue. He had won her sympathy, her mother love . . . he sensed the reality of the situation, he had won her confidence and all her secrets. Frau Muller must be used. He would pile her ruin upon that of the minds of fresh lads from the hills and vales of his highland home . . . The massacre of the innocents!—their minds, not their bodies. He ceased.

"My Ulrich has felt like that, too. His brain and inventive genius degraded to the service of futility. You know him well: his fine character. From what you say I can see that you were comrades, close and intimate. How he dreaded the summons to war! It was not his courage that ever failed. His work in the mines had proved that. He feared only the enslaving of his skill to the machine of war. But when the summons came, he faced it bravely."

"I know, I know," interposed Grant, "we were together."

The widow continued: "I remember when he was summoned to army headquarters by the chief engineer some eight months ago. He was glad, but afraid. They needed his brains, a great engineer. He left me for three days. Then he returned—so proud. He remained for just a week. Daily he went to a disused mine near Hattingen. He experimented in secret. They placed several hundred prisoners, French, English, Russian miners at his disposal from the big camp at Elberfeld. I have seen them, poor devils. They worked in long shifts. The escorts kept the inquisitive far from the pit head. They came and went in silence. And Ulrich would sit late at night working on his plans. I would not leave him. While he worked I sat with him. He begged me to go to my bed, but I should see so little of him. I sat and watched him working: and I, too, worked. He must wear the uniform of a major of Imperial Engineers. The tailor came. I worked its appointments. The week was all too short. Then one day he had completed his tests. He told me he must go to the army headquarters. His workings were placed in my little bureau. When the war was over he told me he would use them for the industry which was his pride, his life.

"And then he went away. He has not been back since. He has written often. I have his letters, too, in my bureau. I do not understand the war : I cannot even guess. Then he remains in one place, so it seems, for his letters come more regularly. He is working hard. He is confident. He tells me his great work for the fatherland is nearing completion. The plans are perfected, but I cannot know what is his work." The widow sighed. "I am lonely. I have my flowers, my housework, the church. I feel alone. Ah, Wilhelm, it is good of you to have come. You will describe him to me, his work, his pride. I need to feel him. He is all I have. I have his last letter. It is in my bureau in my bedroom. You can tell me what it means, fill in between the lines. I am old and lonely. I want to feel him again."

"So," reflected Grant, no longer under the spell of his own reflections, "the bureau is in her bedroom. Muller's papers are there."

Frau Muller rose. She glided quietly from the room, Grant holding the door to let her pass. There was colour in her cheeks, her eyes bright. She smiled at Grant as she passed, grasping his arm lightly and pressing it affectionately.

Grant was alone. He had time to think, to formulate some scheme. He must obtain the plans from the bureau upstairs in Frau Muller's bedroom. He listened acutely for her steps above; one . . . two . . . three . . . eleven steps along the corridor upstairs, the latch of a door clicked; he could hear her moving overhead, not directly above, but towards the front of the house. He could find that room . . . up the stairs, along the corridor, eleven short paces, a room to the right. He heard the jingle of a bunch of keys. Then a drawer was opened.

He must secure those plans . . . at any price. He would take his time. He heard the *madchen* humming a doubtful marching ditty. He looked carefully round the little salon. Portraits of Ulrich, an illuminated address to Professor Muller of Bonn University. That would, doubtless, be the husband of the *Witwe* Muller—a fine head. He examined the bookcase; it was lined with scientific works—mathematics, geometry, chemistry. Professor Muller was a scientist. His mantle, then, had fallen upon Ulrich.

Grant opened the case; and, haphazard, he chose a work upon statics, the author, Heinrich Muller. It was well thumb-marked. He hurried over its pages. There were pencil notes upon stresses and strains, perhaps in the handwriting of Ulrich. That might be important. He would hold the book in his hand when Frau Muller returned. She would probably volunteer information. Footsteps came along the passage, twelve this time, the rustle of satin as the back of her dress swept the stairway.

Frau Muller entered. Grant was standing before the open bookcase, Heinrich Muller's text work in his hand. To his unspoken question she nodded and smiled : "My husband's," she said.

"Of course. To me, also, that is a very interesting little library," he remarked. "No wonder Ulrich gained distinction : his genius inborn. I see Ulrich has been a keen student too. His handwriting?" he hazarded.

"Oh, yes, he used my husband's work for his plans. He frequently referred to this book. It is a great treasure. I know little of these things. My life was for my husband—entertaining his little family of students, many of whom, his favourite, the most able, visited our house in Bonn. Then he was taken from me. I moved to this quiet village. It was sufficiently close to the mines for Ulrich's studies and apprenticeship. Before he finally went away he used my husband's book as I sat with him. His handwriting, you ask? Oh, yes; Ulrich produced his master scheme from my husband's theory. He called it the W plan, and then, you know, of course, it was his jest—inverted M."

"I know, I know," interposed Grant. "We have worked upon it together."

"Ah, I guessed that would be so. All his heart, his whole mind was in that scheme. He left me and went to the front in order to put it into operation. That was seven weeks ago. He reckoned that it would require ten weeks to give effect to the whole plan. He complained that the prisoners would not work : they were too slow. He experimented at Elberfeld, and arranged his time schedule by their performance. The engineeer-in-chief would give him no more than ten weeks. He complained that even so many entailed risks were too long. The English must be trapped. They would soon be reinforced.

"Ulrich worked furiously, long hours, to perfect his plan, and now it will not be long before all is ready. You have been with him, working with him. How you must have needed respite before the final stage of the plan is completed! That will end the war : Ulrich was so confident. The English will be taken unawares, thrown into disorder, their lines penetrated in a dozen places.

"But," she said wistfully, "I am sorry for the English. I have had an affection for them. We have received their professors from Cambridge at our home in Bonn, and students too. We have a lady in this village—Fraulein Maurer—she frequently visits me, who has spent several years in England. She taught our language and our music—Bach, Schubert, Beethoven—Germany has the world's music—in the home of a Scottish nobleman. They are different, the Scotch—so she always insists. But there is so much hate in Germany for the English today."

The old lady rambled on. "She insists that the Scotch are different. They have fought against the English. I have suspected that perhaps she may have loved a Scot. She returned to Germany four years ago. She is ill. She would not go to her home in Koln. She preferred, she has told me, to bury herself among the people. She nurses voluntarily in the prisoners' camp at Elberfeld. No matter her illness, there are few willing—they need those who can speak English. In the evenings she comes often to my house. She lives in a flat by herself near the Stadt Baurat. And she is much alone, perhaps her health is worse than I know. We two are alone, so she comes and plays to me and we talk together. She had her secrets, perhaps as I have said she had a lover. I know not. I do not care to ask. She plays to me, and I feel less lonely."

The widow sighed, then continued :—

"Ah! but I have Ulrich's letters. Read his last for yourself, you can tell me. He hopes to visit me within a month. Would that mean the end of his work ? He has scarcely slept. He is confident. The work goes forward. Everything is quiet. Our airmen—are they not gallant?—they keep the enemy away. The English cannot observe; dare not attack. He meets friends everywhere : but he may not talk. Few know of his work. The English make raids. They are repulsed, so many English taken prisoners, others lying dead.

"He says the prisoners are often fine specimens, but young and badly led. The officers untrained. They throw themselves away. They do not understand technique. He is a technician. He observes that always. War is a technique like mining engineering. Ulrich is an engineer : he does not pretend to understand warfare. But we have our experts, have we not? He likes to listen to them. His plans must harmonize with those of other experts. And the English, they are brave, but everything haphazard. They kill their men with their own artillery, their machine-guns are without organization, they play at soldiers—see, he says it—as they play at their football."

Grant nodded an assent. How bitterly he understood. "But it is horrible, this war. Everyone is infected with its fever: morality has died. God is forgotten. The workmen clamour always for more money. Prices go up; there is extravagance, no control. I live alone : my *madchen* comes every day for a few hours. Then, at six, she goes home. She was a good girl; but now, well, I have my fears." Grant recalled the dirty ditty. So the *madchen* would soon be gone. That was good. He could still wait.

"Ulrich has written regularly. Every four or five days I receive his letters but there has been no letter now for nine days. See the date. Today it is the sixth of June. His last letter is dated the twenty-fourth of May. I was afraid.

"Then last night I have received the telegram. He is missing." Frau Muller leant forward and clasped Grant's hands. The colour had departed from her cheeks, her hands were cold. Her eyes searched his own. Involuntarily he shivered. "But you have brought me news," and her fingers tightened upon his wrists.

"Yes, yes. I must tell you his story," he stammered. "He is safe. He has brought honour to your house." Her grip relaxed, the faded colour crept back to her cheeks.

Grant's capacity for improvisation must produce a story—"We were working together in the battle zone, just behind the firing line. My engineers were weary. The English had been shelling the front line and support trenches. It was heavy shelling. I lost many men, some killed, others wounded. We were expecting a surprise attack. The infantry and machine-gunners were ready. We had orders to withdraw.

"A heavy shell burst in the trench just beside us. Its walls collapsed. It was dark. We extricated ourselves. I thought that Ulrich was with us, as we withdrew. When we reached the reserve line, we sought shelter in the galleries. Ulrich was not with us.

"I asked my lieutenant. He said that Major Muller was safe at the headquarters of the battalion holding the line, in a deep dugout. When dawn came there was a roll-call of our men. There were some known to be killed, others had been reported wounded through the aid posts, a few unaccounted.

"I telephoned to the battalion headquarters for Major Muller. He was not there, had not been there, he was missing. The lists were drawn up. The clerk reported the names as was his duty—killed, wounded, missing. Of course that of Major Muller was among them.

"But, have no fear now, Frau Muller. I went out at once to find the truth. I was distracted. I searched the lines where we had been. I found Ulrich. He had been crushed by the falling parapet. He had lain there the night through at the bottom of the trench—no safer place—his leg pinned by the weight of earth, but he was safe."

"*Gott sei dank*," murmured the widow, crossing herself devoutly.

Grant continued: "These messages take time to pass through headquarters. Your telegram is three days since the event. In a week maybe, or soon, you will receive another communication . . . perhaps sooner than you think. I will tell you more. You must know of his life and of his work."

3

ACROSS FOUR YEARS

Alight step was heard on the red brick path leading from the road to the house. The sun had sunk low behind the little village, and the room was deepening in gloom. Grant looked up.

"It is Fraulein Maurer," said the widow. "She will be glad to meet you." The latch of the green front door was lifted. A light step passed across the little hall and the door of the salon opened.

In the dim light, almost behind her, too, as she entered, Grant could see little of the woman's face. She was of tall stature, elegant in her carriage, but thin, almost emaciated. The shaft of light from the setting sun caught a wisp of her hair which had escaped from the careful plaits arranged on either side of her head. The hair was like spun gold.

"Ah, my dear, I must present to you Major Schaeffer, Ulrich's friend. He is visiting me and has brought good news. Ulrich is safe."

The girl stepped forward, her hand outstretched. Grant, following the usual courtesy of the country, drew his heels together, bent his head, meeting her outstretched hand with his lips, while he touched it with his fingers. Her hand was thin—he felt the bone, so cold, even upon this warm summer evening. Frau Muller took the girl's cold hands in her own.

"Play for me—a prelude of praise: then you shall hear Major Schaeffer's story. I, too, will hear it again."

Fraulein Maurer choked a little, then sat before the keys . . . her fingers dwelt upon the keyboard. "It shall be Liszt," she said. "He played and prayed, perhaps the greatest of all pianists, pathfinder in music, big-souled philosopher, triumphing out of sorrow—Liszt—It shall be the 'The Mountain Symphony.'" She was now facing the window, the last light of day playing upon her tired face, her glorious hair deep gold but softened here and there with a streak of silver.

Grant, deep in his chair, was wrapt in thought. Plans were taking shape in his mind. The general's odd obsession was the master-key.

The music swept through his soul—warbling birds, rippling streams; the hills mounting higher and higher, crag upon crag, boulder upon boulder, even as a ladder to Heaven; the sweep of eagles' wings, a soft breeze singing through the pines, laughter and echo . . . The girl appeared buried deep in her music, her head sometimes pressed affectionately over the instrument, listening, inquiring for those deep, true melodious notes with all their variation of light and shade, which were interwoven by a master in the mosaic of the symphony. The music of Liszt was enthroned.

The widow sat forward in her chair, her face transfigured with joy. "Never have you played like this, my dear," she said softly, then relapsed again into silence. The weariness had passed from the face of the player.

Grant raised himself to see her better. The eyes were closed as if in sleep, her fingers finding the notes with certainty. A rare beauty enriched her pale face. The mouth was upturned in a wistful smile.

Rosa . . . the piano which sang. A rush of memory over four intervening years . . . Rosa, the same glorious hair, the bewitching smile, figure, form, atmosphere. Rosa, his flower bud, the same, yet how different. The little *fraulein* in a widow's house, a faded flower, so pale, playing music which charmed the ear and lacerated the heart. She stifled a cough; it shook her emaciated bosom. She played on, a glorious soft melody which she filled with the shy sweetness of a wild rose—Rosa.

He moved from his chair to sec her more closely. It could not be . . . not the same Rosa. He leant his arms gently upon the piano, his head between his hands. His eyes searched her. He could see now how thin, how drawn, almost haggard she was; the bones in her neck stood out.

His eyes dropped to those skilful hands, fingers of velvet, yet when they conjured a rising crescendo, a torrent of sound, as if forged of bronze. Fingers, on one a ring—diamonds clustering a single ruby. Rosa, his ring. Her eyelids lifted. Her eyes, deep blue, met those of Grant . . . Her fingers trailed from the piano . . . the notes ceased. Frau Muller rose. She crossed to the piano, her hands outstretched. She touched the girl delicately upon the shoulder, kissed her lightly on the brow.

"Thank you, Rosa. Thank you. How happy I am tonight with you and Wilhelm. I will fetch the lamb and prepare a little supper, you will both tonight sup with me. Wilhelm can tell you the story of Ulrich's escape. Then, perhaps, after supper, unless Major Schaefrer must depart—and I have not even asked him where he is staying—we may have a little more music. I am so happy. God is good to me."

Frau Muller moved from the room, a smile of sweet ecstasy upon her face. Grant's mind was in a torment—the plans and . . . Rosa. What to do? He must go, wait in hiding; watch for the departure of Rosa, return upon some pretext, take the papers from the bureau— by diplomacy, by force if necessary. And here was Rosa, his Rosa . . . impossible, yet...

"I cannot trespass further," he stammered, "and my time is so short..." He hurried after Frau Muller into the hall.

Rosa still sat as if in a trance at the piano.

"But you must remain for supper; is that not right, Rosa?"

"Major Schaeffer—will remain," a voice so low as to be almost inaudible was heard from the salon.

"Very well," he said. He stood for a moment in hesitation in the hall. Then slowly he returned to the salon, closing the door behind him.

"Duncan, I felt, I knew it was you. I do not understand. Why are you here? It is for me you have come? I do not understand." A sob shook her frame, ending in a cough which racked her whole body.

Grant moved forward swiftly. He pressed the shaking body to him, buried his face in her hair.

"Rosa, poor Rosa," he murmured.

A hollow cough rent her body. Duncan held her. Her body was limp in his arms, she gasped for breath. Then he looked into her eyes, taking her thin hands in his own. Their eyes met. Years were swept away . . .

It was an evening just such as this, a summer evening, the sun dipping into the sea, painting it a vivid gold. His uncle's home, overlooking the beauty of the loch. The casement windows of the music-room were thrown wide open, revealing a stretch of cool green lawn leading down to the inlet from the Moray Firth in which some boats lay lazily, the idle water rippling gently against their sides. Away across the water lay the purple hills of the Black Isle. They had rambled across the moor and through the pine forests all the afternoon, tea with great scones and cookies with dear old Miss Aitken in Ardesier, then slowly walking back to the home. Three weeks they had been together. Her sweet voice trilled German songs on a Scottish hillside. How she had rejoiced in his knowledge of her country's literature and art . . . the daughter of Graf von Gleiwitz—the name Maurer with which the widow introduced her to him he could not understand.

Then that day he had discovered his love; the serene beauty of her character, the magic of her art, the glory of her beauty enslaved him. So they had wandered back to the great, grey stone house at the water's edge.

His uncle and the children had driven into Inverness. The house was empty. Rosa and Duncan had passed into the music-room. She played with her polished technique—Schubert, Beethoven, Schumann—light and shade with all the emotions, her passion volcanic in Rachmaninoff's Prelude, thunder and lightning; the tenderness of her touch melting the heart in a passage from Beethoven's Sonata Pathetique.

Duncan was leaning over the end of the grand piano, as he had today, feasting his eyes upon her, the rise and fall of her breast, her hair, her sweet almost childish face, the eyes lowered upon the keyboard. Then as she looked up their eyes met—as today. Her face was transfigured in rapture. He could see her now as she was then—Rosa—they had kept their secret for a little while. They had journeyed one day together to Inverness, to hunt for books, and there together, they had chosen a ring, a ruby . . . red, red rose; set in diamonds . . . the dew-drops of purity.

He knelt now beside her, his arms entwined round the poor, thin body. Her fingers played with his hair. "Duncan," she murmured, and bent her head. So they remained for many minutes as the light faded, and a quiet gloom stole softly over the room.

A footstep sounded in the hall, a light flickered under the door which opened. Frau Muller carried an oil lamp in her frail hands. Duncan had moved towards the door.

"Twenty minutes to half an hour, my dears," said the widow, "I am preparing the feast and you can well entertain each other." The spell was broken. Facts must be faced. There was much to tell. Grant must tell the truth. He could trust Rosa. He would not ask her aid. He must tell her . . . everything.

"Rosa, I will tell you my story quickly. You will believe me, I know. I am here in disguise. No one knows. I am seeking information. It is my duty. War is horrible. This war . . . my God! I have a duty. It brought me here. No matter how. In a day or two I shall have gone away again. Then I shall return to our own lines . . . That is all."

There was a pause.

"I can understand," said Rosa slowly . . . "all." There was silence in the little room for a while, then Rosa spoke again.

"You are in danger, every minute, every day. I must aid you, if I can. I know nothing, want to know nothing, of your plans. Perhaps I can help you, not in them," Rosa covered her face with her hands, "but to keep you safe. I have known you were at the front. Every day I pray for you—even now the bell rings for vespers—I pray for you, Duncan. Let me help you. Tell me what I must do."

"Rosa, Rosa, I cannot ask you to help me. You may, perhaps, be of service to this poor widow in her grief."

"Her grief?" she questioned.

"Oh, yes, Ulrich Muller is dead."

"But you have told her . . ."

"I know, I know. That is part of my plan . . . a ruse . . . diplomacy, call it what you will; and . . . it has served her well. Better for her to have this news broken gently than for her to nurse the fears of the unknown, or the shock and anguish of a sudden discovery. He was taken prisoner. He died of wounds on the second of June. I have seen him. He is buried at Neuve Eglise. One day, after I have gone away, you will tell her gently, and tell her also that I am sorrowful. When this war is over I will come to see her, if she will, and will tell her the whole truth. Today, not yet, she must not know. You will do this for me, Rosa."

"I will. Poor little lady . . . she is to me as a mother."

"Rosa, dear, I have waited for this day all these years. I have a little time. Can we not talk? Why did you leave me, my sweet rose ? You loved me, ah . . . how I knew it, but you left me to my sorrow. Four years I have waited and now . . . I want you as before. You remember our hills at Black Isle . . . Rosa," and he knelt again beside her, tenderly stroking her wasted arms and hands.

"But you are ill, Rosa, you have been ill for long. I know. And you toil in the camp. It is not fit; you must leave this work for others. There are plenty of women with nothing to do. Rosa, I implore you, make yourself well. This war will not last for ever. We shall meet afterwards . . . I will take you home. My rose."

"Duncan, I cannot do this. You ask me why I left you. I will tell you. I could not marry you. I was ill. I fought it. There was no cure . . . I cannot live long. That is true, Duncan. I can still serve, so I work where none others will, and where at least I can aid those who need it most.

"So I left you . . . I hoped that you would forget me. I had your memory and your ring. I took the name of Maurer. No one knows, but my sister. She is mother superior in the convent at Santa Maria near Geneva. She sends me the money my father left me in trust. He is dead, and my mother too. So what does it matter? I am Rosa Maurer, the nurse who speaks English and visits the prisoners' camp. I can help there. I have had news of you once, Duncan dear. I was glad. Do not ask me to promise anything. I was content; and . . . now that I have seen you again and felt you near me, I am happy. Dear, dear Duncan. But, Duncan, I must help you. We will leave the house together soon after supper. We may talk a little together then. You will . . ."

"Now come along, my dears, the feast is served. Bring the lamp, Wilhelm. We shall require more light."

Frau Muller seated herself at the head of the table in the high-backed arm-chair, Rosa to her right, Wilhelm at the left. A bowl of freshly-cut roses stood mirrored upon the polished board, old point lace mats supported die dishes. There was a decanter of Rhine wine and tall-stemmed glasses whose iridescence caught the light of the lamp, claiming, too, the delicate tints of the roses. A vegetable soup with mint and flaked cheese opened the feast.

"Pray serve the wine, Wiihelm—Echloss Johanisberg, a rare vintage . . . I seldom take it." She raised her glass, inclining her head first to Rosa and then towards Wilhelm. "Your very good health, my dears."

"God keep you, little mother," Grant smiled at her.

Then he studied Rosa's face. Her lips moved. She sipped her wine, looking deeply at him across the brim of the glass, the colour of whose golden contents fought for mastery with the reflection of her hair.

The widow was in high spirits. She prattled on, of Ulrich, of her home in Bonn. Both Duncan and Rosa were relieved, sunk in their own thoughts—the love that had been and still was, and Duncan with his plans. The dinner was a high success. The soup was followed by a dish of beaten eggs with asparagus tips. The widow would hurry to the kitchen, while Grant reset the table for another course. Then tiny fillets of veal— "the meat was hard to secure"—and then a sponge trifle, spiced and warm with Kirsch. Some strawberries completed the repast.

"You will like to smoke?" asked Frau Muller. His hand went instinctively to his breast pocket—Muller's cigar case! He remembered only just in time.

"I seldom smoke. No, I think not, thank you."

Now to his task; he must cast the die. "Ulrich requested me to bring his plans—his workings from the experiments. I had almost forgotten . . . your kind hospitality makes me forget." He avoided Rosa's eyes. She was looking at him : he felt it, reading his motive. She had detected the purpose of his visit to the little home of Frau Muller.

"Why, of course, but the papers are so many. I have placed them in my bureau. Have you to depart tonight? Perhaps tomorrow; you will come tomorrow as you wish. You may then go through the papers. You will know which relate to his work. Tomorrow." It was, of course, a widow's plea to preserve her joy. She wanted Wilhelm to return. The balm was working wonders. She could not lose Wilhelm so soon.

"Tomorrow morning, Wilhelm ?" she asked.

"Oh, yes, tomorrow will do." He laughed with gaiety, a little forced. Rosa was watching him. "And now, little mother, it is late. I must return to Barmen. I shall like the walk in the cool of the night; and you must rest, little mother. Perhaps I may accompany Fraulein—Maurer to her home."

"We will go now," said Rosa. "It is past nine. It is late for me, and I have my work tomorrow." They rose from the table. "Play to me once more, Rosa," requested the widow, "before you go. I shall like to go to rest with your music in my ears. I am happy, so happy."

They moved to the little salon. Rosa seated herself at the piano. She sighed, closed her eyes, then her fingers sought the keyboard—a refrain from Beethoven's Pastoral Symphony—the sun painting the waters of Moray, red and gold . . . Rosa and Duncan alone in the music-room of the grey stone house . . . distant purple hills.

"Good night, little mother, until tomorrow. Sleep well, and thank you. Good night."

Grant held the door as Rosa passed out beneath the little porch. Then he closed it.

"Rosa," Grant was agitated. "Is it possible for you to see the priest tonight? Tell him to say nothing to Frau Muller. Yes, he knows that Ulrich is dead. He must not see her."

"I know what you have come to seek, Duncan. I will help you. The priest will not see Frau Muller. Take me to his house. I shall not go to the prisoners' camp tomorrow. I do not always go. Sometimes . . . I am not well enough. Tomorrow, they will think I am not well. I shall come to Frau Muller's. Then we will talk.

"Duncan," Rosa grasped him tightly by the arm. "I must help you . . . my Duncan . . . I can help you . . . we will meet tomorrow. Now take me to the priest."

They walked in the darkness of the silent village street, his right arm round her, Rosa's two hands clasping his arm. They reached the priest's house. A light burned in the window.

Grant raised her face to his own. "Good night, my love, my sweet rose." He kissed her lips, a long kiss . . .

"Now go, Duncan." Their hands fell apart. She knocked at the door while Colonel Grant strode on into the night.

The door opened. "Father, I have just left the *Witwe* Muller. The major, Ulrich's friend, was there. I know the truth. He could not tell her then. He will come back tomorrow. He tells me you know of Ulrich's death. Do not see the widow. I pray you. There is time yet for her sorrow. I see her often. I am a woman, and, how well you know it—with my sorrow, too. I can aid her as only a woman can. Then later I will send for you. You may help her with the comforts of Mother Church."

"I understand," said the priest. "You are wise. It is good of his friend. There is always time for bad news. In these days I have carried so many sorrows and there are many sick. You will tell me, *fraulein,* when the poor widow needs my ministration."

"And now, good night, Father . . . I am not so well tonight. I need rest."

"Good night, *fraulein,* do not work too hard. We have need of such sweetness as yours today."

The door closed. Rosa walked slowly to her little apartment at the Stadt Baurat.

Grant paced quickly down the road to Barmen. He lit a cigar . . . and in a moment had cast it away. He must think. His mind was in a whirl . . . his plans . . . his safety . . . his Rosa. A vague uneasiness had settled upon him . . . his thoughts danced and distorted themselves within his mind.

He entered the hotel. The large hall was filled with people, a babel of sound . . . shrieks of forced gaiety coming out of the restaurant. He sat at a little table . . . weary and preoccupied. But he desired conversation . . . He must talk . . . sing . . . shout . . . do anything. He nodded to a heated, over-fed man mopping his brow at a table opposite; then called for a bottle of sparkling hock.

Several women passed him with questioning eyes. Then he observed that older woman whom he had noted at luncheon. An old man, coarse, and a little tipsy, pressed his blandishments upon her boredom. She caught Grant's eye. With a bare apology she left the gross one to his mutterings and his wine and threaded a passage through the crowd to Grant's table. He waved her a seat, called for another glass while he lazily toyed with the scintillating stem of his own. The wine, brilliant in the glare of the lamps, poppled into her glass with beaded bubbles floating and winking at the brim.

"*Prosit! Herr Major* . . . You are on leave?" she queried.

Grant would be cautious. These creatures were everywhere, international, in every capital, in every town, without home or fatherland. They gathered like vultures; money, excitement, and drink to drown their sorrows, to banish the haunting shadow of mother love, a childhood and other happier days. Spies, too, many of them . . . in the pay of both sides . . . the older, the more experienced, the underworld of the diplomatic corps, secret agents. Perhaps this creature was a spy . . . setting a thief to catch a thief . . . What a jest! Perhaps even she intrigued for his own Foreign Office.

"Do not let us talk of the war," parried Grant. "Amuse me; I am bored."

"Poor boy," lisped the harlot, quickly scenting money, the supreme incentive, relapsing to the tawdry of the *maison meublée.* She stretched a smile at him. An effort, Grant noted.

"Staying in the hotel ?" she asked.

"A bird of passage," he said. "Tell me about these people, that old devil who was chucking kisses at you." He refilled her glass.

"Oh, that's Herr Messer, president of the Messer Werke. He's made a pile of money and lost two sons in the early days, killed by the English. Christ!" she chuckled, "you should hear him revile the English. The shock killed his wife . . . that's where I come in. He's hard, though; he won't part with a mark. That's his youngest son, the pale-faced kid with crutches—had his leg shot off in the air—no use for me, a sanctimonious little devil, but tolerates me for dad's sake. He's trying to reform him." She giggled.

"I'd like to have a yarn with the lad," Grant said.

The woman rose and went across to the young officer. Grant beckoned him to come over; then realizing his disability walked over to join the pair. The lieutenant attempted to rise. Grant acknowledged the courtesy, and waving him back drew up a chair. The woman had already seated herself and called for wine. Conversation fell to the war, aerial domination, the spirit of the army, developments. The young man had a keen intelligence. Grant did not particularize. The woman was either bored, or pretending to be so. Finally the possibility of easier money lured her away from a conversation growing too technical to a Herr Messer with the simpler vocabulary of Bacchus.

"My father," indicated Lieutenant Messer, waving his hand towards the woman's companion.

"Poor devil! there are many such. Don't worry too much. You can put that right when this dirty business is over."

"I live with him—I'm the ewe lamb," and he laughed a little. "Poor dad. I'm the only one left. He's got his work. That was fine . . . before war made it too easy for him. Then he lost his sheet anchor—my mother. But you don't want to hear our family troubles?" and he broke off for a moment.

Resuming, he said: "Funny thing, this morning. I get up early . . . force of habit . . . and my leg won't let me sleep much anyhow. I fancied I heard an aeroplane overhead. They come sometimes, and I always have my field glasses handy. I like to see the types of machines . . . improvements and so on. The sound died away going east.

"It was a gorgeous morning, and I sat in my chair marvelling at the changes in the sky and watching the stars go out one by one. My window faces east. I had been there just over half an hour when I heard an aero engine again. It was coming nearer. I got my glasses and hopped to the end of the veranda, and I could see the machine distinctly." He glanced round him, lowered his voice and bent forward. "It was about two miles south, and going in a westerly direction rising all the time. I raised my glasses to obtain a better view. I judged the height then to be about eight thousand feet." His voice sank to a whisper. "It was an English aeroplane, English markings on the under wings, going like the devil. I told dad. He laughed at me. 'Dreams, sonny,' he said, 'just dreams.' But I can swear to it. I know an English machine when I see one . . . My God, I've been in a few dog fights! What do you think, *Herr Major!*"

Grant considered for a moment. So Mayne had been observed! "Very probably you are right, my lieutenant. Strange things happen in war. An English aeroplane perhaps, probably: but have you considered? . . . an English pilot? It was very early in the morning, you say. You should tell no one of what you have seen. Probably a new ruse for observation. An early start keeps the inquisitive in bed . . . like our friend sitting with your father. I never trust that type, but their line is the gossip of beer halls. I suppose it has its value and its price. Take my advice and keep what you have seen to yourself."

"Very good, *Herr Major*. You will excuse me now. I will ask the porter to call dad's chauffeur. I must take him home."

"I, too, will retire." Grant rose and yawned, a little more obviously than good manners would have permitted him, in order to impress the lady.

"Good night, sonny. Don't fret yourself. Look after your father. He will need you. Get well soon." They shook hands. Grant held the lad's hand in his own firm grip, and tightened it as he whispered confidentially: "Remember to keep what you have seen to yourself . . . Goodnight."

Grant moved towards the lift, and, passing the waiter, said: "Waiter—the wine to my account." He must get some ready money. It was awkward. Twenty marks to the woman would make her less inquisitive; a tip to the waiter would keep his tongue from gossip. Rosa—she had offered help. No, he could not take money from her . . . Yes. Rosa. How necessity drives! He went to the lift and straight to his room. He threw off his clothes— Muller's clothes. Thank God . . . clean, new pyjamas: the ecstasy, the purifying of a bath. He jumped into bed, switched off the light—Rosa, sweet music, evening sunlight upon a loch, purple hills, a kiss, Rosa...

* * * * *

Grant awoke, refreshed. It was after eight o'clock. He jumped out of bed, bathed and shaved, and dressed rapidly. He rang for coffee, and drank it, munching rusks as he dressed. He put on the clean underclothes, the others he threw into a drawer. He went straight out, taking the high road again to Hatzberg. He was in high spirits, his step buoyant. Soon he would see Rosa. By half-past ten he had reached the little village. He went straight to the little gate. He knew that from some window Rosa was watching for his approach.

As he walked down the red brick path he called cheerily—" Frau Muller! Good day to you, little mother!"

"Is that yourself, Wilhelm? Come into the salon."

Grant hung up his cap : then crossed the hall to the salon. Frau Muller rose from the table which she had cleared and set in the window. It was covered with documents, some tied with tape, others piled with brass ornaments set as weights to prevent the breeze from the window disturbing them. The widow came across to him, raising her hands which she placed on his shoulders. She raised her face to him affectionately. He kissed her brow lightly. She clung to him and buried her head on his bosom. She wept a little. Grant felt a sharp pang of embarrassment. He had made up his mind to keep sentiment at arm's length. His duty summoned him to a different task . . . a little diplomacy, all that was necessary . . . and he had much to do. He felt an impatience, but he must be tolerant of the widow.

"There . . . there . . . little mother. Now let us look at the papers."

"I have them all here. I used to collect them into bundles for Ulrich, and after he had gone, I carefully put them altogether. See, I have set them out upon this table, just as I did for Ulrich. I can explain when you wish. In this bundle are the markings upon the W Plan." She laughed a little: "Inverted M, I should say. You will find the plans complete. Ulrich went through them: these he wished to use in his work after the war. In this pile are the results of his week's experiments with the prisoners at Elberfeld : you will find these also complete. Here tied in the green ribbon are the results of his tests with various explosives.

"I do not understand these things, but they concern, I think, the different charges, angle of laying and density of soil to be blown. In this pile you will find a number of maps of the front with some notes; and here in this roll tied with the red ribbon is the model of the W. Plan. There are two maps.

"Among these papers are the notes which he made towards the end . . . they are not complete. Ulrich took his notes with him," she smiled. "And now I will leave you for a while. You are familiar with the subject and will be able to go through the papers and select what you and Ulrich will require from them. You will stay to lunch. I will see to this and go about my household duties."

Grant seated himself before the papers. He was no engineer. This was a large task even for one with high technical qualifications. First he would rapidly examine each bundle. He selected the maps, the easiest task. With topographical plans he was familiar. He unrolled them. One was a large scale map of the whole front upon which was pasted a transparent plan. The transparency bore fine black lines in the form of almost regular trellis work, broad at one end, narrowing down to two points. At the points of the trellis on the wider end were red spots. Grant pressed the transparency down upon the map and read.

The network covered a front of some fifteen miles—Poperinghe, Abeele, Flêtre, Strazeele, the River Lys. A number of lines crossed and recrossed the tracery to which there was a key at the foot of the map. Muller, reflected Grant, was captured at Scottish Wood, just east of Dickebusch. This was important. He turned to the other map. It was a large scale repetition of the former, masses of figures, a time table, many more lines drawn direct upon the map, but all conforming in general plan to the trellis tracery. He rolled them up, but as he did so the triangles of the tracery remained in his mind's eye—a series of W's.

He rapidly unrolled again the second plan. Quite plain, the letter W, intersected, one after the other, conforming to a definite plan. Inverted M . . . Grant chuckled with joy. He tied up the maps and put them on one side. He took up the bundle tied with green tape. He slipped off the ribbon and rapidly turned over the papers. Charge I, Charge 2, and so on, many of them detailed workings: lower down, instructions to engineer in charge of Section 1, 2, 3. He counted seven of these. At the bottom some plans in pencil referring to charges showing the angles, charges required, time schedule of detonations. The plans were in Section, each one conforming to the shibboleth . . . W. He would examine these later.

So it was, of course it was, a mining plan on a large scale. Ypres to the Lys. But what the hell for? That didn't get the Germans very far. After all, we blew a few mines at Fricourt to open the Somme break-through. What a fiasco! . . . held up at High Wood after fifteen days, and bogged at Les Boeufs up to the present day! Anyhow it was interesting, but nothing yet to cause G.H.Q. to become unduly agitated.

He selected another dossier—experiments with prisoners at Elberfeld. This was quite straightforward. The papers were pinned together, first day, second, third, fourth, and fifth. He looked over the first day : two hundred and fifty men, task of digging and clearing a shaft and laying narrow gauge rail track; cleared X tons of soil from shaft. Another calculation showed a time schedule using the Messer excavator and single track running gear. Only forty men used in the shaft, the balance utilized for emptying track wagons, except for trained miners employed in propping the shafts.

He rapidly glanced at the fifth day's workings—Messer excavator used almost entirely. Large numbers of men employed on emptying wagons and removing soil from endless winding gear . . . miners engaged on expert work. "Scottish the best workmen and well disciplined" was a note which met his eye. Hell! the native genius of his race and the discipline which he himself had helped to inculcate being utilized in some foul scheme against his own country. Grant's pulse quickened with excitement and indignation.

He was collecting and putting aside the papers when his eye fell on a single sheet of foolscap not attached to the rest—the names and addresses of a number of women. Dear Ulrich had been careless, reflected Grant. Mother wouldn't like this little list—but where had he seen a list like this before? . . . Ulrich's pocket book! He whipped it out of his breast pocket, ran through the pages. Emilie Gartner, Malapaner Strasse 15, Breslau. The same upon the foolscap. The names and addresses in the notebook tallied exactly with those on the foolscap. Well, he wouldn't require evidence twice, and the mother wouldn't like it. He folded the foolscap, and placed it in his breast pocket, replacing Muller's book.

He then took up the first pile of papers which Frau Muller had indicated as the completed plans. They revealed an analysis of the experiments with prisoners and with the Messer excavator.

Messer! how stupid not to think of it before . . . the bloated old man at the hotel! That is how he made his pile. Grant wondered how much his mistress knew. At any rate, she hadn't made much use of her knowledge. The Foreign Office hadn't an idea. Perhaps she was only in the stage of finding out. She complained the old man was hard . . . perhaps even tighter and shrewder with his secrets—business instinct, even ex alcohol—than with his profits. However, he wouldn't need the papers, a bulky lot, relating to the experiments with prisoners. "Scottish the best workers, well disciplined." That stuck in his throat! However, here was a summary. The plan, the Messer excavator with prisoners to be employed . . . the W Plan—vertical and horizontal—time schedules, storm troop concentration in short galleries, mine charges, excavations by Mont Kemmel and Steenwerk.

Grant pondered the situation as he had left it . . . no wonder the Boche fought like cats at Kemmel and pushed the French out at the end of April! "The first among all causes of victory," says Clausewitz, "is to pursue a great object with energy and perseverance." Germany needed, must have, Mont Kemmel at any price—the backbone of the W Plan. He turned to re-examine the papers. The plan was taking shape in his mind. He must take away these papers and study them. He reached again for the maps of the W Plan.

Deep in reflection, he had not heard the step of Rosa. She entered quietly. Grant glanced up from his work. Rosa . . . God, how ill she looked, but how beautiful! He caught a sob, and hurried to her. A feeling of great pity swept over him. He clasped her to him. Then he coloured with shame. She had seen his work, his treachery to the widow. Rosa knew what was passing through Duncan's mind.

"My dear," she said. "I knew what your work would be. I have come to help, if I can. I have told them at my apartment that I am going away for a little rest. I am free to do your bidding. If you have nothing for me to do, if you cannot, will not, use me,

I will sit here. Shall I play to you? . . . but I want to help you. Duncan, say I may. Tell me how I can help you."

Duncan placed her in an arm-chair and seated himself upon its arm.

"Rosa, I do not want you to help me. Perhaps your aid might soil our love. I have my duty. It is not a woman's work . . . not women of your type. I want as clear a conscience as I can have. The war has already sufficiently degraded my instincts, my sense of honour. That is a duty—right or wrong, it is not my part to question —but our love is apart."

"My dear, if I cannot aid you now when you may need my help most, of what use is our love? Remember I abandoned it once." A cough racked her. "Duncan," tears welled to her eyes, "let me help you."

"Rosa, this is a sordid business. It will defile the purity of your nature . . . I have nearly completed my plans; but . . . there is still much to do . . . and so little time..." He paused and regarded her searchingly. "If you wish it, Rosa . . . yes . . . you can help me."

"I do wish it, Duncan," she replied earnestly, the colour flooding her face and neck, and then very quietly she sighed : "For better or worse, Duncan. Can't I give myself to you, dear . . . feel you close to me . . . replenish these barren years of your life . . . and of mine . . . Duncan. I am yours . . . do with me what you will..." She looked up into his face . . . "I need you, dearest. Give to me your love . . . As your wife I may help you, as Rosa von Gleiwitz, I cannot."

Duncan relinquished his hold of her, stepped back, and regarded her. After many moments he spoke: "Rosa . . . you have my love . . . as my wife you shall help me . . . We can go to Barmen this afternoon. We will go to the hotel. You can veil yourself. I will explain later. And, Rosa," he laughed, "what a confession! . . . I have no money, not a blessed mark. Bring all the money you can."

Rosa smiled. They kissed. "Now get on with your work, Duncan. I will play to you for ten minutes—Mendelssohn, the Wedding March." She seated herself at the piano and struck the first chords.

Frau Muller entered. "Why, Rosa, I did not hear you come in. I am preparing luncheon. You play . . . how delightful . . . but why the Wedding March?"

Rosa continued to play, and smiled at the widow wistfully.

"You can keep a secret, little mother. Wilhelm and I are old very old friends."

"Wilhelm?" A look of astonishment crossed the widow's face.

The march swept on to a triumphal end. The last chords seemed to quiver and vibrate for a moment about those in the room . . . then faded away.

"You will bless us, little mother," said Rosa. "We shall need your blessing." Frau Muller sank upon her knees, her head buried in the cushions of the settee. Her frail body shook. Intense emotion swept her...

"Dear little lady," said Grant, as he bent over her, "it is true: but Rosa will return to you. You two will comfort each other."

When the echo of the last notes had died away, Frau Muller joined the hands of the two lovers, kissed them, and then bustled away again to the kitchen. "Another feast, Rosa and Wilhelm."

"It is a secret, little mother," Grant called after her. "Now, Rosa, go quickly, and prepare."

With heightened colour, the light of happiness in her eyes, and buoyancy in her step, she waved him farewell.

Duncan gazed from the window until she had passed out of sight, then turned again to his task. It was nearly completed. He gathered together the files, discarding one pile and some odd papers; parcelled and tied them up in a large piece of paper which Frau Muller had thoughtfully provided for the purpose. Then he wandered into the little back garden, and lit a cigar.

It was just past noon. He must reflect. It would take him time to go through the papers, to study the technique of the operations planned. He must take them to some quiet spot, master them, and then go to the front area and discover what was being done. There might not be much time: he must allow, too, for accidents. Eight days in hand : then he must return to Barmen and slip away at dawn with Mayne. He had the plans, he would take no unnecessary risks, but he must assure himself that they were being operated. The facts were of vital importance. The wits of one general were being pitted against those of another. Colonel Grant's task would utilize all his skill, his resources, reserves, mental and physical. He was a spy—more often than not a title to which stigma and dishonour are attached.

But the profession of espionage probably demands more varied attainments, harder work and greater courage than any other. The physician not only has the whole-hearted co-operation of his patient, but suffers no penalty for error: the barrister, however unskilfully he may conduct his case, enjoys the protection of the law and cheerfully collects his fee : the soldier has the support of the nation; the clergy the privilege of their cloth; the business man the backing of the bank: while even the journalist is entrenched and camouflaged in an anonymity.

But the spy has no protection, no privileges, no entrenchments, no cover. He spends every hour of his existence in launching the attack, and from the moment he shows his head he is liable to attack. He is bombarded from front and rear, he is enfiladed and walks between fires. He is eternally committed to the offensive. For him there is no retreat, he must advance or perish. He must be a linguist of the first order. He must be forceful yet persuasive, both simple and subtle. He must be an advocate, a logician and a diplomat. He must be as versatile as a politician and as consistent as tempered steel. He must be a judge of form, of colour, and have a ripe knowledge of human nature. He must possess a fighting instinct, and he must have invincible courage. He must be opportunist, tactician, strategist. He must be confident and he must be cheerful, and he must have the saving grace of humour, but he must be neither a braggart nor a buffoon. He must be dogged, yet never dogmatic. He must be an optimist, but he must not inhabit a fool's paradise. To sum up he must be a metaphysician, psychologist and philosopher, in a word both Man and Superman.

The province of an Intelligence Service is sufficiently wide to embrace the whole earth, and engage the whole life, experience and knowledge of the spy. It demands the complete surrender of every social and diplomatic quality he may possess. It demands every moment of his conscious hours, for the born spy is he who from dawn to dark—and long after—each hour and each day, whether of work or leisure, keeps his mind receptive to every impression, every thought, every chance human contact which may add conviction to his argument, supply the missing link in a chain of evidence. If he does this successfully he has found the Philosopher's Stone. But always he must be alone. Every man's hand is against him. He is fearful of substance and of shadow. He has no friends, but everywhere enemies, alone, always alone.

Grant passed slowly up and down the little garden path. He smiled to himself; he laughed aloud; he inhaled the air deeply; his heart was pulsating; he dug his hands deeper and deeper into his pockets and slapped his thighs with delight; he was almost in a seventh heaven, if there be such a thing: he felt almost overcome with exhilaration; he wanted to shout aloud like the Greek philosopher in his bath—Eureka! . . . he had found the Philosopher's Stone.

Rosa and the plans, the plans and Rosa.

He discovered himself humming the words to the first odd ragtime ditty which escaped from the maelstrom of his mind. Life was good, extraordinarily good; he possessed everything he wanted in the world. He thrilled with excitement when he thought of leaving with Rosa that very afternoon. Here, indeed, was romance!

He perceived Rosa through the casement windows. She had returned, a smile of triumph on her lips. Grant called to her softly and she came into the garden. Then came Frau Muller—luncheon was ready. Rose petals had been strewn upon the table. The little party was silent, each preoccupied with thought. Frau Muller would weep a little, then gaily apologize. Little justice was done to the dexterity and industry of Frau Muller's feast. They went into the salon. Rosa played again, happily and lightly.

Then the widow kissed them both affectionately; and secretly to live as husband and wife they left the little village of Hatzberg on the road to Barmen.

4

MEN LIKE MOLES

"DUNCAN, dear, we must send the announcement to *The Times*. All the best people do that," exclaimed Rosa with that old gaiety which Grant remembered so well.

"And, Rosa, we're going to talk home language for just one little hour. My grandfather always used to tell his London friends that the Inverness cabmen speak better English than Mr Balfour or Lord Rosebery. We'll talk the best English—from Scotland. And now for your announcement. What is it to be ?"

"Here we are," cried Rosa, "listen! The betrothal is announced between Lieutenant-Colonel Duncan Grant, Inverness Highlanders, only son of General Ian Grant of Culbokie, and Rosa, daughter of the late Graf von Gleiwitz."

They laughed together, and then leaving the high road crossed to a pine copse upon a little knoll overlooking Barmen.

"And now, Duncan, the help you need. That must come first. Let us discuss your plans and tell me what I can do."

Grant told the bare story of Ulrich Muller, of his flight and of the landing at Viersberg. And then he told her of the hotel clerk.

"Suppose," he said, "I had told him I shall be joined by my wife, would he have believed me? I doubt it. But all will be ready for us. And you have married a penniless—markless—man.

I shall need money. It silences the curious, and gives freedom from anxiety."

"I have brought six hundred marks."

Grant was silent for a moment. "Rosa," he said, "Rosa . . . how good of you." Then he laughed. "I was anxious about the hotel bill. Suspicion would be aroused if I left without paying it. A young lieutenant, Messer, son of Messer, the steel magnate, knows that a British aeroplane was over Barmen on the fifth. I advised him to tell no one. But there might be a hue and cry. Things would move quickly. Muller—who was Muller? . . . from Hatzberg. But no, surely he was reported missing. And Major Schaeffer, who was he? Answering to the description of Muller of the Hotel Imperial. Whence did he come? Who was he? Rosa, how I have needed your help! But you, too, are in danger, great danger. Rosa, dear, I hadn't thought of it. Rosa Maurer and Wilhelm Schaeffer. Who is this Schaeffer? Suppose questions are asked? We must think this out together. I have asked too much of you, Rosa, dear."

"Silly one, do you think I had not thought of this ? I wanted to share your danger, your life. Why not ? And there are many ways. But you will leave Barmen without suspicion. And," she added wistfully, "we will go—together, you and I, for a little while. We cannot remain in the hotel."

"We will go tomorrow. I must read through these papers carefully as soon as we reach Barmen. Then I will plan for the future. There is much to do. This will not be too much strain for you, dear ? Take my arm now. We will take the tramway at the Quellen Strasse to the Neumarkt. You have your veil; you can cover yourself before we enter the hotel, and we will go straight to my room. Then we will plan. Now we will talk of ourselves."

"I remember reading somewhere," said Rosa :

"'Greater than my need of thee
Greater than my misery
Greater than Eternity
My love of thee! '"

She sighed. He pressed her closely to him. "My beloved, I have almost learned to bless the hour you left me. If I have lived alone for this hour, I am happy—Rosa." He kissed her lips.

Then with her arm pressed lightly upon his, they walked slowly through the wooded way to the outskirts of the town.

A short rest upon a seat; and then came the rattling tramcar, filled with workmen and girls. They made way respectfully for the officer and his lady. They had no bitterness towards the man from the front and the lady, so delicate, pale and beautiful. With good humour they exchanged jests. At the Neumarkt, Duncan and Rosa alighted. Rosa drew the veil, one of thick buff lace, over her face, then took Duncan's arm and they walked across the square to the hotel. It was after five o'clock. A few were drinking beer and wine, but the lounge was almost deserted. He drew up a chair for Rosa.

"I will tell the clerk that my wife has arrived. She is tired after her journey; we will dine in our room, perhaps, later. That will give us several hours, undisturbed for work." He strolled across to the reception desk. The clerk received his message with an ill-concealed smirk. Grant felt a strong desire to strike the man; but he forced a smile. He must comply with war's convention and licentiousness . . . nay, more, and he passed ten marks across the desk . . . After all, the clerk had anticipated it and Major Muller had readily accepted the suggestion. Rosa and Duncan went to room No. 23. He turned the key.

"Now we will make ourselves comfortable." He took her hat and coat and threw off his tunic. Then he drew out the table, placed two chairs, and unwrapped his parcel.

"Here are all the plans. I must completely master these tonight. Will you take notes—in German—in this pocket book? It was Muller's."

For two . . . three hours . . . more . . . with scarcely a word exchanged between them . . . Grant re-examined the plans, charts, schedules and maps. Rosa helped him by making an occasional note and by rearranging the papers.

And this is a summary of the plan as Grant discovered it and realized it. Every German effort to break through the cordon of steel around the frontiers had suffered defeat. The Germans had struck through Russia and Italy. They were thwarted. The effort to strangle Belgium and Romania both by invasion and with every diplomatic artifice, with the object of disrupting the allies, of weakening the blockade, and of creating difficulties in the eastern theatre of war, had failed. Money, men, experts had been poured into Asia Minor in order to create a diversion, without success. It is true that a treaty of little value to Germany had been signed with revolutionary Russia. Doom had overtaken the depravity of a sunken nation, and Russia was in every consequence no ally for a Germany fighting for its very national existence. Rather was the treaty of Brest Litovsk a dangerous, insidious drug, though it might temporarily relieve German pain.

The two main theatres of war were in the East—Russia . . . that was disposed of; and, in the West—England, the French and Belgians on a front of over two hundred miles. The French were weakened : men spoke of mutiny, of wholesale desertion. Belgium was invested, her army infinitesimal. America had declared upon the side of the Allies; the first troops, raw, untried, led by inexperience were already coming into the line. England stood firm, though weakened, with a growing political faction clamouring for peace.

The offensive at Verdun, fought with matchless gallantry on both sides, had been broken by the stubborn, heroic defence of the French —"They shall not pass!" cried Marshal Foch, with courage unquenchable, great in leadership . . . The massed assaults against the British in bitter fighting had been checked before the Belgian hills—the jagged tower of the Ypres Cloth Hall still kept its eastern watch. The British, stubborn as their mules in defence, vigorous and fierce in attack, were yet unconquered and as unconquerable as had been the "Contemptible Little Army."

The Allies were girding their loins. Germany must act. To break the English lines and gain sight of the Channel ports . . . that was the supreme task, the final, the only objective. Unless England were broken, the Allies on the Western front divided, the doom of Germany was sealed.

Germany must make a discovery. The Imperial State and its commanders must summon to its council any who could help solve the insoluble riddle—statesmen and diplomats; military, naval and air chiefs. The plans of the strategist are determined by diplomacy and where strategy ends, tactics begin. The silver threads of continuity of strategic and diplomatic purpose runs throughout a campaign, drawing in its train not only commanders-in-chief but all subordinate leaders.

Therefore had the English front received the deepest consideration. The line from north to south ran through from the ghastly Passchendaele salient, thence east of Mont Kemmel, through Méteren and Merris, crossing the River Lys by Merville, then Givenchy and Cambrin, west of Béthune to the battlefields beside Arras, and farther south through the wastes of the Somme fighting, with Bapaume and Peronne as names to mark the debris. No especial tactical advantage lay with either side except at Mont Kemmel. Here the Germans by a supreme effort, with extraordinary tenacity of purpose and heroic courage, had wrested this dominating hill from the French.

The tactical advantages lay with Germany. The British defences and communications were overlooked for miles. Mont Kemmel was a vantage point of immense value, and the king-pin of the tactical and strategic position. The breaking of the English line on a sufficiently wide front at this point, would imperil the Channel ports, would gravely interrupt the main line of communication and supplies, and followed resolutely would throw the English back upon the Channel and drive a wedge between them and their French Allies. This was the task.

A plan had, therefore, been formulated by the chief engineer to undermine the English lines by a series of galleries on a wide front and to force a passage for the storm troops. That was the genesis of the idea. To accomplish this practically was a different matter. This task appeared a superhuman feat, involving the construction of a vast number of galleries several miles long, the concentration of great numbers of troops below ground probably for many days, the draining of a wide area, the surface of which in great part was permanently a swamp.

The foremost engineers of Germany had been summoned in conference. Ulrich Muller, engineer from the Bismarkhütte, and recently appointed as a chief engineer at Dusseldorf, had been included. Alone he had said that the project was possible. The time factor was his difficulty. He was prepared to stake—the older engineers had laughed—his young reputation upon it. More, for that was of little importance, his plans were fully prepared.

Ulrich Muller had recently thrown out some experimental shafts at the Bismarkhütte with the object of penetrating the rich and so far unmined coal seams of Kreis Pless. His object had been to utilize the existing organization, elevators, railway power, sorting screens, administration, welfare establishments at the pit head, and bring coal by mechanical process, five, possibly even thirty miles underground by a new process and method of shaft sinking, drainage, ventilation and haulage. He had tested all the necessary apparatus over two or three years of arduous work and the whole of the working plans and experiments had been reduced to a series of formulae to which he had, for lack of any other comprehensive term, given the name of the W Plan. The project of the chief engineer could be accomplished. It would take some three months to prepare; but, granted the necessary skilled labour, unlimited resources in machinery and a free hand, Muller declared definitely that the project could be carried out in its entirety. These facts were briefly stated in the notes. The scheme was accepted. Muller was provided with a week in which to finalize his plans. Thus the project took shape.

Two shafts were to be sunk just east of the Mont Kemmel group of hills. Galleries were then to be thrown forward undermining the British lines on a front of fifteen miles and penetrating westwards for eight miles. The galleries were to be so constructed that large numbers of men, artillery, ammunition, supplies, could be concentrated in them. Drainage was carefully provided. The galleries ended with long arms reaching obliquely across the lines, and finally quitting their depth terminating near the surface, while throughout they were connected with each other by a series of shorter galleries thrown also obliquely and almost at right angles to the main gallery, meeting each other at a right angle bend, part of which thrust towards the enemy lines westwards.

Thus did the general concept in plan conform to a series of the letter W, linked together by and at the extremities of the outer arms.

Underneath the main galleries, which ran horizontally east and west, were constructed another series of galleries conforming exactly in dimension to those above, and connected with the upper tunnels by yet another series of similar shafts thrown vertically downwards, but conforming always to the W Plan. This was the trellis work plan which Grant had noted.

Troops, ammunition, guns were to be concentrated in those galleries which formed the angle connecting the two long arms of the letter, the latter being kept clear as roadways to permit the different arms and services to be hurried forward as required, in conformation with the battle plan.

Where the long arms terminated to the west, penetrating far behind the British lines of organized defence, namely the last line of entrenchment, and concrete strong points, a series of mines was shown each of which was connected by electric cable with a point central in the trellis work. The mines would be blown, and in their craters machine-gun strongholds would immediately be established to cover with enfilade crossing fire the deployment of the hidden troops from the points formed by the angles between the two connecting arms. The main arms of the upper system, which in series formed continuous roads converging to a central point of communication and control, would then be utilized for the rapid transit of artillery, wagons and stores, while the intersecting angle arms would be used for the passage of infantry and cavalry.

The main arms of the lower system would be similarly used, but with reserve troops consisting for the most part of armoured cars brought from the Russian front and light troops, whose objective would be to sever the lines of communications running south from the Channel ports through Bailleul, Arras, Amiens, and to capture the Channel ports.

The vertical section was to provide a system of rapid and easy lateral communication, while the angle of slope was so arranged that troops, mounted and dismounted, could pass from one section of galleries to another, utilizing the short angle roadways without interrupting the progress of the westward traffic along the main arms.

The scheme was one of astonishing ingenuity. Nothing had been overlooked. Every detail had been carefully worked out with mathematical precision. From the minute that the mines were blown a steady passage of men would begin to defile from behind the main British lines—horse, foot and guns—an army complete, a whole expeditionary force coming like moles from underground. The plan was made possible by the utilization of the Messer excavator and single-track, endless winding gear, capable of mining and clearing thousands of tons of soil every hour. An additional contrivance was arranged for the automatic erection of props to secure the roof and sides of the galleries, but here the plan required the eye of an expert. The angles of the W system—and as a harmony much depended upon angle—

provided for the blowing of the craters as the means of exit, while a further series of much smaller W galleries constructed at the extremities of the long arms would prevent blow back and provide safety for the hosts secreted in the galleries.

The necessity to success, as in every other military operation, was secrecy—a secrecy which must be preserved for two, possibly three, months. Elaborate precautions had, therefore, been taken to ensure that the work should be carried out so that a leakage of information was impossible. The troops in the line, at that time the 31st Division from the Rhineland Province, were relieved by a whole corps of Jägers, troops tried, dependable, with the highest fighting reputation. The number of rifles in the front and support lines was trebled in order to defend them against enemy operations which might be designed on a minor scale to improve his tactical position. The most urgent orders were conveyed to local commanders to suppress all raids with the utmost energy, and in any case to prevent them penetrating through the support lines.

The Jäger Corps consisted of three divisions. Two of these were placed in the front lines. All leave, even of the most urgent nature, was stopped. Generals of brigade, even the divisional commander and his staff, were placed in the forward area, and west of the heads of the shafts. The division in reserve was placed in a wire enclosure at Courtrai; while thick wire entanglements were thrown out from west to east on both sides of the sector and enclosed in the rear, so that the divisions in the line were equally shut off from outside communication.

An order was published declaring that the Jäger Corps had been specially selected for intensive training and as an iron example to the nation, the object being to promote the will-to-win spirit through the armies. The overthrow of the Russians on the eastern front was, with a purpose, stressed. This order was cleverly conceived and cunningly phrased with the object of diverting suspicion, and it was allowed to fall into enemy hands and into those of any persons suspected of Allied sympathies. It had the further object of discouraging British raids upon the sector, since the name of the corps and the intention was stated, while a raid upon a sector so strongly held would hardly invite an enemy anxiously conserving its man power. The corps responsible for holding the front would, therefore, have no knowledge of the mining operation proceeding in its rear, while the internal relief of the divisions could be carried out without fear of secrets being revealed to an inquisitive population with no sympathy with its invaders.

Instructions had been issued to the officers commanding prisoners' camps to select all miners from the ranks of ordinary soldiers of whatever nationality and dispatch them without delay to Mors, the centre of the Lower Rhenish coalfield. It would be assumed that the miners were to be utilized in coal production. The Guard Grenadier Regiment was dispatched to Mors and a cordon placed round the railway station.

The prisoners in large batches with interpreters were herded into covered wagons as soon as they reached Mors, strong guards placed in charge of each wagon and train loads dispatched to Menin. After each train load reached a point in the open country some twenty miles from Mors, it was halted, and the prisoners were served out with fresh clothing and the uniform of the Reichswehr. Any who showed truculence or refused were instantly shot by the guards. A staff formed from the Intelligence Service was placed in command of the camp, and dummy orders were formulated and promulgated daily to allay suspicion. The formation, consisting of nearly ten thousand men—British, French, Italians, Belgians, Poles, Russians— was designated the 15th Composite Reichswehr Division.

In addition, any German soldiers under sentence of death for desertion or mutiny were dispatched to this camp for work to remove them wholly from their comrades, but to conserve a depleted man power. Indents for rations, supplies, clothing and all the varied requirements of a large body of men under active service conditions bore this nomenclature.

A double barbed wire entanglement, electrified, was thrown up round the camp, and the Guard Grenadier Regiment gradually transferred with each train load to prevent the individual escape or mutiny of any of the prisoners. Upon arrival they were formed into battalions and companies by their nationality and an interpreter placed in charge of each group.

Thus was quietly and with the utmost secrecy formed a division of miners from prisoners of war for the purpose of constructing the W breach. Rigid orders were issued that any attempt to communicate, or any speech with any person outside the confines of the camp would be met with instant death without the formality of court martial.

The camp itself was well furnished and equipped—a large canteen, tobacco, a daily ration of wine, musical instruments, gramophones, reading matter in various languages, good food. The General Staff exercised every ingenuity to promote bodily well-being and mental satisfaction. With the exception of the orders as to communication and the strictest obedience the men were accorded the utmost licence. *Pro formae* of the orders were included in the notes.

Grant marvelled at the comprehensiveness of the scheme, its thoroughness, its ingenuity. As a military operation, albeit, without doubt, a flagrant breach of International Law, it was a masterpiece. And as to Hague Conventions . . . an eye for an eye, a tooth for a tooth!

The experiments at Elberfeld demonstrated that this vast work could be accomplished in sixty-eight days. Muller had allowed a further week in case of accidents or any hitch in the provision of the necessary machinery. But the date must be reckoned from the capture of Mont Kemmel and its surrounding hills. Grant was able, therefore, to determine how far the work had proceeded, it being assumed that it had already commenced.

He remembered the fierce fighting for Mont Kemmel. The French Chasseurs d'Alpin, picked troops, were thrown back, and the Germans established themselves well to the west, their posts being thrust out into the half water-logged country, a feature of which is the Dickebusch Lake. That was on the twenty-eighth of April. He might assume that it would require a week at least before operations could commence, though in the quiet lull on both sides which followed the fury of the battles of the Lys in March and April, an enemy ready to commit itself to an operation behind the battle area could quickly and without fear of interruption put it into operation. He might assume, therefore, that mining had commenced about the fourth of May. He rapidly figured . . . all would, therefore, be ready by the first week in August, possibly as late as the sixth.

The plan provided, also, that drainage of the galleries would be accomplished by the sinking of further vertical W-shaped shafts below the second tier of galleries ending in deep sumps. The water level would be retained below the apex of the letter, preventing a flow back, and a subsidiary system by utilizing the Speyer method of rapid absorption with tranium. Vast quantities of earth, hundreds of thousands of tons, were to be excavated. It was arranged that this would be automatically unloaded and spread on the slopes of the main hills. The fact of the hills and their irregular topography would prevent detection of the increasing elevation, while by a careful spread of the excavations they would not be observed obliquely by aerial observation. The air defence by day over the whole of the British front was strengthened so that it would predominate in order to prevent low flying observation.

The whole of the Seventh Army from the Russian front was to be dispatched to Mons for special training, refitting, equipment.

The general plan of the staff provided then that orders were to be issued to these corps to concentrate ten days prior to X day in the Forêt de Mormal, east of Maubeuge. Dummy arrangements were to be made for their reception, billeting, and the skeleton move. Advanced troops, a few men from every formation, would be dispatched and the Intelligence Staff arrange that the civilian inhabitants and the troops occupying the Peronne sector be well informed, so that with all necessary speed the enemy would obtain knowledge of the concentration.

It was plain that the purpose was to draw suspicion from the Ypres-Lys sector farther south to the Somme, and to encourage the concentration of British reserves in that area. The operation of the W Plan would, furthermore, separate these reserves from their main bases at Dieppe, Boulogne, Calais, Dunkirk. The forest of Mormal itself and its scattered valleys would prevent observation. Similarly, orders were to be issued to the Third Army occupying the front between the Rivers Scarpe and the Somme to strike towards Amiens as the objective, as a feint to weaken the British front and reserves in the Ypres area. The British would conceive that an attack on a very large scale by two armies was intended to drive a wedge between them and their French allies as had been previously attempted and had so nearly succeeded. The French would be drawn to meet this threat, acting upon British information, and then the dramatic discovery of its falseness would, without doubt, give reality to the whispered dissensions between the Allies.

Muller's function was simple—to provide the necessary galleries and shafts—the technique of the engineering plan. The notes were the strategic and tactical elaboration of the General Staff, utilizing the W Plan as the fulcrum of a general campaign. But the plan was perfectly clear : nor was Grant concerned with the more intricate details of the installations of Messer equipment and of Speyer absorption.

The plan was almost diabolical in its conception and thoroughness. That it would succeed, Grant had not the least shadow of doubt. That if it were carried through, it would certainly overthrow the British and destroy for ever the Allied cause he could at once understand.

He selected the essential plans and notes—now reduced to very few. He re-examined the maps. He noticed what he had not previously noted, namely, that each rectangle formed by the trellis was numbered. These numbers were keyed at the foot of the map and against each number was the name of a town. The red points at the tips of the long arms—now known to be the main galleries and exits and the positions of the mines—were lettered, not in sequence, but, as it appeared, haphazard. He ran his eye over the list of towns then quickly took from his vest pocket the list of names which he had placed there to keep them from Frau Muller's eyes. The names tallied—Berlin, Dusseldorf, Coblenz, Worms, Stuttgart and so on.

He read the names over carefully, checking them with any lettering which might appear on the map. The letters at the red points were similar to those of the initial letters of the ladies' names. The initial letter of the name of the street conformed to a letter denoting a main arm gallery running south-west—M.R.B.H.N.V.—and the final letter denoting one running north-west—B.F.M.A.K.C. It was a simple code.

Muller had copied it into his notebook obviously to refresh his memory as he supervised the progress of the plan, and had coded it in this simple fashion for security. The code had been safe enough . . . up to this moment, it had expressed nothing more to Grant than a list conveniently to be forgotten, and, in any case, to be hidden from its author's mother.

Each complete rectangle in the trellis was numbered in sequence, but there were other numbers, namely, those in the list of addresses . . . what of them? For example, Malapaner Strasse, 14 . . . Fraulein Emilie Gartner, Malapaner Strasse, 14. That was the rectangle on the extreme left . . . Emilie . . . E.—that indicated the culmination of the first mine at the end of the main gallery . . . *Malapaner*—M showed the main gallery from the shaft to the end, and R, another gallery for troops and communication culminating at O, the apex to be utilized for the first exit of storm troops. The street numbers would indicate complete sections.

Grant re-examined the plan carefully, and it was clear to him that three or four of the galleries, together with the connecting angles, by now were complete.

It was already past nine o'clock. Grant's immediate work was finished.

The element of surprise is the keystone of success. Thus, the scheme in its entirety was a masterpiece, a supreme combination of all the forces contributing to striking power—infantry, artillery, cavalry, engineers, transport, the air, the mine, mechanics, chemistry. It was a plan proceeding from great generalship similar in its essential character of surprise to Napoleon's passage of the Alps before Marengo; Lee's flank and rear attack at Chancellorsville, Marlborough's march to the Danube before Blenheim. War, Grant recalled, is "first and foremost a matter of movement." Great God! The Germans were about to give a practical demonstration of that principle. Afterwards "War is a matter of supply, destruction and well-organized co-operation against a definite objective." The stagnation of the western front was to be ended. Germany intended war, and one which fully complied with every canon and precept of its science.

Grant rose and stretched himself.

"Rosa, dearest, I had forgotten you. We have had nothing to eat since lunch time, and then neither of us ate anything at all. You must be famished. I will place all the papers inside my tunic and we will go to a little restaurant away from this hotel and have dinner."

They went out, Rosa veiled as before. Grant observed that their exit was followed by the jealous eyes of the harpy. He waved a sign of recognition to Lieutenant Messer, who was seated with his father and a group of friends.

"Tomorrow, I must leave for the front. I will take the train to Brussels. I must see what I can see. On the night of the fourteenth I will return. You will keep all the papers and we will meet at this restaurant at nine o'clock. If I do not return, take the papers. You must write what report you can—you know almost as much as I do now—then when the aeroplane comes down at Viersberg . . . remember—I have given you a little map showing the landing place . . . hand the papers to the pilot. I want you to keep Muller's instruments and chronometer, and when you judge right, give them to his mother. I shall not need them. We cannot go together, but we will meet again on the fourteenth, my dear."

They returned to the hotel. Muller settled his account, remarking: "We leave early in the morning..."

* * * * *

"Duncan . . . I love you." He entwined his fingers in her glorious hair now spread like cloth of gold over the white linen. "Dearest heart, we have found each other. Let me feel you near me, Duncan . . . your life and mine. I can live now."

"Rosa . . ."

5

SEEN FROM A BARLEY FIELD

At six o'clock in the morning Grant awoke. Rosa was still sleeping, a smile on her lips, her pale beauty encompassed by the golden halo of her hair. Duncan kissed her. She stirred and was awakened by the passion of his embrace. She clung to him. "I am happy now . . . content," she sighed.

"Paradise—lost and regained," murmured Duncan.

They rose. Grant rang for coffee and dressed rapidly. By seven o'clock he was clothed. They left the hotel together. The railway station was crowded—workmen and girls coming in from the suburbs to the textile and engineering workshops, others departing for the short daily journey to the loom, the pit, the bench and the office; business men carrying dispatch cases and a number of soldiers in uniform returning to the front.

The people, Grant noted, were much like those of any other provincial town in western Europe, good, honest, plain folk, preoccupied with the small affairs of life, laughing in little groups; a maid and her man; a tearful peasant woman, the mother of a stripling weighed down with pack, accoutrements and rifle. Transpose the scene to Edinburgh, Leicester, Bristol—it would scarcely occasion comment.

He booked his ticket for Brussels, and entered the train. A change would be necessary at Dusseldorf. In his carriage were already seated two or three civilians, professional or business men. They bade him good morning. The train would leave in a quarter of an hour. He stood with Rosa. Few words were exchanged. She placed her hand through his arm, he held her fingers lightly in his hand.

"And now, Rosa, you will return to Hatzberg. The image of your beauty remains with me . . . our little hour."

Grant entered the train already panting with impatience. He held her hands and kissed her lips, a stray wisp of her hair caressing his cheek. "*Auf wiedersehen.*" He leaned far from the window, his hand reaching towards her until a bend in the track hid her from view. He then seated himself in the corner deep in his own reflections. The short journey had no event—his companions solicitous and friendly. The change at Dusseldorf brought him back to his task.

After a short wait he embarked on the journey to Brussels. The train was full: his compartment crowded, officers and civilians. Grant was glad indeed that his companions were his junior in rank. This contributed a natural defence against embarrassing questions. The conversation was of small experiences. He had been wounded in the fighting on the Somme in April. Now he was returning. He lent a ready ear to criticism of the English gunnery, the effect of tanks—how the English had bungled that!—to the detailed history of the great German offensive in the battles of the Lys and the various impressions it had made by its victories . . . and disappointments upon the populations of those areas in which the officers had their homes; and of the impression made in battle contact with English, Scottish, Australian and American troops. He heard lewd tales of brothels in Brussels, Lille and elsewhere—flotsam and jetsam of war. It was all valuable. The younger officers found a ready listener, a mirthful companion, a senior officer with sympathy, and their tongues wagged eagerly.

The terminus was at Brussels. Grant with his light haversack sought the first hotel and commanded a room. He must now quickly reach the forward area. He must make certain that the plans now clearly focused in his brain were in fact being pursued. He could not approach the front in the uniform of a field officer. He would excite attention. A change of rôle was a necessity. As a civilian he would be immediately suspect. He must appear now as a common soldier, one of those hundreds of thousands all so much alike passing hither and thither upon a thousand different missions and engaged in a thousand diverse capacities. He would pass unnoticed, he would mingle freely in the towns and billeting areas, tramp the roads, seek shelter in a base camp, any way-side farm house. He could take his chance almost anywhere. The back areas of the battle zone were honeycombed with every kind of formation, men passing to and from leave or the hospitals, transport, laundries, bakeries, road menders, railway guards. He would pass unnoticed.

One condition only was necessary. He must possess himself of the uniform and of the papers, field service book and equipment of an ordinary soldier, and he must obliterate forever the physical facts of Major Muller and of Major Schaeffer. He wandered out into the streets. There were many soldiers. The taverns and pavements were crowded—a hostile civil population mingling freely and easily with a crowd of soldiery.

A project quickly sketched itself in his mind . . . He would procure a motor car: then upon some pretext or another he would induce—and the offer of money to the ordinary soldier would, he considered, prove a sufficient inducement—or command, a likely looking lad, to accompany him. He would drive out into the country and then . . . Grant considered. He could not commit the horrible act which forced itself upon his mind. Murder . . . murder in cold blood. He could not do it.

He reconsidered the whole plan. Perhaps he could successfully make the man hopelessly drunk. But that would take time. A drunken man's company is a heavy liability, nor could a major of engineers be observed in company with a bibulous soldier.

His conscience battled with the problem. Duty as an advocate came to its aid with keen cross-examination. In how far did the killing of a German soldier by a British officer differ from the coldblooded assassination of a thoughtless sentry by a concealed sniper? Was not war, after all, a matter of killing? Did it matter where or how the killing took place so long as it was achieved successfully? Would there not be one soldier less to fight the British? Was not shelling the killing of the unseen by the unknown, and did not the heavy gunners glory in their work? Did not our airmen only last week drop bombs upon Tourcoing? Was this not cold-blooded murder? The risk involved to his whole scheme would be immense if he did not silence forever the man whom he proposed to rob. He would kill him. Then he would dispose of the body . . . and the motor car, too, and the uniform of Major Muller.

Having once overtaken the qualm of his conscience, he faced the problem with keen interest. He would strip the soldier's body and would array it in the uniform of Major Muller, place it at the wheel of the car, start up the engine, put it in top gear, leap clear of the car as it gained speed, and permit it to wreck itself. He could choose a place where an incline on the road would encourage a triumphant smash. His own underlinen was new: he would remove any marks of the place of purchase . . . and he would himself set fire to the car after the smash, so that the authorities might spend anxious days with inquests, and, he chuckled, would not be able possibly to affix a name to the headstone of the grave of the charred remains. Safe-guarded by the soldier's papers, he could entrain for the forward area, and make his inquiry and observation. But he must first discover a soldier drawn from the area north or south of the sector occupied by the Jäger Corps. He could then approach sufficiently close . . . but not too close.

He went first to his hotel and interrogated the clerk—he must have a motor car . . . but that would be difficult . . . they were requisitioned . . . but for the major, possibly . . . he would inquire. He passed ten marks to the clerk . . . an automobile could be found. . . yes . . . a Benz . . . he would telephone to make the appointment. Grant went out to the garage in the Rue Dolfus, where its proprietor was ready. He drove the car away, leaving fifty marks as good faith with the proprietor; and stationed it in a quiet square near the hotel.

Grant then left the main boulevards and walked into the narrower streets in which the soldiers were accustomed to congregate. Feigning a little inebriation, he entered a tavern. A group of soldiers rose from a table. He waved them back to their seats and commanded a bottle of wine. He called for more glasses and wine. They were good fellows. He would drink with them. They were going on short leave. The trains ran irregularly—no accommodation until the following morning.

Two men were from the 139th Saxon Regiment occupying the Passchendaele front. One of them, a lad of some twenty years of age, was about his own build. He measured him with his eye. He was a soft-eyed lad, wavy hair, smooth-skinned, two red, wet, full lips, the lower of which sagged sensuously.

Grant turned the talk to home, always an open sesame with soldiers proceeding on or returning from leave. Letter-cases and books came from the recesses of tunic pockets. Photographs, leave papers, tickets were produced—all the trivial trinkets of a soldier's prized possessions. But they would be short of money? The major was well paid. How much had they drawn? Field Service pocket books containing the pay entries were shown. He passed each of the seven men several marks apiece, and then turning to the lad whom he had selected, said: "My servant is not with me. Come and help me with my kit. You can rejoin your companions later." An elder soldier laughed loudly. Flattered by Major Muller's notice and selection, the youth accepted the suggestion with eagerness.

"Good night, comrades, enjoy yourselves."

Major Muller, followed by the soldier, smiling sheepishly, left the tavern. He walked quickly to the waiting motor car.

"I am billeted outside the town," he said, licking his dried lips. The horror of what he was contemplating obsessed him. As the car passed through the pleasant suburbs he chattered hysterically to defeat the ravages of conscience upon his peace of mind. The air was warm, but the rush of the speeding car brought a fresh breeze to his throbbing temples.

They left the long rows of little red-roofed villas set down in square gardens, then the more pretentious mansions with their broad acres in the suburbs, and passed into the open country, travelling at a high speed. Beyond Assche, Grant observed a side road, a rough track from which the ground dropped abruptly to the left side. He slowed down, and, remarking that he had nearly missed the turning, backed the car to the crossing, and thrust his way up the track.

Two hundred yards farther on he stopped the car. "It seems as if there is a puncture in the tyre—offside hind wheel. Jump out and have a look."

As the young soldier turned and scrambled out of his seat, Grant bent down and seized a heavy spanner which he had placed in readiness by his feet.

"My God, I can't do it," said his conscience. "An eye for an eye," said the advocate.

The soldier bent a moment to examine the tyre. He fingered and punched it, dusted his hand . . . then looked up. Grant was kneeling on the driving seat, his trunk twisted, muscles gathered and arm raised to deliver the blow. The insipid smile faded from the face . . . the sluggish intelligence slowly grasped the pending tragedy arrested for a moment in mid air . . . the jaw dropped, the eyes wide with horror gazed into the face of the merry man suddenly turned murderer. The arm descended.

The unholy fire in Grant's brain had died. He looked down. Something lay sprawling grotesquely—almost ludicrously—beside the wheel. No sound, no movement . . . silence.

Swiftly he unclothed the body. The light, thank God, was failing. Poor devil! He exchanged his clothes with those of the soldier—the name was Otto Gedern, 139th Saxon Regiment. It was an unpleasant business, but at least the clothes were warm. He hesitated a little and then clung to his new underclothes: they would comfort him against the obscenity of this new masquerade. He was now fully and properly dressed, and realized that it is a considerable physical effort to clothe an inanimate man.

The task was complete. He raised the body and with difficulty placed it in the driving seat, the right foot on the accelerator, the leg slightly bent from the knee—the pressure of the limp, unrestrained leg would effectively depress the pedal. He swung the engine, and, standing on the dash-board, bent over and placed the car in gear, first, second, top. The car was moving nicely. Pulling the wheel hard over with his left hand, he jumped clear to the right, rolling on to the grass. Grant jumped up. The car had plunged over the embankment, and had overturned on to its side where it was held by two young birches which bent to its weight. The grotesque figure had slipped from the driver's seat, and was lolling limply over the side. Grant pushed it back into the seat, locking the right arm in the steering wheel. He dug the man's bayonet into the petrol tank and from its squirting filled a tin with spirit. He threw this over the figure, and drenched the fore part of the car. Then he struck a match, lit a wad of paper and threw it into the car. Grant ran, then climbed the bank. The flames greedily licked the spirit. Grant could see the horrible figure as it were at the stake. The tank burst with a loud explosion : flames mounted with renewed violence. The figure was encompassed, then lost in a sheet of flame, dimmed by columns of smoke.

Grant ran—Muller and Schaeffer had disappeared. Soldier Otto Gedern remained, with nine days' leave of absence, blessed freedom.

He rejoined the high road and turned west, hurrying from the glare of the burning car. He could not be far from Alost. He was in high spirits—Otto Gedern would have a good time in Belgium. He had no desire to expend his leave in his Saxon home, enough sorrow and unhappiness there. He possessed the larger portion of four hundred marks. He had wished to visit the gaiety of Brussels, and having satiated his desires, he was now seeking the quiet of Belgian villages where his money would prove the best passport to hospitality. That was the plan. In an upside-down world, the idiosyncrasies of one soldier wouldn't worry anyone. He was as free as the air—his papers were in order. He could spend his leave as he liked, provided he reported back to the 3rd Echelon of his regiment upon the prescribed date. He was free.

He walked the road happily. He must now reach the forward area quickly. He only wanted confirmation of all he had learned. He would return by train to the forward area, using Otto Gedern's pass. It was June 8—how he had lived! He had seven clear days left to complete his task. On the fifteenth at dawn he would meet Mayne again, and . . . on the fourteenth—Rosa. Seven clear days—if everything went well more than time enough; at any rate, ample. He would make for Tourcoing. It would probably take him a whole day, the lines would be sure to be congested. Tourcoing would be a good jumping-off place; the 139th Regiment was quite sufficiently far away, but he was near enough, as a soldier proceeding on leave, to pass without comment. He struck a match and examined the leave pass. Ten days granted from the sixth. That was two days ago, and the poor devil had already wasted one day. His leave expired on the sixteenth at 3rd Echelon . . . so did that of Grant, but at Viersberg. From Alost he would board the first possible train for Tourcoing. On the fifteenth he would be able to tell little Mayne from personal observation what kind of mess he had made with the "eggs" he dropped last week.

Grant wandered into a dismal looking inn near the station. A sour-faced Belgian told him he had no accommodation. Grant produced five marks. Acquisitiveness overcame prejudice . . . the innkeeper would see what he could do. Grant accepted the offer in stuttering French and German—the lingua franca of the invading army. He ordered a simple meal and turned in. He was tired, an exhausting, nerve-racking day. He awoke at six, dressed and quickly walked across to the railway station.

He was accosting a blue-smocked railway man when a corporal of military police touched him on the shoulder. For one brief second Grant experienced all the horrors of a criminal apprehended in crime by the majesty of the law. "Show your pass," said the corporal. Grant produced it. It was examined. The photograph of a girl slipped from between its pages and fluttered to the ground. Grant stooped and picked it up. He fingered it in half guilt, his eyes cast down. Damn it all! he hadn't noticed it before—taken in Dresden. He looked up : the corporal was grinning at him.

"You're a long way . . . from her," commented the soldier, jerking his head towards the photograph, "and you're wasting your leave. Better get on the next train through Brussels," he said, not unkindly.

Grant hesitated. "No, corporal, I'm going back . . . They don't want me at home . . . she doesn't. I'm going back—have a good time Tourcoing way—I know a girl there—have a good sleep and crawl back on the sixteenth . . . I'm fed up with leave."

"You're an odd one. All right, there's a train at nine-twenty-five, over an hour to wait. Come and have a yarn."

They sat in the little waiting-room, now the military headquarters and post. A corporal and three men, greybeards, formed the garrison—two asleep—the other Grant could see dismally guarding the points by the signal box, a carbine slung over his shoulder. A dull place, Alost, except when the leave, hospital, and reinforcement trains passed through.

They had been busy last month with wounded from the great offensive, and later division after division from the Russian front had passed through. The corporal was glad of a change of companionship. He had been severely wounded in the lungs at Verdun . . . a bloody business that! . . . now he was cursed with the companionship of men old enough to be his father. Soldiers . . . it made him sick!

"Your train is signalled . . . Good luck," cried the little garrison.

Grant climbed into a train crowded with soldiery. He thrust himself into a seat, yawned and closed his eyes. He feigned sleep for two hours, listening to the conversation. They took him for granted. The men were returning from leave. They had travelled together from Hanover, men of the same division, except one gunner who was too drunk to participate in the desultory conversation. Grant stretched himself and nodded. He lit a cigar and joined in the fragmentary talk, which, as the heat grew, faded away. The train with many delays wandered through the peaceful countryside.

It was after three when it dragged into Tourcoing. Grant got out. He showed his pass at the barrier and walked out into the streets, mingling with their crowded soldiery. He went to the Catholic rest house established in a temporarily disused factory. Then, greatly daring, he wrote a little letter—just love—to Rosa. It would cause no suspicion. Then, regret tugging at his heart strings, he destroyed it. The act might be taking a chance with Fate. He was getting irregular in his meals. He dropped into the canteen, gorged himself, and then joined a group in the billiard-room. He moved about from one group to another: then out into the streets again; drinks in a tavern . . . he was popular, for he had money to spend.

From this group and from that the evidence which he had gleaned from the plan was partly confirmed—the Jäger Corps, disciplinary troops, were occupying the Kemmel sector. There was a rumour that a new Army Corps from the Russian front was going down to the Somme area—so the bluff was being noised abroad.

There was other news too . . . the British bombing raid of the past week had made a devil of a mess of the remount depot, hundreds of horses blown sky-high, and very many others had to be destroyed. Another bomb had narrowly missed the area commander's quarters, and had killed several women employed at the laundry. Several of the bombs, fortunately those which had been best placed, had proved to be duds . . . curse these profiteering manufacturers, was Grant's mental comment. One was embedded in the Rue de Lille. All traffic was diverted and the houses in the near vicinity had been cleared. The town engineers, Belgian civilians, had orders to unearth the bomb and remove it. "They fairly had the wind up," sniggered a staff sergeant who had never heard a shot fired.

Grant knew enough . . . he would strike the road for Wervicq and hope to obtain a lift in a lorry. He must see more. This information was hearsay, good confirmatory circumstantial evidence, but not sufficient. He set out to walk. It was hot and dusty. No lorries came along. Otto Gedern's boots pinched his toes, the heels mocked him at every step, chafing the flesh. The mental strain had been enough : he was beginning now to feel its effects physically.

He reached a wayside inn, now half-past seven. He called for a *bock* of beer, and took off his boots and socks. Both heels were blistered. He stretched his toes. He could not proceed much farther in this condition . . . Blast the fellow's boots! He sat in a shabby chair beside the road, drinking beer.

Grant was admirably fulfilling the rôle of common soldier. Otto Gedern—fed up . . . and far from home—the silly expression appeared as a rainbow on his mental horizon. He grinned. Well, life wasn't so bad—even as Otto Gedern . . . though his heels were sore. He heard the sound of heavy wheels and a motor engine. He put on his socks and boots quickly and stood in the road, boot laces trailing, tunic unbuttoned, typical soldier returning from leave.

He hailed the lorry driver, who pulled up. Grant offered him a drink of beer : then requested a lift anywhere a bit farther on. The driver in his shirt sleeves, face smothered in dust and streaked with sweat, got down from his seat. He mopped his face with an oily rag. They drank beer. Then both men got up on to the driver's seat. The lorry was going to the Guard Grenadier store depot—load of electric cable.

"Very particular, the Guards," commented the driver, "this bloody stuff has to be unloaded and then reloaded into the Guards' own wagons."

He would be at the job half the night, and had orders as soon as unloading had been completed to return straight to his depot in Lille. He had been for a damn joy ride half round Europe already. He would drop Grant at Garde Dieu—that would be about two miles short of the Guards' store, reflected Grant. He would dearly like to see the store depot and get confirmation of the Guard Grenadier Regiment. It might be a risk.

He inquired: "Don't you usually carry a relief driver?" . . . That was true . . . The relief had gone sick: there was no one else available and they were in a hurry. Grant volunteered that he was accustomed to motors and spoke of technique. The driver allowed him to take the wheel . . . he was satisfied and drove on.

"My leave's nearly up," said Grant. "I ought to reach Armentières first thing tomorrow morning. Can't you take me on with you to the depot? I can help you as second driver, and you could drop me on your road to Lille." The driver agreed.

"Take off that tunic and put it under the cushion." He took over the wheel again.

"You must look the part," said the driver with a gruff laugh, passing him the grease rag, with which Grant smeared his arms and hands, and then reaching the dash-board added dust to his make-up. They drove on. Night had fallen. A half curl of moon climbed up over the horizon : a swift car overtook them. They came to a crossroad : the driver pulled up and inquired the road of the military policeman who checked his pass. He was given directions—about half an hour from the cross-road. He drove on.

The shaded beam of a lantern showed down the road. He reduced speed to a crawl. A voice rang out. "Halt!" The lorry was pulled up. A sentry came forward. "Your pass and direction order." The driver produced his oily pass and order. "Spare driver with you," said the sentry, nodding his head at Grant. The driver acquiesced. "All right, go ahead slowly—two hundred yards. There's another sentry there." The lorry moved on and was halted again. "What is your load?" asked the sentry. "Electric cables." "Turn in to the right." A sergeant jumped on the dash-board and blew a whistle. A party of about a dozen men ran out handling a run-way. They placed it against the tail of the lorry, then swarmed into it and slowly lowered the great wheels carrying the cables. Grant had had ample time to examine the men. Guard Grenadier Regiment all of them. He slammed up the tail board. The sergeant wrote out a pass. "Hand this to the second sentry. Turn the lorry here and get out quick."

Grant climbed back into his seat. He could see a number of lorries and loading parties but could discern no encampment. This then was only a ration and store dump. The dummy division took wise precautions. The lorry turned out into the road. The sentry repeated: "Hand your pass to Post No. I." Grant delivered the pass to the sentry, adding "Good night." The courtesy was not returned: Grant remembered . . . no communication outside . . . penalty death. These Guards adhered to that order to the letter. The lorry returned to the cross-roads where the driver inquired the road to Lille. Directions were given, and they drove on into the night. The driver indicated a tumble-down village on the Armentières road. Grant pulled out his tunic and equipment and slipped from the footboard, thanking his friend.

The lorry rattled on, its noise reverberating through the silent village. Grant stood for a moment in meditation. He must turn in somewhere for the night. He walked down the village. A light showed from under the doorway of a large barn. He listened— voices speaking German. He knocked at a small door inset in the great gate. It yielded to the pressure.

"*Wer ist da?*" cried a voice. The light blinded him.

"Returning from leave. I've lost my way. Can I sleep here?"

"Come in," shouted several men.

The focus of his eyes were adjusting themselves to the lamp light. A jeer greeted his appearance, and Grant suddenly realizing that he was in a motley of grease and dust stood grinning broadly. He saw some fifteen or twenty men in various postures of ease, clothed and stripped, reading, smoking, playing cards and engaged in that perennial entertainment of rounding up the ubiquitous louse. He was told that he could find a corner in the straw, the corporal adding that there was a pump in the yard outside.

Grant threw down his equipment, divested himself of his tunic, shirt, boots and socks and went out. The French soap from G.H.Q. was balm but he had no towel. He came back dripping : someone tossed him a towel. Then he drew up to the light of the lamp to examine his blistered feet. His right heel was angry red and raw. A kind soul offered him lint and iodine.

It is a universal habit that when man engages in the self-application of that universal antiseptic, his fellows always watch with intense interest and excitement. Men revel in the iodine comedy. Every head looked up. Grant dabbed the iodine on the wound, winced . . . whew! He had played the comedy well. Everyone laughed.

He was in good company, soldiers in reserve, resting from their tour in the line. He shared a blanket in the straw and slept happily —physically tired. The men were early astir and woke him. He redressed, carefully packing the offending boots with lint. The soldiers passed him part of their breakfast with strong coffee. He was a very smart soldier indeed when he left the billet, and moved oft in a northerly direction. The day, the tenth of June, was overcast, a strong north-westerly breeze had arisen and drove the scudding clouds before it. He was only some ten miles from Kemmel. He must see for himself the prisoner division somewhere on the road, and if possible obtain some nearer view of the activity behind the hills. He had a mental picture of what he was seeking.

He took the road for Houplines passing through L'Epinette and skirting Armentières. Grant felt quite at home . . . Back in Armentières of all places . . . and he laughed . . . billeted inside the lunatic asylum during November in the first months of the war : and then, in the Rue de Nieppe—literally blown from his bath by a crump! . . . living like a water-rat, leg-bound by mud as thick as treacle, while continuous rain poured from Heaven as from a bucket . . . rain fell upon June the tenth . . . Grant, a veritable Jonah, was back in the boat!

The line was very quiet. No one took any notice of him. He walked on, going due north. He came to a canteen and filled his belly. Continuing north, he struck out towards Ploegsteert—"Plugstreet "of bitter memory. He must not go north of a line lying roughly between Kemmel and Courtrai, and he must give the appearance of leaving or rejoining his regiment, which lay in the sector some miles north-west of this line.

He sought shelter with an engineer group engaged in road upkeep . . . yes, he was a bit off his beat . . . he would have to make a detour . . . The Jäger disciplinary division. They laughed uproariously. They had been engaged keeping a section of road in good repair for three years. Life was pretty good, food, warmth, comfort, entertainment, and buxom Belgian girls in the village . . . Roll on the war! . . .

But the Jägers, and, of course, the silent division quartered with the Guard Grenadier. No one knew anything about them . . . from the Russian front, new allies; possibly released convicts—God knew! Each day a large party went up the line for training with the Jägers . . . the ideas of the staff were crazy, the ways of authority to be marvelled at . . . no, they did not work that section of the road but he would cross the Menin road at Wulverghem . . . The camp would not be far from there.

Grant went out again into the rain. Heavy dark clouds had gathered and the rain was descending heavily. He was soaked to the skin. He came to a rest camp—fragments of every regiment and corps. He would shelter for a while. He saw some men of the 19th Saxon Corps, but not the regiment of Otto Gedern, deceased. He avoided them, and mingling with the crowd, laid aside his equipment, and took off his tunic to let it dry. He purchased a flask of cognac and ample food at the canteen and again set out. He reached Gapaard cross-roads where he learnt that the main Courtrai road was "*Verboten.*" That probably would be the way to the camp of the 15th Composite Division.

He must secrete himself and watch the road. He walked about two miles north, then leaving the road, passed through fields of corn, now bowed and dripping with the rain. He could see the telegraph poles along the forbidden road leading diagonally across his path to Courtrai. He followed a trench which divided the fields, corn from barley. The high, yellow barley stretched to the edge of the road to which it yielded with reluctance. Grant plunged in among the wet stalks, and moving carefully forward so as not to disturb their appearance from above, crept to within about ten yards of the roadside, from which position through the stalks he could see clearly, being shielded from above by the thickening ears of the barley and veiled by the criss-cross of whiskers.

He lay down to wait. The rain had slackened to a steady drizzle. The barley ears dripped steadily upon him . . . seven . . .

eight o'clock. The road remained deserted. He was cold and chilled to the bone. The rain had ceased. The flying clouds opened fitfully to admit a shaft from the setting sun. Dusk crept about him and the road remained silent. He took another nip of brandy and chewed bread and cheese. His limbs were stiff, he was cramped and began to shiver with cold. Night fell. It was very dark. Grant stood up, flinging his arms cabman-fashion to revitalize and warm his cramped, cold limbs. He slapped his thighs with his hands, beat his chest and had another nip of brandy. He was prepared to stay all night, if necessary all next day. He was at the end of his task. Identification of the 15th Division was vitally necessary. Alternately he sat in the midst of the wet barley and stood up for exercise.

Then he heard the heavy thunder of a column of motor lorries approaching along the road from the east. That would be from the encampment. He stretched out among the barley stalks, dragged himself a little nearer to the roadside, and bent the stalks above his head.

The column was quite near. The lorries carried no lights. The first drew level. He dimly saw the outline of the covered wagon, the driver and the silhouette of a soldier seated beside him. A second, a third, four, five . . . twenty-five lorries passed at a few yards' distance from each other, moving steadily. He could see nothing but the dim shadows of the two men on the driving seat, and the outline of the wagons. Twenty-five lorries. That would mean five or six hundred men, if they contained men. Grant cowered down again in the barley, stretching farther forward. More lorries began to pass . . . two and then . . . an open wagon. Four . . . five . . . more and more . . . Grant could see the silhouetted heads of men, bodies packed tightly on the floors of the jolting wagons.

Twenty-seven wagons passed, mostly uncovered—a host of men. Then all was silence. Cold banished fatigue. The hours, with intermittent rain storm dragged by, Grant punctuating his boredom with brandy, cheese, chocolate, and humid bread. The wind had relaxed and Grant's clothes hung heavily from him, those next to the skin clinging with a clammy embrace. A cock crew in the village, then another. Light, shadowy and unreal, stole upon the deserted countryside. Grant, to warm himself, ran along the grass flanking the road. Then he heard the muffled sound of motor engines, the trundle of wheels to the west.

He fled back, re-entered the field by the trench dividing corn from barley, and crept back to his hiding-place. The roar increased. He covered his hands, sank his body to the earth, scarcely dared raise his eyes, his green cap pressed down over the forehead. He noted the driver : close to him on the near side sat an armed soldier of the Guard Grenadier Regiment. The wagon, a covered one, had passed. Followed another, a similar soldier; then . . . another. The back of the wagon was open. Grant could see heads, bearded men mostly. Another wagon . . . Grant's eyes were for its tail end. It was closed. Another; it was an open wagon, twenty, possibly thirty heads, some bearded, the shoulders were dirty, earthy. The back of a man rested on the tail board. It was streaked with clay. Grant knew that clay . . . its yellow, mawkish colour. Lorry after lorry passed. Grant failed to count. These were no ordinary soldiers, bearded and dishevelled, the spruce Guard Grenadier in charge so different. The column passed on.

Rain fell again. Grant had had sufficient confirmation. It was the twelfth of June. He was shaking with ague. He took out his flask of cognac . . . the smell of spirits always made him shudder in the early hours . . . he drained the flask. Its stream warmed the course of his throat. He was seized with sickness, retched and sank limp with perspiration, fatigue and chill against the side of the ditch. He must get away from this place. Precaution fired him to action. He broke into a jog-trot across the sodden fields. He would rejoin the Tourcoing road, anywhere. He stumbled on, avoiding the index of telephone posts indicating roads proceeding north. So he went on for an hour, or more. It was after six o'clock. The weather looked more hopeful, but it was still overcast. A strong flight of aeroplanes passed overhead going back to their hangars. Others, high up, droned their warning patrol.

He came to a farmhouse. It was astir. A thin wisp of smoke curled lazily from the crumbling chimney, to float awhile in the still air before fading into the dim haze above. Grant walked in through the tiled porchway. The inviting smell of coffee smote his nostrils. Madame *la bonne femme* was busy with her pots; bowls were upon the table. A yellow-haired youth sat blinking at the table, two little girls were seated upon a bench, the elder weaving her younger sister's tousled hair into plaits. He bade them good morning, and asked for coffee. He threw down some marks upon the table as the first move in the game of diplomacy.

He told them he was going home on leave . . . Poor boy, he was tired, hungry, yes? . . . and from the *sales tranchées* . . . his mother, wife, sisters, sweetheart, would be glad to see him? She prattled on. The sight of the marks had worked wonders with her day-today heart. He was wet through, yes? . . . he must draw up to the fire. She poked it vigorously. Grant took off his tunic. A cloud of evaporation was drawn off. He must dry everything . . . he would catch his death of cold.

So, with gladness, he divested himself of all his clothes, and naked yet quite unashamed, for the first time since he set out, Duncan Grant, lieutenant-colonel, without camouflage, uniform or decoration, as God made him, mothered and fussed over by this Belgian housewife . . . he sat before the fire sipping hot coffee, the clothes of Otto Gedern, soldier deceased, steaming before a cracking fire.

The farmer came in from the cow byres. His wife nodded to the marks still lying upon the table. They were a passport. He extended a welcome, drank his coffee, ate cheese and bread and went about his daily task. The woman brought him a blanket and she wrapped it around him. He slipped forward in his chair; his eyelids were heavy. He blinked at the glowing embers, then pulled the blanket closely round him. His head sank upon his chest. He slept. His work was done. Back to Barmen . . . and Rosa.

* * * * *

In the snug warmth of the blanket before the blazing fire, the exhausting nervous tension of the past few days relaxed, the physical hardship banished, Duncan Grant had slept deeply.

A light hand shook him. He was roused to that half-consciousness which, in the warmth of blankets, is so infinitely pleasant. Thoughts chase each other by selection through the quietness of the mind. He drowsed with visions of green fields, and waving corn, soft lapping seas and shingled coves, the cottage and the stook, rolling hills, glen and moorland stream. His mind refashioned the days when all the world was young, the smell of the loam, the music of the stream, the tang of the myrtle berry, the caress of the upland breeze, and the sight of the rolling purple hills. He recalled schooldays in the pleasant vales and cottages of Berkshire, shrouded in a blue film of smoke and haze; the minarets, waving palms, and placid waters of the Nile, the red-roofed villages of Surrey; the snow-capped peaks, forests and temples of the Indian foothills; the whole kaleidoscope of a regimental soldier's joy days, hunting, fishing, shooting, in good company; but always he bent his wayward mind to that picture of shady glens, purple hillsides, and triumphant peaks of the Highlands which formed the background to a face set in a golden halo . . . Rosa.

The housewife shook him again; the sleeper awoke. It was high noon. A savoury smell greeted him. He blinked at the hot embers, stood up, yawned, and stretched his limbs, the blanket falling from his well-knit frame. A loud laugh greeted him. Little heads turned, and, remarking his nakedness, sniggered and buried themselves in plates of steaming vegetables and bread. The man, returned from his farm work, was engaged upon his midday meal, the children, too, at the table, the good wife busy with the cooking and service, snatching a bite, or a sip of coffee, in the intervals of her work. The man, munching a husk of bread, spluttered in his deep guttural: "*Ne dérangez vous, c'est tout égal.*"

Grant was at home. The woman tossed him the dried garments and trousers, into which he slipped, and then set before him soup, bread, cheese, and coffee. Grant was amply rested, his spirits high. He permitted his command of the French language to excel the dictates of caution and conversed merrily. They were fed up with the war, its restrictions, impositions, requisitions . . . otherwise things went on much as usual . . . the messes were good customers with good money, and . . . there was always the washing done for officers.

Grant nodded with delight. Here was a nation divided in twain by two invading armies of different races, with no common language. The peasantry were suffering untold hardships and inconveniences; they knew little of the causes of the war, nothing of its strategy and wide-flung campaign; but it had its compensations— vegetables and eggs at famine prices to the invaders, and . . . there was always washing to be done for officers. He rocked with laughter. The midday meal over, he placed ten marks on the table. Ah! he was a *bon garçon* . . . God would protect him. That, too, was amusing ever—the conception of God as some kind of unseen, remote, charity organization society handing out His Divine protection to those who paid in good cash for small earthly services and often grudging hospitality. The peasants were like the gypsies on a Derby Day . . . "Gawd bless yer pretty faice, dearie," as the shillings passed from the smooth, small hand of the lady to the horned, dirt-engrained paw of the woman of the caravan.

Grant put on his tunic; then sat to gird again his feet in Otto's boots. In the soggy dampness of the leather, they had passed unnoticed. Now, dried before the hot fire, they resisted his feet as would a small size in steel armour. Madame bent her muscular frame, and seized the obstinate footwear. Her strong thumbs kneaded the hard leather with tallow. Her sinewy arm basted toes and heels. They resisted a little less; and, Grant hoped, the shrinkage would try his heels the less. He slung his pack and equipment, and went out into the day. The sun shone again, but not too hotly. He had all the appearance of a soldier from the trenches, unshaven, unwashed, his hair tousled, uniform coated in the mud from the barley field in which he had lain. Specks of rust tinted the steel of his rifle and equipment. He was going on leave. It was the eleventh of June. He still possessed three days of freedom and . . . he had been delayed . . . *une affaire* . . . a little too much to drink . . . a little sickness. But much could be done with three days' leave.

He struck the road to Tourcoing. A light railway, used for carrying stores, engineering apparatus and artillery ammunition ran beside it. An empty train with odd details of men, sick, lightly wounded, the miscellaneous from the battle front sat on the empty trucks. It puffed busily along. Grant ran: willing hands took his rifle and pulled him into a moving truck. Now he would have a little peace from Otto's boots. The train rolled into Tourcoing. He went down to the station and presented his leave warrant. The transport officer jeered at him for a fool, then more kindly bundled him into a waiting train filled with soldiers. They were in merry mood. Grant now familiar with the front could without restraint take an easy part in the conversation. He was enjoying himself.

The train was bumped into sidings, where it remained for hours, while convoy after convoy of wagons, propelled by panting engines, pushed past—material of war, guns, limbers, men, always more men of every formation and from every kingdom, principality and district in Germany. The stage was being set, reflected Grant. The merry spirits flagged. The night was spent in jolting and shunting with little eastward progress. It was the morning of the twelfth and the train rumbled into Brussels. Six hours' delay. Grant sat in the canteen, listening to chance gossip. He dared not go out into the streets for relaxation.

Evil thoughts preyed upon his mind which the activity and interest of the past forty-eight hours had banished . . . the murderer revisiting the scene of his crime . . . he must occupy his mind. He would buy a new pair of boots. So he went out and fitted his feet with the extravagance which every gentleman loves—good, well-fitting boots, not quite adaptable to the grouse moor, a little too . . . well, they lacked the square toe, homely, intimate, leathery appearance of the brogue or shooting boot from a bespoke maker in one of those shy turnings off Regent Street or the Strand. A little too flashy, made to look the part, to proclaim a shooting boot—he thought of Tartarin—but they were well-formed, soft, clinging, and comfortable—good, comfortable boots. No longer would he be dogged by the footsteps of Otto, nor would his feet at every step chant a *Danse Macabre*, in requiem to a battered figure at the stake.

The qualms and fear which afflicted the conscience of Duncan Grant were becoming doped by the advocacy of reason, of logic and of duty. No one ever truly lives who carries a load of self-denial ordinances and penances. They are the dugouts of cowards, the funkholes of the afraid. All progress depends upon untrammelled mental ability and activity. The smaller things of life, lived thus, fall into their proper perspective—a killing at a cross-road to frustrate a devilish design, to enable a victory with consequences which would reverberate throughout civilization and amid remote savagery. Poof! . . . Grant had no rabbit-hole for his conscience . . . and the haunting boots had gone.

He returned to the canteen. There was a further delay. Two o'clock on the twelfth. How he longed to tell Rosa that he was coming probably a little earlier. He dare not. The train would leave for Dusseldorf at seven o'clock in the evening. He busied himself with chance gossip—a tale here and there. Each yarn brought confirmation to all he had read and seen.

He boarded the train, empty goods-wagons returning to the great arsenals at Dusseldorf, Crefeld and Elberfeld. There was a two days' congestion of leave : men were herded into the wagons. They sought rest anywhere on the wooden floors, packs stacked as pillows against the creaking sides, rifles and equipment, sufficiently haphazard to irritate a neighbour and to devastate his chances of peaceful sleep. The train drew out from the station, fitfully, making loud protest and raining showers of coal dust upon the wagon roofs. There was little ventilation. All the confused smells of unwashed, well-fed humanity rose to choke the heat of the night—sweat, tobacco smoke, damp, unwashed clothes, food, spirits, wet leather. Some were drugged and slept fitfully in their corners, or against the wagon walls. Those less fortunate who occupied the centre of the floor kicked by restless sleepers, discomforted with equipment, cursed freely and perspired . . . the stench appalled.

Daylight after the long night was welcome. The exhilaration of anticipation again gripped the men. The train rumbled over the points, then came to a standstill. The wagon doors were thrown open—Dusseldorf. The soldiers, thirsty, hungry, unwashed, mud-soiled, and their eyes blood-shot with fatigue and the suffocation of the night, hair tousled, partly dressed, swarmed out upon the platform where coffee, soda water, ginger bread cakes were prepared and waiting. Kindly, quiet women, from some voluntary organization, ministered to the wants of these elemental, rough and roughly-used men, but whose blasphemies were strangely stifled in their presence. As hunger and thirst were appeased, each collected his equipment, and the grey-green mass disintegrated into small groups bound for their several destinations.

Grant examined the direction board on the main platforms. There was barely an hour before the first train to Barmen, a workmen's train, similar to that which had carried him to the front. He washed, shaved off a two days' growth of beard, and then seated on the platform cleaned his rifle and equipment. The train drew into the platform. He climbed in with a score of mechanics and artisans. In less than an hour he was in Elberfeld. He alighted and was lost in the hurrying crowd, waving his leave warrant to the blear-eyed official as he passed through the ticket barrier. He entered a restaurant and partook of a very good breakfast. And now for his final plans . . . and Rosa.

Mayne would meet him in two days' time. Supposing he did not come, or there was an accident in landing . . . two possibilities. What then? . . . supposing the aeroplane was wrecked, or shot down on the return to the British lines . . . what then? The information which he possessed was of supreme importance. At all costs it must reach the Commander-in-chief within two or three weeks at the latest. At any rate Grant must improvise two lines of communication with G.H.Q. A memorandum outlining the plan must be prepared in duplicate. He himself must take one, the other . . . ? There was no one but Rosa. But how? What could she do? And the effort and strain were far, far more than she could possibly undertake. He pondered. He paid for his breakfast, then entered a shop and purchased writing materials and carbons for copying. He would find a quiet place to prepare his memorandum and draw the sketch maps. Perhaps an idea would occur to him as to how Rosa could help. But she would know best; she would have ideas but he dared not enter the village of Hatzberg. Perhaps he could send her a note by a messenger or telephone to the Stadt Baurat asking that a message be given her.

But Heaven knew . . . Rosa might already be under suspicion, even in difficulty. Grant struggled with the desire to see her, prompting always his designs and plans. Then he discovered himself unreasonably creating barriers against such a meeting, when more than probably their brains—and hearts—in co-operation could find a solution of the problem. Grant decided upon communication. He went to the public telephone . . . could he speak with the Stadt Baurat? . . . Why, certainly . . . was it possible to speak with Fraulein Maurer? . . . Oh, yes, it was important—a friend with news from her sister. But Fraulein Maurer was not well, she was in her apartment . . . Grant insisted that the matter was important . . . they would bring her to the telepone . . . He must tell her somehow in the first breath of conversation that it was himself.

"*Fraulein Maurer?*" he inquired, eagerly awaiting the sound of her voice.

"*Ja, hier Fraulein Maurer.*"

"Is all well with the widow?" That sentence would surely indicate himself.

"Yes, yes." Grant intervened rapidly . . . She must say nothing. "I must meet you quickly, important news of your sister. At the tramway terminus by the Quellen Strasse, twelve noon. You can do this?"

"Yes."

"And no one knows?"

"No one."

"*Auf wiedersehen,*" and he hung up the receiver. Rosa again, blessed news. He went out, took the tram car to the Quellen Strasse, and with two hours to wait, crossed into a shady clump of trees and shrubs, took off his equipment, unpacked the writing materials and settled himself on his stomach, elbows resting on the ground. The memorandum must be concise, definite. It must briefly set out the simple facts. He commenced writing.

Grant considered his notes. He could say no more. It was impossible to convey in words the magnitude of the operation, the seriousness of the situation, the threat to the safety of the British lines.

Then he re-wrote his memorandum carefully stressing the main points of the message in capitals, and underlining the passages commanding action.

URGENT. IMMEDIATE ACTION.
VERY URGENT.-To G.H.Q. W PLAN.

1. Major Muller, buried Neuve Eglise, June 2, was engineer in charge gigantic offensive operation.
2. Germans have extensively UNDERMINED sector from YPRES to LYS using new engineering (Messer) process.
3. UTMOST SECRECY has been kept. Jäger Corps know nothing of this operation.
4. MINESHAFTS are sunk East of MONT KEMMEL and STEENWERK. Exact location undetermined. (See plan.)
5. Underground GALLERIES extend from KEMMEL and STEENWERK westwards for about six miles.
6. Plan provides for SEVEN EXITS approximately at LOVIE CHATEAU, The POPERINGHE-STEENWOORDE Road, ABEELE Railway Station, KRUYSTRAETE, FLETRE, STRAZEELE Station, LA MOTTE.
7. Three EXITS are probably now complete, at LOVIE CHATEAU, FLETRE, KRUYSTRAETE.
8. Galleries are in two strata, upper and lower, intercommunicating.
9. GENERAL OFFENSIVE IS PLANNED TO COMMENCE FIRST WEEK AUGUST (possibly a little later). SIXTH AUGUST the date by present order.
10. ATTACKING TROOPS WILL EMERGE from UNDERGROUND at Seven Exits preceded by explosion of MINES.
11. Two ARMY CORPS with armoured cars and cavalry in advance will be utilized.
12. Concentration of two army corps in the SOMME area is a skeleton blind. A feint attack will be made against AMIENS.
13. Objective of Main Offensive—CUT COMMUNICATIONS from CHANNEL PORTS and Capture the latter.
14. Whole resources of German Armies to be thrown into this offensive.
15. 15th Composite Reichswehr Division is conducting whole mining operation. This consists of PRISONERS of

WAR— British, French, Russian, Italian. IN GERMAN UNIFORM. Guard Grenadier Regiment are with them as guards and German soldiers as interpreters. Encampment is west of TOURCOING. Exact location undetermined. Large parties proceed to and from Shafts by night in motor convoys. Route passes GAPAARD X Roads.

16. Sketch plan attached.

WHOEVER RECEIVES THIS MESSAGE DISPATCH SECRET UTMOST URGENCY TO G.H.Q. TO G.O.C. IN C. AT ALL COSTS.

Transmitted through two sources at 5 a.m. June 15 by the man who went to find the W Plan on June 6 last.

URGENT URGENT URGENT

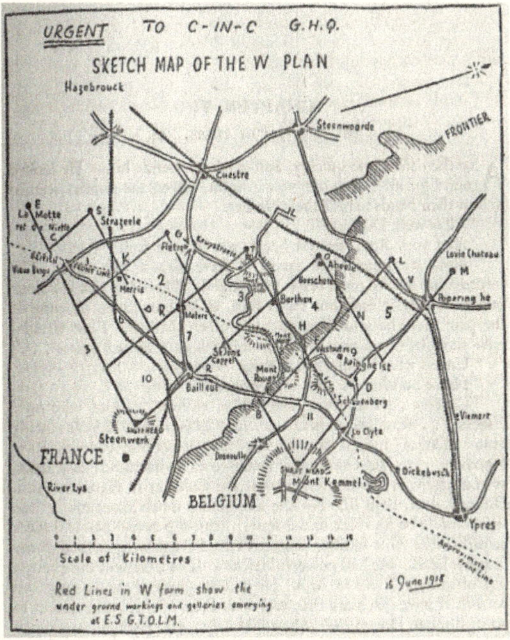

The memorandum was completed. Then he prepared the map in outline. The details he could not supply without the aid of the plans and papers in Rosa's possession. Would she bring them with her? He had plenty of time. He folded the papers, placed them in two envelopes, and secreted them in his tunic pocket. Then he repacked his equipment, and wandered down to the seat at the tramway halt. Twenty minutes still remained. He lit a cigar, thrust his hands into his pockets, thrust out his legs, and with his head thrown back idly watched the smoke curl into the air and drift away in the light breeze.

6

THE GREATEST OF THESE...

And then she came quickly, and sat down beside him. He looked round guiltily. No one was in sight. Even the poplars seemed to bow their heads to hide their blushes.

"All is well, Duncan?"

"And you, Rosa, dearest heart, you too are well?"

"Now we must plan again. I have almost two days. The information I have must reach the general. There is a risk if I alone possess it that it may not reach him, at least in time. A copy of the plan must be sent through some other channel. I am afraid I have thought of no way in which this can be achieved unless . . ."

"Unless what?" intervened Rosa.

"I have no idea . . . no . . . none."

"Confess . . . confess," she smiled at him. "And why not? Unless . . . Rosa has an idea . . . now listen to me. I have already quite decided—indeed it was my first news for you—to leave Hatzberg . . . and Germany. I will go to Switzerland. My sister, as you know, is Mother Superior at the Convent in Geneva. And, Duncan, dear, I am ill. No one will bother much about me, a little sick *Fraulein* of no value to the state. I can slip away; nor will there be difficulty. Our family, von Gleiwitz, have privileges though my father is dead. He had powerful friends.

The trustee of the estate is in Dortmund. I will see him. He will recommend the passport and permit. I have discussed this, too, with Frau Muller. She desires to go with me to Dortmund. She could help. Her husband was much respected and well loved: several of the leading engineers have studied under him. She will help me if necessary. That has been my little surprise. Then quickly I will go. I will be near my sister and live quietly in the mountains. My sister has asked me many times to go, but I have not cared. I have had strength for a little work—which I have loved—service which no one else would do. From Switzerland," her eyes brightened, "I could write to you, dearest, and you to me. We should be near to each other."

Rosa spoke slowly, wistfully; she choked a little. "Perhaps . . . I could . . . live for you, Duncan, and I could carry the plans to Geneva—is that what you wish? . . . Duncan, can I do that . . . for you ? It would not be difficult . . . for Rosa von Gleiwitz. Then I can . . . yes, I can pass them through to the English Legation."

"Rosa . . . dear, what a wonderful idea . . . one of perfection . . . but I fear it will not be so easy to obtain the necessary pass. It will take time, of course. But do not . . . promise me . . . harm yourself in this endeavour . . . you will promise, Rosa?"

"I promise, Duncan, to do my best . . . for you."

"Then you shall . . . we must discover a quiet retreat. I am on leave. You are my wife . . . Rosa? We will go to the Barmen Wald. You will perhaps know of a little inn where we can stay. The tramway will take us. We can sit in the wood, you and I, Rosa, we may plan . . . and love. And you have brought the plans with you, Rosa?"

"I have everything."

Hand in hand they sat under the shady poplars, the leaves beating a merry tattoo in the light wind, two lovers, almost unnoticeable, the soldier and his maid sitting beneath the trees, at the head of the Quellen Strasse. The tram came. Rosa and Duncan seated themselves shyly amid approving and smiling faces. Alighting at the Neumarkt they crossed to the south of the town and boarded the light railway to the Toelleturn. The woods greeted them and soft hills rose in salute. They found a little inn, the Schutzen Haus, an unpretentious wooden structure with a large restaurant, a popular centre upon Sundays and holidays. They were most welcome . . . for one or two nights . . . why certainly. The good *haus frau* was delighted . . . nay, honoured . . . The soldier had come from the trenches . . . and now with his bride . . . they should feast and be given the best guest-room. The patriot rose in her buxom bosom . . . more, it should be the room of honour. So they lunched; and then taking the plans wandered into the wood.

Duncan made a little nest of pine needles, a cushion of moss for Rosa, and there seated, on a summer afternoon, the light of a high sun dancing a fairy ballet through the close leaves, they examined the plans afresh. The memorandum in its two envelopes was rediscussed. Rosa would take one copy . . . she would fold it and secrete it in her clothes . . . she would think out a method . . . she would sew Duncan's copy into his tunic. He took it off for her examination. It would, she considered, be safest in the stiff lapel of the collar. This could be unstitched and the memorandum and map inserted on either side. She would finish that in the evening. Duncan opened up the haversack and brought out the writing materials. Together they drew the W Plan upon a sketch map showing the threatened sector. The drawing of the plan occupied some two hours. Each had a copy. They were folded and placed in envelopes.

Grant considered. "Rosa, what will you do with Muller's papers? You cannot take those with you."

"No, that would be unwise."

"I think I will take them," said Grant, after reflection. He placed them together, and slipping them into his tunic buttoned them securely in.

"Now, Rosa, as to your plans . . . not one day . . . even for ourselves, should be lost."

Rosa sighed. "Tomorrow . . . not today, Duncan . . . I need you for a little hour . . . then I will go back to Hatzberg. I will tell Frau Muller that I am ready. We will go to Dortmund the next day; and, then . . . Duncan . . . I will do my best . . . I cannot say . . . But I will reach Switzerland."

The evening hour closed in. The long shadows stretched themselves upon the grass, the warm glow of the setting sun gently caressing two lovers who had forgotten all but the serenity of devotion which now filled four barren years.

At twilight . . . the little inn: and night . . . so quiet, so peaceful.

* * * * *

Duncan walked with Rosa to the little station. A lover's farewell . . . and he was left to his own thoughts and plans.

Less than twenty-four hours remained. He would wander slowly to Viersberg through the woods. And he would hide among the trees and shrubs, first disposing of his rifle and equipment which made him now perhaps an object of curiosity and remark. He plunged into a lonely pine copse. With his bayonet he dug a trench, and laid in it his rifle, covering it with earth. He walked on to another clump of trees and similarly disposed of his bayonet, pack and equipment. Then he strolled on.

He partook of a meal at an inn, purchasing bread, cheese, dried meat and a bottle of Kirsch. He plunged again into the woods, moving south-east. As night fell he walked rapidly to the course of the upper stream. He could not tell precisely at what point he had met it, but judged his position to be north of the rendezvous, and the moon was not yet up. He waited for some hours in darkness. By the light of the moon he followed the pathway, which followed the course of the stream, walking in a southerly direction. Everything was well. He passed the saw-mill at the water's edge, finally reaching the marsh. There he paced up and down to test its surface after the recent rains. The level of the river was considerably higher and the marsh a little spongy to the tread. He paced its surface carefully. He must find the place of most severe resistance for Mayne's landing, as far up river as possible. Even if the aeroplane landed well it might have difficulty in gaining sufficient speed to rise off the heavy ground. This reconnaissance of the ground took considerable time.

Grant was glad to be able thus to pass the anxious hours. He found his nerves in a state of high tension. The creak of a branch made him start, the sound of a snapping twig chilled him. He placed his cap to mark the best position for alighting. Very early in the morning he would flag this point with his shirt and Mayne would see the signal. The night dragged on. Grant munched a little bread and cheese, and swallowed a mouthful of Kirsch. His nerves were on edge . . . anti-climax was setting in.

He watched for dawn. He felt it slowly coming, though the stars persisted in their brilliance. Alternately he watched them, and the east, for a paling of the dark pall of darkness. Almost suddenly it seemed to grow lighter. He listened, straining his hearing. He re-examined the ground, then taking off his shirt laid it out upon the tufted grass.

Light was wading in upon the darkness. He listened. He strained his eyes to pierce the bluer blackness. The stars went out one by one . . . an orange streak painted the horizon . . . he could now discern the trees, the curve of the river.

He gazed up into the vanishing night . . . Dawn . . . the sun rose triumphantly. He searched the heavens anew. Light painted them orange, yellow, deep blue, paling to cerulean and cobalt.

He began to fear. But Mayne would come . . . must come.

The sun as if by great bounds mounted before his straining eyes . . . the skies were clear . . . the trees threw long, fantastic shadows on the ground. The sun mocked him. He began to tremble, prayed incoherently . . . Mayne must come, he almost screamed. My God! He stifled a sob. The hour of safety had passed . . . yet hope remained. He gazed up into the limitless roof of Heaven, hand to ear—no speck in the sky . . . no drone of an engine. He grew cold, the perspiration of fear drenched him; hoping without hope. The sun climbed always up, now painting the landscape in all its summer clothing. He stumbled back to the trees . . . hope had vanished. Colonel Duncan Grant wept.

Then hope came again to his rescue. Perhaps the date had been mistaken; or something had gone wrong. He would wait. Tomorrow Mayne would come: the sixteenth. The marsh would be drier still under the heat of another day's sunshine. He pulled out his flask and drank deeply of the Kirsch. The warming spirit buoyed him. He put on his shirt, marking the landing spot with a large stone. He would wander in the woods, or watch a fisherman higher up. There were peasants and woodcutters. He could obtain food. He sauntered up the river bank. It was deserted. Four miles up he met an old man accompanied by two lads. They were rolling logs towards the swollen stream. He was on leave . . . nothing much to do . . . he would help them for a while. The physical energy required would soften his nervous tension.

He worked hard, furiously, the thoughts playing mad hide-and-seek in the recesses of his mind . . . Rosa was leaving for Dortmund, and Mayne would come tomorrow . . . a log splashed to the river's edge. That was a heavy one . . . But why hadn't Mayne come today? Hell! . . . he laid his shoulder under the end of another log, raised it with all his strength, every muscle taut . . . it tipped on end . . . almost like tossing the caber at the Inverness games . . . Rosa . . . purple hills . . . the sun, curse it!. . . painting the loch, orange and red . . . and, as he threw the log forward . . . Mayne is coming tomorrow.

It was midday . . . the men drew out their meal. He would share it? The physical work had been as a tonic. Hope now ran high. He toiled all day happily, then returning in the evening with the peasants to their wood-built home. Plenty of food was hidden within the house. He told them stories of the trenches : the old man nodded . . . he remembered 1870 . . . the boys sat agape.

Before dusk he bade them farewell, and wandered back along the river's edge to keep his silent vigil. Clouds had drifted over, curtaining the stars. A light drizzle fell and the night was muffled in black. Grant made a covering of pine needles, and propped his back against a tree trunk. His eyes were heavy with sleep, his heart with disappointment and bitterness. His courage was ebbing . . . he wanted Rosa. His head dropped forward . . . This was surrender . . . he forced his eyes wide open, staring into the darkness. He must not sleep. He must think clearly. Suppose the aeroplane did not come tomorrow or . . . was it yet today? He must discover some new way out . . . he was wide awake now.

He must make an appreciation of the situation . . . what a bright idea? . . . Just like being a kid again. Appreciate the situation . . . dear old Sandhurst, cavalry sketching board, a bicycle, canvas case fitted with many coloured chalks, his whole body hung round like a Christmas tree with field glasses, clinometer, map case, and . . . a pub with good beer at Frensham . . . appreciate the situation . . . "The Blue force holds the line from—" Bunkum. . . Why! they hadn't even visualized a war of three dimensions, in the air, upon land and sea . . . and . . . underground . . . the W Plan.

He dared not wait indefinitely for an aeroplane, not even after tomorrow. But, of course, Mayne would come. But . . . suppose he did not. One line was secure . . . Rosa would be able to get through to Geneva, but . . . Heaven knew when! If the wheels of the German bureaucracy turned as slowly as those of Whitehall, the pass might be granted in two, three or six months' time. Slow, yes, but sure . . . if in time. And if Rosa could go through Switzerland so could Colonel Grant, or Otto Gedern—but . . . in a different manner.

Did it matter if he were interned? He would declare himself a British officer. The Legation would substantiate that. Then he could hand over his information. Interned . . . Grant began to wish for that—on parole with Rosa beneath the shadow of the great white peaks in which he had climbed, and loved so well. His mind fashioned a new life of love and perfect tranquillity. He must reach the Swiss frontier.

But Colonel Grant had been transformed . . . the spectre of wretched Otto Gedern loomed before him . . . Otto, soldier of the 139th Saxon Regiment whose leave expired on the sixteenth of June . . . tomorrow.

What a jest! . . . Mayne was coming and Otto would take French leave . . . to France.

Always it came back to him—appreciate the situation. Mayne . . . Mayne might not arrive. Grant must reach the Swiss frontier. At Bâle would be the nearest point. Trains would be running but he could not enter a railway station. He no longer had a valid pass. He must board a train going south, always south, following the course of the Rhine . . . it must be at least two hundred and fifty miles—so many miles full of danger, of the risk of detection. He could board a goods train in a siding; that would be safer than a passenger train.

Perhaps he could change his rôle . . . as a plate layer this time, and hop from train to train. He yet possessed an ample supply of money—a little palm oil would accomplish wonders. At least he could cover a large part of the journey by rail, probably by goods train . . . that would be the way of least resistance . . . no curious officials or inquisitive police scrutinized the passage of a goods train. The engine driver and the stoker were fully occupied with steam pressure, coal and signals; the guards were concerned with brakes. He could discreetly make the necessary inquiry as to the destination of the wagons, secrete himself amid the miscellany of a goods siding near Elberfeld and board the train as it slowly moved out. The stations were well marked. He could note these and jump off as the train slowed down before signals, or, in shunting operations, if it turned at a junction in a false direction. The process could be repeated, or perhaps later he could steal a bicycle. There were many ways, but he must avoid the towns and the inquisitive . . . But, of course, Mayne would come...

The dark night passed slowly, the trees dripping a tattoo upon the hard ground. Grant stood up, yawned widely and stretched his limbs, drank Kirsch from his flask. He discovered a day's growth of beard on his chin . . . he was dirty and disreputable, hardly a credit to the Inverness Regiment . . . not even to the 139th Saxon Regiment. A distant cock called a strident note, the first herald of a new day. An hour and a half, perhaps two hours more, he judged. He gazed up through the dripping branches: the rain had ceased, though the pines still wept great tear drops. He left the belt of sheltering trees and re-examined the landing ground. The rain had soaked the tufted dry grass, but, underneath, the earth surface remained firm.

Through the mist of the passing cloud the stars peeped down upon him shyly. Cock crew again, answered by a jealous neighbour. Mayne was coming . . . he would soon pass overhead flying down towards the Ebbe Gebirge . . . he would wheel round and land . . . then breakfast, blessed breakfast, for two, and later . . . a bath, blessed bath. The auto-intoxication of high hope touched him. He paced to and fro upon the landing ground. He sought the stone: the darkness was breaking . . . he found it readily. Mayne is coming! Clouds and rain might have held him up a little.

The east paled, then light began to steal upon the western world. Mayne is coming! . . . in a few minutes now. He strained his eyes to pierce the cloud.

He heard a drone, surely an aeroplane . . . but, no . . . he had always heard that sound . . . damned monotony . . . only the rush of the stream. Mayne must come! He clenched his hands until the bones stood out white. They were raised in supplication.

"God! . . . speed Mayne," he muttered in anguish.

It was light.

He spread his shirt again, and paced the landing track, angrily kicking the tufts of grass as they rose and defied his footstep. Grant prayed, then cursed. Mayne must come! He walked almost in a delirium of fatigue and mental anguish. Half an hour passed.

He stood still . . . Blast them! He was forgotten! . . . but . . . little Mayne . . . he would come! No aeroplane appeared. Hope . . . courage . . . deserted him. Tears welled into his eyes, a great sob choked his throat; something unexplainable, unknown, undiscovered . . . snapped; and Grant abandoned himself to his grief, stumbling back to his little nest among the pines . . . he was forgotten.

Sleep, that kind, unseen nurse of the broken, whose soft ministrations bring new hope, new life to the mourner and the afflicted, gently took him, pillowing the weary head upon the pine needles, closing the hot, anguished eyes. Duncan, the child who had lost his plaything, cradled in his nest beneath the trees, slept the sleep of utter exhaustion.

* * * * *

He sat up and rubbed his eyes. He was refreshed, infinitely so. He looked out through the trees. There was his shirt, laid out to dry. He jumped up and shook the clinging pine needles from his clothes. Of course, Mayne hadn't arrived. There was no time to lose. He must begin the adventure over again. Everything seemed so very long ago . . . Frau Muller . . . and Rosa. All like a dream. He had been asleep. Otto Gedern . . . dirty dog who had overstayed his leave.

He went down to the river, and splashed the cool water over his head and breast; and scooping it in his hands, drank. He put on his shirt. There were the plans, the bulky parcel of papers thrust into the inside pocket of his tunic. He could not carry these any longer. They would have been useful. But he had all he wanted . . . the essentials. He would burn the W Plan. He re-entered the wood. The thin curl of smoke would not be observed above the tree tops. He struck a match. The papers, plans and maps burnt slowly. He watched them . . . then as they warmed, a sheet of flame gripped the mass—how like his last conflagration on a small scale—it twisted the blackened papers . . . smoke enveloped the flames. Grant fanned it with his hands to dissipate the incriminating signal above the tree tops.

The fire flickered, then went out. The W Plan had disappeared.

He threw earth over the dead embers, stamped upon it, then, turning on his heel abruptly, strode westwards. He would not be worried in Elberfeld; everyone was too busy. He picked up the light railway and followed the track to Barmen, left it outside the town, threaded his way through the pleasant gardens of the southern suburbs of the town, and strolled across to the Bahnhof Steinbeck. He peered over the fencing at the sidings, busy with shunting and loading. He joined a group of workmen loafing beside a gateway giving entrance to the goods yard . . . casual labourers . . . there was always a job in the goods yard . . . short of men. Then having crossed to the station and filled his pockets and haversack with refreshments and another flask of spirit he rejoined the group.

A call came for loaders. He pushed his way among the workmen, taking his check-in pass from a railway official at the pay-box beside the gate. With two others his task was to load drums containing chemicals. He examined the chalk marks, indicating destination, drawn upon the wagons. They were consigned to Crefeld, He edged away from his task and sought another working party : they were loading pit-props—destination Courtrai. He returned to the task, working hard and methodically, chaffing his fellows for their tardiness. He sidled away from them, the task more than half completed, and strolled round the yard. Four men were loading large barrels into an open wagon. The destination was Mainz. The barrels were heavy. Grant lent his aid. He peered again at the chalk marks . . . "Despatch 16th June" . . . today. Mainz . . . that would be well on the way. The barrels were empty— tallow vats—a musty smell pervaded the atmosphere—nauseating, rancid. He struck, as if accidentally, the top of a barrel as he thrust it up towards a man standing in the wagon: the top tilted a little under the force of his blow. Grant had decided he would travel to Mainz in a tub . . . the cynical wisdom of Diogenes . . . the cunning of Forty Thieves.

The task was completed. He noted the exact location of the wagon in the sidings. He must give up his pass, then he could scale the railings later, and under cover of darkness board the wagon and clamber into the tub. He accompanied the men to the gate. He must conserve his rations, so entered a small restaurant beside the station, filling his stomach. He lounged about the station until dusk, then hastily looking around to see if he was observed, pulled himself to the ridge of the fencing and jumped lightly to the ground on the other side. He waited in the shadow of the fence, holding his breath. He had not been observed. He ran quickly, threading his way through the wagons. He broke into a walk as he passed some railway men engaged upon a routine task. Scrambling under some covered wagons he reached the siding. He spied the truck which he had been loading in the morning. He clambered up quickly. The tops of the tubs did not show above the level of the wagon line. How the place stank! . . . tallow.

As an engine noisily shunted he beat open one of the tubs and climbed in. The stench nauseated him, but . . . he would get used to it. Another long wait—agonizing, uncomfortable, beastly. Then the wagons were shunted together. He was jolted horribly in the tub. Men came and hitched the couplings. After hours, as it seemed, the long line drew out. The journey had started. During the night he could sit at ease and in comfort on top of the tubs, or lie at full length. By daytime he must be careful . . . no looking for men, honest or dishonest, at midday . . . wise Diogenes would merge his personality into that of one of the Forty Thieves . . . he would forsake Greece for Baghdad . . . and, if only he could, escape at last from the appalling stench of tallow!

The long convoy struggled fitfully, yet it continued with little delay. Night passed. Grant wriggled into the tub. By pressing his knees against one side and his back against another he could rest in comparative comfort. He pulled the top lightly over his head. Playing at Diogenes was really rather fun . . . if only the barrels had been clean. From time to time he would cautiously tilt the top of the tub and look over its edge, straightening his body. He stood upright and could peer over the edge of the wagon and note the names of the stations. They were following the course of the Rhine, had passed through Koln and Coblenz, and were nearing Mainz. Grant peeped out and noted Bingen. He would be alert now. When the train slowed down, or preferably halted, as undoubtedly it would before Mainz, he would emerge from his tub, clamber along to the brake van and jump off from its lower step.

The train was passing through the market gardens, and beyond he could see the domes, spires and chimneys of the fine capital city of Rhenish Hesse. He pushed up the lid of the tub, sliding it upon its neighbour. He looked round and saw that he was unobserved. He jumped, pressing up with his arms, and scrambled along the tops of the tubs, upon which, for a moment, he lay at full length. The train was slowing down with brakes applied. He ran quickly to the brake van, swinging himself into it and jumped down upon the metal step. He glanced out and forward, to the left and to the right. He chose a place to alight which afforded the almost immediate cover of a clump of poplars and low shrubs. The train was slowing down, the couplings of the wagons, as they were jerked and compressed, making a deafening sound. Grant jumped. He stumbled against a sleeper, recovered his balance and, running for cover, threw himself among the shrubs. The long convoy of wagons was passing. No guard looked his way as the train vanished towards Mainz. So far so good . . . now he must move on.

He leapt up and began walking towards the city, striking the road at Amöneburg. The hour was now after six in the evening. He was about to enter a small restaurant when suddenly he met his appearance in a mirror advertising a popular wine. His face was grossly unshaved, his clothing creased and marked with stains. The restaurant was filled with people taking the pleasure of a summer evening away from the busy city. Grant turned and hurried away, but . . . he was hungry.

He entered an inn, unkempt and poor in appearance, its ragged façade and windows covered in dust. Three bicycles were leaning against the wall. He pushed into the dimly-lighted, rudely furnished *wein stube,* and called for wine. The workman lounging against the counter nodded to him. Grant requested supper, throwing upon the counter a twenty-mark note. The slattern cut bread and dried meat, piled the plate with fresh green vegetables and potatoes and passed it over to him. He ate greedily, reflecting, and feeling sorely tempted by the bicycles . . . but there would be an immediate cry, and he was in such thin company as to be too noticeable. He took up his change, and sauntered out, proceeding towards Mainz.

He entered the suburbs and replenished his pocket rations at a shop and, having inquired the way to the railway station, walked in the fading light down the Mombacher Strasse to the Haupt Bahnhof. He hoped there to discover another train proceeding south through Baden. Grant considered that it would be an advantage to be shaven. He would still pass as a soldier on leave as long as he avoided the possibility of scrutiny and examination by police or other officials. But he must not permit the time taken over such a luxury to militate against the immediate journey.

He sauntered up to the busy railway station and passing it walked upon a bridge from which he could view the metals and rolling stock, and probably discover the way of entry to the goods yard. He perceived long lines of wagons being loaded, and crossed over to the goods yard, walking beside the high fencing until he came to a gateway. It was closed. Through the crack, Grant could see a small box lighted by an unshaded electric bulb. A railway official was seated reading a newspaper, obviously on guard over the gate in order to prevent intruders.

Keeping his eye to the crack, Grant pushed the gate very gently. It began to yield to his pressure. He pushed it a little farther. The man looked up over his paper. Grant felt his eye meet that of the guard, who leaned forward a little. Grant held his breath. The man resumed his reading. Grant waited, then pushed the gate again. Damn! It creaked on its hinges. The eyes looked up. Then the man rose from his chair, newspaper still in hand and looked out of his box. Grant stood very still. The guard laid aside his newspaper and crossed over to the gate. He observed that it was opened. Then he looked round the gap, observed the unkempt dirty soldier, told him to go to the devil and slammed the gate. Grant heard the key turn on the inside.

Curse it! He must find another way. He could, of course, pass through the main entrance of the station, then slip down upon the track and make his way to the goods yard. That would entail risks, but he would adopt the habit of a wounded man from hospital and cultivate a generous limp. He approached the main entrance walking slowly, his right leg trailing with assumed difficulty. The main hall was thronged with people, men and women and soldiers, of all classes and grades. He limped through the crowds to the turnstiles leading to the platforms and track ways. He noted that at those barriers conducting to local train services the officials were perfunctory in their duties, while at others leading to the main lines, the tickets and passes were carefully scrutinized.

It was of no importance to Grant from which platform he dropped down upon the track. If he were held up at the barrier he could readily excuse himself that he had no ticket, and, of course, he could purchase one for a short journey. He joined a crowd of workmen and artisans at a barrier. As he limped a man offered his arm. Grant took it, while those in front allowed them precedence of entry. The official allowed them easy passage.

Grant was now on the platform, and thanking the man for his courtesy, sought a seat. He would jump on to the track at the end of the platform when the train had passed out. It came in, waited for a few minutes, its carriages filled, then a whistle blew and the train steamed out. Grant rose, and forgetting his limp, walked to the edge of the platform.

He felt that he was being watched from the barrier. He slowly turned his head. A soldier was looking at him . . . one of the military police. Grant feigned an unconcern which certainly he did not feel. He lit a cigar and strolled up the platform out of sight of the barrier. He would wait a minute, then run like the wind and disappear.

A step echoed from under the archway. Grant's heart beat in his throat. He dared not turn his head in the direction of the footstep. It approached slowly. Grant turned and confronted a military policeman, a domineering, big man. His thumbs were thrust into his belt, his legs wide apart. A cynical smile smeared his red, meaty face.

"So, you're a wounded soldier, are you? . . . And which leg hurts the most?" he guffawed . . . "Show your pass," he ordered abruptly.

Grant measured him under his eyelids . . . the man was big, certainly, but the spread legs made him a fair target. Grant unbuttoned his tunic pocket saying: "It's all right, corporal," and withdrawing his pass with his left hand, swung his weight behind the right with closed fist, and struck the unbalanced man full under the jaw. His great legs sank and he dropped.

Grant turned and ran. He jumped from the platform down upon the track. He heard a savage voice shouting after him. Grant fled towards the goods yard. The voice followed him. A man jumped out as if from nowhere to impede his progress. Grant swept by him. He could hear the voice in his wake . . . he was being followed . . . a cry had been raised . . . the warning whistle of a train blew behind him . . . he looked over his shoulder and saw the bright red lights of an engine with steam up bearing down upon him . . . he jumped to one side . . . a passenger train was passing, gaining speed, a yard from where he paused . . . a crowd yelled behind him . . . Grant leapt to the train . . . his fingers found a handrail . . . he pulled himself up on to the footboard . . . his face was against the glass of a carriage window, through which he could discern the travellers. They looked up in astonishment at the sudden apparition. Grant pulled himself to the forward side of the door, and opened it . . . hands helped him in.

"Nearly missed the train," he gasped, for lack of a better introduction with which to excuse himself.

"Karlsruhe train," said someone.

"Thank God," breathlessly gasped Grant.

An official came for the tickets. Grant still possessed ample money and to spare to cover the journey—Rosa had ensured that. The collector eyed him suspiciously. After leaving Worms the official entered the compartment, and scrutinized him closely. Grant began to feel very discomfited . . . the train was moving too swiftly for him to jump off again . . . and perhaps, he was unduly anxious . . . the train was proceeding fast . . . At Karlsruhe he would be well on his journey . . . from there it would not be so difficult . . . the train drew up outside Karlsruhe station by a signal. Grant considered quickly . . . he would jump off . . . he had had enough of railways . . . he would bicycle, or become a civilian, unsuspected and respectable.

As he was thus sunk in reflection the collector reappeared. Close behind him was a sergeant of the military police with an escort. Grant looked up. It took him a second to reach for the door handle. He bounded for safety. Hands like a vice gripped his right ankle. He pitched forward, striking his face against the foot-board. He was dragged back into the compartment from which the other passengers had fled and now stood in the corridor excited and anxious. Grant's face was bleeding freely from a severe cut. His wrists were handcuffed behind his back. The sergeant thrust him into a corner of the compartment nearest to the corridor. Grant smiled at him through the blood which dripped from his cheek.

The sergeant spoke. "We've had a message about you from Mainz. Let's have a look at your papers." He reached forward unbuttoning Grant's tunic and took from his pocket his leave pass and other papers. "Leave to Dresden," he commented, "Soldier Otto Gedern, 139th Saxon Regiment; leave expired morning of the sixteenth. So that's it, is it? Posing as a wounded soldier at Mainz, struck the military policeman on duty at the station, and now we've got you at Karlsruhe.

"You're a deserter. You'll be charged with desertion, and with striking your superior officer in the execution of his duty." He smiled broadly. "You haven't got much time to live, Otto Gedern. We don't waste much time over these matters nowadays."

Grant said nothing. He was at the end of his resources, a captive. Sickened by the blow which he had received, he continued to smile stupidly through the clotting blood on his face.

The train drew into Karlsruhe. The sergeant hustled Grant out of the compartment, and handcuffed him to the escort. A crowd gathered—one or two soldiers who looked on sympathetically, curious boys pressing close about the escort . . . in Karlsruhe this was all they saw of war and they liked to register its rare impressions—some unlucky devil handcuffed to a policeman, hustled and hurried through the streets . . . a sleek, comfortable man shook his fist in Grant's face; a fragile woman caught in the crowd turned her head not to see his bloody face; a workman laughed. The sergeant strode ahead, pushing aside the gaping, curious crowd which closed up again behind the escort and its victim as they passed from the station to the military barracks on the outskirts of the city.

The sergeant dropped back and walked beside his prisoner and escort. Now that his duty was accomplished he was beginning to feel a common humanity with his victim. He spoke to him. "What's the game anyway? . . . Trying to desert?"

"No," said Grant.

That, in fact, was the truth, and he very fully realized not only the ignominy of his position, but the impossibility of extricating himself from it. The sergeant would have to make a report, the more complete the better for his reputation... "Did you strike the corporal of military police on duty at Mainz Station?"

"I did," said Grant.

"What for?" queried the sergeant.

"Oh, I don't know," said Grant wearily, "perhaps I didn't like the look of him." The sergeant laughed.

"Even if you aren't a deserter, as you say, you'll receive sentence for striking your superior officer . . . in the execution of his duty. You know that, don't you?"

"Yes, sergeant," replied Grant, yawning. "When I've had a sleep I can tell you all about it . . . Let's leave it till the morning."

They entered the barracks. A group of young soldiers was lounging by the gateway. "Make way there," shouted the sergeant. They withdrew on either side, gaping at the unshaven, dirty, bloodstained figure as it passed. Grant was taken into the guard-room, his wrist unfettered from that of the escort. The sergeant of police went through the formality of handing over the prisoner to the sergeant of the guard. Grant was pushed into a narrow cell, its only light proceeding from the barred grille above the door. The handcuffs were taken from his wrists. He asked for water. He drank, and then sponged his face, drying it with a soiled handkerchief. Then taking off the stained tunic and folding it under his head, he stretched himself on the plank bed, and slept.

7

SUNSET AND SUNRISE

The morning sun of the sixteenth of June painted the façade of the creeper-clad mansion and its gardens with all the vivid tints and quiet shadows of an early summer's day, bright emerald melting into deep olive greens, scarlet and crimson offset by opaque purples, yellow and orange piled upon russet and browns.

An elderly butler, clad in a green apron, watering-can in hand, moved with spongy tread among the flowers and ferns, which banked both sides of the porchway leading to a massive, double-fronted door. A host of additional, though small, duties had fallen upon him, since the general mobilization of men for service; but, with the help of the head gardener, whose age and years of devotion to the Blesch household vied with his own, he filled in the mosaic of a day's duties with serene composure and exactitude.

Hearing the sound of footsteps, he pushed the watering-can upon one side among the flower pots and hurried busily into the house, closing the door quietly behind him. He bustled to the pantry, stripping off the green apron, and quickly slipped into the black coat of his higher and appropriate office.

A bell rang. The doors of the Blesch house never opened quickly to the unexpected caller. Having allowed a few dignified minutes to elapse, the butler, who had tiptoed across the marble floor of the great hall, ceremoniously opened the doors. Two women stood nervously between the flower banks. The younger, advancing, asked if Herr Blesch was at home. The butler, in reply, with dignity said : "The Herr Kommercienrat Blesch receives no callers except by appointment."

"But you will tell him," said the woman, "that it is Fraulein von Gleiwitz who desires to speak with him."

The old retainer stood back shading pale eyes with his hand, and gazed at her. "Pardon me, *fraulein*, surely not the daughter of Graf von Gleiwitz?" he inquired.

"The same," replied Rosa, smiling, "and this is my friend, Frau Muller. We desire to speak with Herr Blesch."

Restraint and dignity fell from the old servant. He stretched out trembling hands in welcome.

"Your father was one of our oldest friends, Fraulein Rosa. Ah! and I remember you so many years ago, our little golden Rosa, but" —he paused, holding her thin hand in his own— "you seem cold, you are not well, Fraulein Rosa . . . You will come in . . . Ah, pardon, I had forgotten myself; pray come into the inner hall and be seated. The master himself is not at home . . . He has great affairs . . . This terrible war . . . He is always busy with immense responsibilities."

He conducted the women across the pillared hall to a wide lounge, from which stairways led to the upper apartments, and offered chairs.

"Herr Blesch is not at home," he explained, "but the countess, his wife . . . perhaps you may know her . . . is, I think, in the library, and I will acquaint her of your visit."

Then he moved away with clasped fingers, a new buoyancy in his gait, muttering cheerfully, in search of the countess.

The Countess von Arenfels, the second and young wife of Herr Blesch, industrialist, sat before a wide escritoire engaged upon a correspondence which increased always with her husband's ramifications in the control of manufactures and of men, and with her consequent duties as hostess. The line of her nostril and the curve of her lip connoted a superiority which the blending of aristocratic inheritance with new-found wealth had amplified, while the restlessness of head and hands implied an impatience and irritability, which gave place to a certain cold charm only when she was the focal point of social activity arising from her husband's affairs.

To Herr Blesch, the social status, youth, classic beauty and ability of the countess were valuable assets. His first wife he had loved; the countess he regarded as capital on the credit side of his estate, so far not depreciating in value : nor had the countess herself any illusions upon the point. Herr Blesch denied her nothing, but his own time and intimacy, and she responded faithfully, if cynically, to the bargain.

The butler quietly opened the door, paused and discreetly awaited the countess's pleasure.

"Well, what is it, Joseph?" she inquired irritably, without looking up from her desk. "I am very busy. I observed two women pass the window. What do they want? You know I never see people of that class. If it's some claim, tell them to submit it by letter through the appropriate organization."

"No, madam. These ladies are not ordinary callers. They desire to see the Kommercienrat."

"What nonsense, Joseph!" interrupted the countess. "I expect you to have more sense."

"I beg your pardon, madam. It is the Fraulein von Gleiwitz, a daughter of the Graf von Gleiwitz, a very old friend of the Kommercienrat . . . in the old days, madam. I remember the *fraulein* as a quite little girl. I felt sure madam, the countess, would see her."

"I'm very busy, Joseph... I have told you. What does she want?" exclaimed the countess tapping a toe with impatience upon the parquet floor.

"That I do not know, madam, but if it is your pleasure, I will show the ladies in. The Graf von Gleiwitz was very closely associated with Herr Blesch, and the *fraulein* seems ill. If I may say so, I feel sure that the master would desire that you should see this lady."

"As usual, Joseph," said the countess dryly, "you are indeed presumptuous. You may be right: at least, I can save my husband the inconvenience of an interview. Show the ladies in, please."

"I thank you, madam." The butler retired, while the countess seated herself again before her desk, ensuring, however, that her back was turned a little farther towards the door, from which, by experience, she realized that her profile could be seen with advantage mirrored in the gilded overmantel.

The door re-opened. In quiet tones the butler announced: "Fraulein von Gleiwitz and Frau Muller to see the Countess von Arenfels," and then closed the door behind them. The countess did not raise her eyes from the desk for some moments, and then glanced at the mirror, meeting the timid inquiry of Rosa and the widow. She rose slowly and turned.

"Ah," she said, "the *fraulein* . . . I did not properly catch the name . . . but no matter."

"Von Gleiwitz and Frau Muller," interposed the widow.

"Why, of course," said the countess, "friends, so Joseph tells me, of the Kommercienrat . . ." she paused, "from the old days . . . We are living in different times now . . . He is, as you may know, very occupied, his days, hours, minutes, engaged in the service of the state . . . Perhaps I can, what shall I say? . . . assist you. Ah, please be seated . . . Forgive me... I forget others, as his wife I have little time for such relaxation.

"I do not recall the name, von Gleiwitz. It is some years since you have seen my husband. Yours, of course, will not be an ordinary social visit. You will have, I presume," said the countess with a slight sneer, "some favour to prefer, an interest, perhaps, relating to my husband's more obscure past. I endeavour, where possible, to relieve him of such small irritations." And, smiling unpleasantly, she added : "You may confide in me."

Rosa was distressed by the chilliness of the reception, and her tongue tied by the querulous austerity of the countess.

Frau Muller spoke. "It is very good of you, countess, to receive us. We had hoped rather to make an appointment convenient to Herr Blesch. It is a small matter that has brought us to see him, but one in which his good offices can greatly assist the daughter of his old friend, the Graf von Gleiwitz. Perhaps you have observed, countess," she continued, "that Rosa is very far from well. She has been ill now for many months, and has been advised to go to a sanatorium for treatment in Switzerland. There are difficulties about passport formalities. We felt sure that the Kommercienrat, by virtue of his high position in the state, could facilitate such matters."

The countess, flattered by this reference to the power of the Blesch household, smiled with genuine pleasure. "I am quite certain," she said, "that my husband can assist you. It is, as you say, a small matter, and you may leave it with me."

Rosa leaned forward in her chair, a new animation lighting and flushing her face. "That is most kind of you, countess. My father and Herr Blesch were colleagues, and I came often to this house. When old Joseph opened the door, I felt just as if I had come home again."

The pleasant smile on the face of the countess withered. "Joseph," she said, "is a veritable encyclopaedia as to the past ages, but a little inconvenient and embarrassing to me with his reminiscences."

Rosa, realizing that she had touched a delicate spot, continued quickly: "I have been urged by my sister, who is the Mother Superior of the Convent of Santa Maria, at Geneva, to come to Switzerland. My health, as my friend, Frau Muller has told you, has been failing. Your very kind offer of help relieves my anxiety. It is most good of you."

The countess relaxed a little. If she had little in common with her husband, at least she studied his interests with meticulous care. This was a small matter. It would please Herr Blesch to assist this pale and sickly child of his old friend. She would unbend and be gracious. "My husband will not return until dinner time. You will be our guests for a few days, perhaps. We are understaffed and a little primitive," she said. "Have you luggage with you?"

"Oh, dear no," replied Rosa, laughing. "Our small requirements are at the station."

"Very well. I shall send for them, and will have rooms prepared for you. It will be a happy surprise for my husband when he returns," added the countess.

Later, while the widow sat upon the veranda dreaming before gay borders and cool lawns, Rosa and the countess walked quietly in the Dutch garden. The two women were of an age, socially of equal distinction. The countess was drawn towards this frail and lonely girl. She surveyed her, and saw that she possessed both beauty and rare charm. She became friendly, took Rosa's arm in her own, and invited confidence. Rosa had desired that Frau Muller should make no mention of her hurried betrothal to the Major Schaeffer, and her secret would certainly remain inviolate in the Blesch household.

The countess, with her own sterile love, breathed sympathy for the beautiful girl, whose illness had removed her from the grand emotions. She expressed, too, her own disappointments and found Rosa a sympathetic listener.

"Ah," she said, "your music must bring you consolations. For myself, I direct my desires into business channels. For my husband I am a kind of female dragoman, labelled wife for convenience. He has no interests outside his affairs. I am his prisoner, but I can never get close to him... I am, I think, on the whole, satisfied. You are free, Rosa: when you are well, perhaps your music will not suffice."

Rosa remained silent, her eyes upon the ground, thinking of Duncan.

"We have much in common, Rosa. It will be a real pleasure to me, as I know also it will be to my husband, to have you with us for a few days, until this matter is arranged. You will, too, be able to entertain a young officer, who will be with us in a short while. His father—you probably know the name—is Herr Messer, my husband's closest business colleague. I do not see him," she added acidly. "You perhaps know of his reputation in Elberfeld; but the boy is a soulful lad." She paused. "He has lost a leg. He has a great future, I believe. Do you know him ?"

Rosa shook her head. "No," she replied, "we have not met. I live very quietly."

"I sometimes think," continued the countess, "his experiences have made him a little light-headed; and, of course, his life at home . . . his mother died from shock some months ago, when she lost two sons . . . his life is impossible. Your music, I am sure, will comfort him. What I have seen of the boy is attractive; he has dangerous views, but he is discreet . . . Now you will like to rest before dinner," the countess concluded, "you will make yourself entirely at home. I have matters which need attention, but I shall look forward to further little talks with you." She took her hands in her own and kissed her with affection.

Dinner was not served until nearly nine in the evening. The ladies awaited the arrival of Herr Blesch in the drawing-room. He entered swiftly, a man of fine presence, over six feet in height, of firm figure and muscular gait despite his fifty-seven years. He kissed his wife lightly, passing with hands outstretched to Rosa.

"Our little sunbeam, little Rosa. How like your mother!" he exclaimed. "The same expression, the same hair. It must be nearly ten years since we met . . . This is indeed a pleasure . . . And Frau Muller, of course . . . your husband was a genius, a great man. We owe much to him in these days." He paused, then in lowered and serious voice continued : "And your son, my dear lady. I trust that all will be well . . . You have my deepest sympathy in what I know must be your present anxiety."

"Oh, dear, oh, dear," exclaimed the widow brightly, "I assure you I have no longer any anxiety. I am . . ." Rosa regarded her searchingly and anxiously . . . "I am quite sure," said the widow firmly, "that he is safe."

"Then you have received news?" asked Herr Blesch.

Rosa intercepted, covering her own anxiety. "Frau Muller," she said quietly, "has her faith, and in that she trusts."

"Naturally," replied Herr Blesch, "faith is a wonderful comfort in these dark days. We few who are familiar with the work of your son must, too, have faith. You have courage, madam, which I am proud to say is an example to myself." He dismissed the subject with a sweep of the hand. "Now let us dine."

The intimacy of the dinner table was a happy one. Herr Blesch, who, as Rosa had perceived, was disturbed by the disappearance of Major Muller, of the circumstances of which he obviously possessed a fuller knowledge than did the widow, was grateful to Rosa for her interception. An embarrassing moment had passed, and he was glad to talk of the little affairs of Rosa's childhood, and of the distinguished days of Professor Muller's occupation of a Chair of Science at Bonn University. But he carefully avoided any further reference to Major Ulrich Muller. As to the passport and necessary visas for Switzerland, there would be no difficulty. He hoped within a few days to be able to conclude the formalities, and would press the matter forward personally through the Foreign Office without delay. He was delighted to have two old friends as his guests again, especially since, as he could observe, Rosa and his wife had already established the intimacy of friendship.

Five days passed in comfort, rest and quietness. Before dinner on the twentieth of June, a motor car brought Lieutenant

Messer to the house. Rosa and Frau Muller were in the garden reading. Herr Blesch would return for dinner. The lad had important letters from his father to deliver, and these would require, perhaps, some verbal explanation. The three women went into the dining-room and were joined by Herr Blesch and the lieutenant some ten minutes later.

"Permit me to present the Lieutenant Messer, a very gallant officer of our air forces, and the son of another old friend, Herr Adolf Messer. Perhaps you may have met him in Barmen, Rosa?" said Herr Blesch.

"I am proud, indeed, to meet you, *Herr* Lieutenant. But we have not met before, I think," said Rosa.

"Fraulein von Gleiwitz lives in Hatzberg," interposed the countess.

"Oh, yes, but I go out very seldom," replied Rosa. "I live near my friend, Frau Muller."

Heinrich Messer bowed to the widow.

"Ah, how interesting!" exclaimed Frau Muller. "You will know my son, Ulrich, perhaps? He has spent much time at the works with your father. He is an engineer."

Herr Blesch grunted assent.

"Surely he cannot be Major Ulrich Muller of the Corps of Engineers?" questioned Heinrich.

"Why certainly! And you know him?" asked the widow eagerly.

"I could not say that," replied Heinrich. "He is a very great engineer. My father says he is a genius; one of Germany's master brains. No, I cannot say that I know him."

"Then perhaps you know his friend, Major Schaeffer?" put in the widow quickly. Rosa looked across at her and frowned, catching her breath, but Frau Muller did not observe the glance. "Major Schaeffer has just been with us for a day or two." The widow turned to Herr Blesch. "It was he who gave me the first assurances as to Ulrich's safety. But, of course, Herr Blesch, as you know, I never doubted."

"I know, I know, of course . . . But who is this Major Schaeffer? I have not heard his name in connection with . . . ah . . . Major Muller's activity."

"Probably not," laughed Rosa, determined to turn the conversation, "there are so many majors of engineers. Just a friend, I think."

"Oh, no," said Frau Muller warmly, "a very close friend. His most intimate. You do not do him justice, Rosa. Major Schaeffer was with him everywhere in his work."

"I think I should tell you, Frau Muller," interposed Heinrich Messer, "that I was not right in giving you to understand that I have not met Major Muller. Certainly, I do not know him. But just a few days ago, an officer spoke with me, very kindly, in the lounge of the Imperial Hotel in Barmen . . . only for a few moments... I did not know his name, but he was a major of the Corps of Engineers . . . He was very courteous and friendly to me... I observed that he was a resident in the hotel, and I asked the clerk his name... I then realized that I had been honoured indeed . . . I saw the signature at the reception desk... It was Major Ulrich Muller."

The widow leaned across the table towards Lieutenant Messer, her face animated with excitement. She caught the look of fear in Rosa's eyes. There was a still silence for some seconds, then a fork dropped with a tinkle upon the widow's plate, and she fell back limply in her chair. The countess hurried to the widow's aid, and sought to compose her. Herr Blesch was speaking; Rosa, pale as parchment.

"You spoke with Ulrich Muller in Barmen, Heinrich?" he questioned. "Are you sure? Major Muller has been missing since the fifth of June. You observe the shock which you have given to his mother. Are you sure? For me and for your father, the fate of Major Muller is of the utmost importance."

Heinrich appeared bewildered at the consternation which his remarks had caused. "Of course it was Ulrich Muller. I saw his signature in the register."

Rosa had been thinking rapidly. She must protect the identity of Duncan at all costs. This inquiry was leading along a difficult path. "There are probably a score of Ulrich Mullers in the army." she said with forced gaiety.

"Describe the appearance of your acquaintance. That will quickly clear the matter up," demanded Herr Blesch.

"He was tall," said Heinrich quietly. "I should say six feet; sandy hair, blue eyes, big boned; hands, large and practical, just as I thought he might be."

"That might be a description of our Major Ulrich Muller," said Herr Blesch grimly. "But you are positive the eyes were blue, Heinrich?" he questioned. "And you noticed his hands? Had he any fingers missing?"

"No, certainly not. As to his eyes, I am quite sure. I marked him particularly. I saw him again the following day with a woman, heavily veiled, and he waved recognition to me as he was passing through the lounge."

"You are sure," pursued Herr Blesch, "that you would have noticed had fingers been missing from his right hand?"

"Positively certain," replied Heinrich, without hesitation.

"You may compose yourself, Frau Muller," said Herr Blesch kindly. "There is certainly some mistake. I am sure your son was not in Barmen; nor could he have been."

"I heard what the *Herr* Lieutenant said," replied the widow faintly. "It is odd. His was a description of Ulrich's friend, Major Schaeffer . . . very odd."

"Or a description of anyone else," added Rosa gaily. "This must have been a practical joke, or perhaps someone wished to hide his own identity from the curious. One can never tell in wartime" —she laughed— "can one, *Herr* Lieutenant?"

"It seems queer to take the name of one's friend, who is, as I understand, reported missing."

"Very queer indeed in the circumstances," added Herr Blesch. "You will excuse me, ladies. I have important matters to which to attend. You will not be anxious, Frau Muller. Heinrich, when you have finished, please join me in my study."

Conversation languished. Both Frau Muller and Rosa were obviously greatly disturbed. Heinrich after a few awkward minutes made his excuses and joined Herr Blesch in the study.

The Kommercienrat was seated at his desk. "Sit down, Heinrich, I want to talk to you. I have already telephoned to the chief-of-staff. There is as yet no trace of Ulrich Muller. The name of Major Schaeffer is not known. I must tell you, in confidence, the facts. Muller was reported missing after an English raid. He was, as you have said, a genius, and responsible for certain engineering plans of high importance to me and to your father, and to the state. His loss has greatly disturbed us. You are positive both as to the name and as to the correctness of your description of the man?"

"Quite positive," replied Heinrich. "I remember, too, my conversation with him very well." Heinrich related his experience of having seen the aeroplane, and of his talk with the major of engineers. Herr Blesch listened with grave attention.

"However painful this may be to Frau Muller and to Rosa, too, I must question these ladies closely. There is something very curious about this matter. It may be, as Rosa suggests, just a practical joke, though I can scarcely believe it. I shall require you to be present. We must discover the identity of this Major Schaeffer. Now let us go to the ladies."

When Herr Blesch and Heinrich entered the drawing-room, Rosa was seated at the piano. Frau Muller sat in a small, straight-backed arm-chair, her eyes closed in quiet ecstasy; the countess reclined upon a sofa turning over the pages of an illustrated paper.

"Rosa plays exquisitely," she remarked to her husband as he entered. "You are fond of music, are you not, Heinrich? We have just had Beethoven's *Pastoral;* now what shall it be?"

"Just one moment, Sophie," intervened Herr Blesch. "I want to ask one or two questions as to Major Schaeffer."

The widow reopened her eyes, and sat up abruptly, clasping the carved arms of the chair in her thin fingers.

"My dear Karl," sighed the countess, "please let us have a little post-prandial peace. This subject is distressing to Frau Muller. Why, Rosa told you it was just a practical joke, and Heinrich has been mistaken. You really are becoming absurdly apprehensive, and very fussy. Take a rest, Karl. Now, Rosa, let us have more music."

Rosa allowed her fingers again to stray bewitchingly over the keyboard.

Herr Blesch had coloured darkly with annoyance. He smoked in silence for a moment and then said harshly, with impatience : "You may play in a minute or two... I am sorry if I pain you, Frau Muller . . . you will forgive me . . . but, no doubt, I can help you further. Tell me," he said, addressing himself to her, "who is this Major Schaeffer ?"

"Karl, do sit down, or go to your study and leave us in peace."

"Who is Major Schaeffer?" barked Herr Blesch angrily to the widow.

"I really do not know," stammered the widow nervously.

"You do not know, what do you mean?" inquired Herr Blesch, his voice rising.

"He is a friend of my son Ulrich . . . He told me so," replied Frau Muller quietly.

"There you are," said the countess. "A friend of Ulrich's."

"Yes, indeed," continued the widow, "and an old and intimate friend of yours, Rosa, is he not?"

Rosa fingered the notes, played a stanza of chords, with lowered eyes, while she fought for self-composure, and reasoned quickly as to her reply. "Oh, yes, of course. There is no mystery about Major Schaeffer. Both Frau Muller and I know him well. He was on leave and came in to see us."

"And," put in Frau Muller, "he told me of Ulrich. Major Schaeffer had only recently been with him. Why," she said with assurance, "I gave him some of Ulrich's papers to take back to him in the trenches."

"Papers," roared Herr Blesch, "what papers?"

"Don't you think we have had enough of this, Karl? You make me quite ashamed. Rosa, play to us a little more."

Herr Blesch crossed to the bay window, puffing his cigar in anger. He passed out on to the veranda. Rosa played, she scarcely knew what; excuses, explanations chasing each other through her mind. Herr Blesch was more than agitated; that was plain, nor would he be baulked in his inquiry. There was danger. This Rosa realized . . . but for herself alone. Duncan was safe. It was now five days since he had returned to the British lines. But could she be sure? He had told her that she would hear the aeroplane and perhaps see it on the morning of the fifteenth. How she had strained her hearing and eyes. She had heard and seen nothing; but Duncan was safe. An intuition told her so; the secret telepathic message of love. She would take the offensive in question, and remain no longer the passive witness beneath cross-examination.

After several minutes Herr Blesch, whose footsteps had been heard pacing the veranda, re-entered. He was calm and smiled as he entered. "It is," he said, "most interesting to me to hear details of Ulrich Muller and his colleague from his mother and friends. Your son's work is known to me and to this boy's father intimately. We are honoured to be his servants."

Frau Muller's face glowed with pleasure.

"I should so much have enjoyed meeting his colleague, Major Schaeffer. That is why, Sophie," he said with a curve of the lip, "I have appeared a little importunate. Perhaps, Frau Muller, you may be able to suggest where I could get in touch with Major Schaeffer?"

"I really do not know," replied Frau Muller. "He returned immediately, or almost at once, to the front, I believe to rejoin Ulrich in his work . . . but Rosa will tell you. She was with him after he left my house."

Rosa had hidden her face behind some manuscripts of music which she had raised upon the rest above the grand piano.

"I have not the slightest idea where he is now. How should I? There is such secrecy in these matters; is there not, *Herr* Lieutenant?" said Rosa, gaily addressing herself to Heinrich. "What do you say ? . . . 'somewhere in France' . . . and that may mean Belgium, Luxemburg, Poland or even Turkey."

"Then he has gone back to the line, Rosa?" questioned Herr Blesch. "What a pity! When did you first meet him, Frau Muller?"

"Oh, only a day or two ago," replied the widow.

"What date?" said Herr Blesch sharply.

"Let me see now . . . it would be about the sixth, no, surely, the fifth of June. I remember well now; yes, it was the fifth of June."

"That was the date, Herr Blesch, upon which I saw the aeroplane," intercepted Heinrich.

"An aeroplane," exclaimed Rosa, "how exciting! He never told us, did he, little mother? Did he come in an aeroplane?"

"It is quite possible that he did," replied Herr Blesch dryly. "So you never met Major Schaeffer before the fifth of June . . . You were speaking of some papers a little while ago, Frau Muller. What papers were these ?"

"Oh, dear me, just the papers Ulrich left behind, after he had finished his experimental work in the mines, before he went to the front—maps and plans. Ulrich wanted some of them, so his friend had come for them."

"And you gave them to him, Frau Muller?" asked Herr Blesch sternly.

"Why, certainly."

Herr Blesch smoked in silence for a moment, then he said : "Will you play a little, Rosa? Frau Muller is tired." When she paused in her playing, Herr Blesch continued :—

"Rosa, dear, how long have you known Major Schaeffer?"

"Quite a long time. Not very well, until recently, but surely you must remember him. It must have been at your house that I first met him, years ago."

"Ah, ha," laughed the countess. "Oh, fickle memory! At last you stand convicted, Karl: it was you who introduced the mystery man to Rosa."

"I am quite certain that this was not so," replied Herr Blesch with some heat. "Perhaps Rosa will describe this major."

For a moment Rosa sat in reflection, then she answered: "He is tall . . . very dark, both in hair and complexion... A striking figure, thin, aesthetic. But surely you will remember him now I have produced this little picture."

"Rosa," exclaimed the widow, "you must be mistaken. Wilhelm is fair, a fine figure of a man, in build much like Ulrich."

"But such a one was the Major Muller who spoke with me at the Imperial Hotel on the fifth," interposed Heinrich, "and I saw him with a lady thickly veiled on the following morning."

"Your happiness must have dimmed your eyes, Mother Muller," laughed Rosa gaily. "Oh, no, Major Schaeffer was dark." Rosa must mystify and mislead now, whatever the cost. The effort of control was taxing her strength. She choked suddenly, then, for a moment, was overcome with a paroxysm of coughing.

Frau Muller leant forward quickly in her chair, then half rose. "Poor, poor Rosa; she is not strong," she said in explanation. "I . . . I do not understand," she faltered, "all this curiosity concerning my son and Wilhelm. I was happy and satisfied until tonight... I do not understand . . . let us leave it . . . Rosa is not well." She appealed to Herr Blesch, whose expression hardened perceptibly.

"Countess," she continued, "this is all very painful. What does it matter if Wilhelm was fair or dark? I am old, my eyes are dimmed... I am sure Rosa must be right..." The widow paused, shook her head as she mused, then smiled softly, "Rosa knows . . . she and Wilhelm are very dear friends . . . they are betrothed."

"Is that true!" cried the countess shrilly.

"I have said so," replied Frau Muller quietly, and she rose and crossed the room to where Rosa sat before the piano, exhausted, breathing heavily and gazing before her with wide, staring eyes. The widow gathered Rosa to her. Rosa whispered : "Wilhelm was dark, little mother." The widow spoke. "Rosa will tell you that she and Wilhelm love one another. It is true! Are you not glad? . . . She has waited for her happiness... It has come."

"I had understood," said the countess with a sneer, "that Rosa's affections were confined to her music. I am sure we must all congratulate her upon this discovery of her attachment to the . . . ah! . . . dark man of mystery." Silence followed.

"Rosa," said Herr Blesch stiffly after a while, "as your trustee, I am glad indeed to be one of the first to congratulate you. Can you now tell us something about this Major Schaeffer?"

Rosa coughed to defer her reply. Then she said faintly : "There is very little to tell . . . I have been much alone . . . he was kind, very kind, to me. Are you not glad ?"

"I think," replied Herr Blesch, "that I must give you some information which perhaps will shock you... I ask you to be calm . . . For me . . . this matter may be of . . . great importance."

"As they would say in Germany's new territory," laughed the countess, mocking him : "'*L'Etat, c'est moi.*' But continue, Karl. I love to hear you in the grand manner."

"Don't be a fool, Sophie . . ." he replied testily.

"Fool?" she sneered, "I've been fooled enough during the past few days by this friend . . . from the old days, Karl."

Herr Blesch lit another cigar, and puffed the smoke in silence, then continued. "The information which I have to give is as follows. After leaving the dinner table, I telephoned to my friend, the chief-of-staff. I asked if there was any further news of Major Ulrich Muller. I am sorry to have to tell you, Frau Muller, that at nine-fifteen this evening, he is still missing: there is no news. Major Schaeffer's encouragement to your hopes was, I fear, unfounded."

"Oh, dear God!" cried Frau Muller.

"But do not alarm yourself. No news is good news, you know, and . . . you have your faith. Take courage, madam . . . Major Schaeffer's story to you was not true . . . the name of Major Schaeffer is not known at Army Headquarters: no man with such a name was at any time associated with Ulrich Muller..." He paused while the burden of this information penetrated the minds of the little audience, now entirely under his control, awaiting the next words with breathless expectation.

"Rosa, tell us, please, is Wilhelm Schaeffer the name of your lover?"

"Yes," breathed Rosa.

"Then Wilhelm Schaeffer is a liar," he said dryly.

"Go on," said the countess quickly, her eyes bright with excitement.

"I am going to ask Lieutenant Messer to tell you of what he saw on the morning of the fifth of June."

Heinrich told of what he had observed, of hearing and seeing an aeroplane. When he had completed the story Rosa leant forward upon her arms across the piano. She had gathered all her courage and strength. Her mind had quickly sought an avenue of escape and of excuse, by question and answer, by self-examination and cross-examination. She must fight for Duncan with every artifice and power at her command, the strength of her mind, the weakness of her body. She must utilize all her resources. The urge to action roused her. The pale cheeks were flushed.

"How thrilling, *Herr Lieutenant*," she exclaimed. "I do wish I had seen it, too. Tell me, if I had been awake, should I have heard the aeroplane, and seen it, too?"

"Of course you would," answered Heinrich, speaking with the enthusiasm of a master of technique. "You couldn't miss it. You could hear the drone of its engine miles away."

The light died from Rosa's eyes—"You could hear the drone miles away," said the airman. Duncan had said so too. She had heard nothing . . . seen nothing. Had the aeroplane come back? Where was Duncan now? Perhaps still in Germany . . . She must save the discovery of Duncan's identity.

"Now," said Herr Blesch, addressing himself to Rosa. "It will be interesting to go over what we have learnt. The evidence will help you, I feel sure. . . . As your trustee I have, too, a duty in your protection . . . Perhaps you may not have chosen as wisely as you had hoped. Let us see. Heinrich tells us that on the evening of the fifth of June, a major of the Corps of Engineers spoke with him, . . . The name in the hotel register was that of Ulrich Muller. It is quite plain that this visitor was not the Ulrich Muller whom we all know... In conversation he warned Heinrich not to disclose the evidence as to an aeroplane . . . This man coincided exactly with Frau Muller's visitor."

"No," cried Rosa.

"Let me conclude," said Herr Blesch swiftly. "Frau Muller insisted before you corrected her."

"I am not sure," sighed the widow, interrupting.

"I . . . am quite sure," replied Herr Blesch. "Wilhelm Schaeffer and the visitor at the Hotel Imperial were one and the same person—the description and dates are agreed. Rosa alone disagrees. This man is to marry Rosa. We do not know when they first met, certainly not at this house; of that I am sure. Wilhelm Schaeffer is unknown to Army Headquarters. He posed as a colleague of Ulrich Muller... He lied... He examined Major Muller's papers. And then we have the story of an aeroplane . . . with English markings . . . Can you not put two and two together? Am I so apprehensive, Sophie?" he asked, turning towards the countess.

"Rosa," he said sharply, the rasp in his voice rudely breaking the silence, "when did you first meet Wilhelm Schaeffer?"

Rosa gasped for breath. Her bosom heaved; she paled with emotion. The evidence was overwhelming, she felt herself being pressed back and back; the space for manoeuvre narrowing, always narrowing . . . evidence, like walls, was closing in upon her; there was no avenue of escape. She had reached the last line of defence; yet not hers . . . that she must surrender . . . Duncan's identity alone could be shielded.

"I suppose," she replied slowly, feeling the eyes of all fixed upon her, "that my first meeting with Wilhelm Schaeffer was . . . yes . . . at the house of Frau Muller . . . no . . . I cannot tell you." She coughed and fought breathlessly for self-mastery, her fingers fumbling the silent keyboard. Frau Muller, whose eyes were closed, had swooned. She lay back in her chair unnoticed.

"You had not then met him before?" pursued Herr Blesch sternly.

"Of course not," cried Rosa, uttering a sound in part chuckle, part sob.

"And your description of this Wilhelm Schaeffer? Was he this fair man or another?"

"I do not quite understand," replied Rosa. "Fair or . . . Wilhelm . . . my . . ."

"Lover," supplied the countess acidly.

"My lover, if you like. He is tall . . . dark. I have described him."

"But we are not certain," said Herr Blesch gravely. "Are you quite sure?"

Rosa's moment had come—she must play her part now. Rosa rose from her seat, triumph writ upon her face. She threw her trump card.

"Quite sure," she said firmly. "Heinrich observed a veiled woman at the Hotel Imperial . . . That woman was Rosa von Gleiwitz... I am quite sure of my lover's description... It was I who spent the night with Major Schaeffer!"

Rosa's words swept on. "You are apprehensive, Herr Blesch . . . you have your secrets, jealously guarded, fenced round with barbed wire and with bayonets... I, too, have my secrets . . . trivial things, little hopes, emotions, fears, desires... I have nothing but my honour to defend . . . You have torn down my defences . . . you are apprehensive? As my trustee, perhaps you have acted within your rights." Her voice rose in staccato tones. "Yes, I slept with Wilhelm . . . He gave me what no one else has ever even offered . . . You have his description. Do you need more?"

Rosa covered her face with her hands and stumbled from the room, her body shaken with great sobs. Duncan's identity was secure. Rosa had carried conviction by the very baldness of her confession. She had stripped herself of modesty, to ride naked through the highways of their cynosure, while the countess played at Peeping Tom. Now, in her shame, Rosa fled.

"How disgusting," murmured the countess, yawning as Rosa passed. "From the old days, Karl . . . a common prostitute . . . yet . . . I could almost be sympathetic with her." She laughed harshly. "Send the little *poupée* away and forget it . . . Stick to business, Karl; it's more profitable . . . Ring for my maid : we will take Frau Muller to her apartment."

Herr Blesch and Heinrich were alone. Both were silent for many minutes wrapt in thought. Herr Blesch spoke at last. "Well, Heinrich, you are a soldier. What would you do?"

"I do not know. Nothing is plain to me," replied Heinrich.

"Not plain? You don't know?" shouted Herr Blesch. "It's as plain as a pikestaff. Someone came. I don't know who . . . a spy, probably. He sought to rob Frau Muller of evidence vital to the state. Frau Muller has told us she had nothing of importance. Thank God, our secrets are inviolate. No one can steal them from us. Who is this fellow? No one knows. He seduced this girl in order to make her a party to his plots. Probably he had accomplices, your fair friend for one . . . The dark man ravished Rosa. She must pay! . . . You don't know what to do . . . send for the police . . . arrest her! She gave herself to a spy, and you don't know what to do? Does a German woman's honour mean nothing to you, Heinrich? Send for the military police. I'll have the woman shot as an example to the others."

The lad had grown very white. He stood up, gripping the edge of the writing table to support his weight.

"Do you suppose," Heinrich stammered through his tears, "I gave my mother and brothers in order to have to listen to venom of this kind . . . When I looked down at the bloody pulp which had been a leg, I thought that was the dirtiest sight I should be asked to see . . . I've seen something more beastly now!"

Herr von Blesch, who had regained his composure, remained quite unruffled. "Be quiet, Heinrich," he said sternly.

"Be quiet be damned!" shouted the lad. "We're not all cogs in this infernal machine of war, going round and round and round, while you and dad, and a few others sit back and rake in the profits . . . you have no right to accuse this woman," he continued breathlessly. "You know nothing of her life, which has brought her little love or joy, except . . . in a work which no others would do. You are dug in here in smug complacency, while the lads, and women, like Fraulein von Gleiwitz, dance in Hell. You call the tune, and, just because you think, only think, mark you, that she's been a party, willing or unwilling, to something which will stand between you and your profits, you vilify her in your own house."

The countess had returned and stood within the half-opened door.

"Heinrich," her bosom heaved as she fought for words. She strode toward the lad, and thrust him roughly into the chair.

"Sit down. I will not have such words in my house. Sit down or get out at once. My husband has his clear duty to the state of which, as you have rightly, though intemperately, observed, he is a major part," she said acidly, with greater calm. "How dare you defend a harlot who gave herself, and the secrets of the empire, for what you call love? You boys don't know what love is." She passed across to her husband and took his arm, standing beside him.

"Lover?" inquired Heinrich, his voice rising and falling as the words in ebb and flow came from him. "My God! I know what love is and what it means. I've seen it in Barmen. Did you use the word harlot? Very well, then, I have my answer. If one word is said against this woman, I will use the influence of an airman who gave a limb, the remaining son of a family well known in Elberfeld, with the workmen. You have strikes and unrest here. We have them in Elberfeld. The fires of revolution are laid among our workers. I can kindle those fires.

"How does my father expend his leisure hours? . . . poor devil! . . . in the arms of every woman in Barmen. He is your friend, Herr Blesch, your closest business associate, the founder of your fortune. I know his profits. If you inform against this woman, I will declare my father's profits . . . your profits . . . to the workmen. I will tell them, too, in what manner he disposes of them. That evidence will recoil on your head. The workmen are waiting for a torch with which to light the fire of revolution. I hold it. You will no longer ride roughshod over us all. If you touch this woman, who has suffered, perhaps more than I, I will light that fire." He laughed hysterically. "Now think of that in terms of profit and loss, Herr Blesch."

"You are mad, Heinrich," exclaimed the countess.

Heinrich remained motionless for some seconds. Quite calmly he continued: "In a sense we are all mad, but I am not blind . . . Every ambition, every desire you have is satisfied. Power immense, complete domination over thousands of men, and wealth untold. You are supported by the whole resources of the state, by law, police, military force."

"What do we get out of the war?" . . . The face of Herr Blesch set itself in an ugly smile. "Yes, I know I'm only a kid," retorted Heinrich, "but I've only got one life, and I have as much title to a viewpoint as you have, Herr Blesch. Every ideal I had has been shattered. My brothers are gone, my mother is dead, my father so debauched that I am ashamed to be his son. Do you really imagine the soldiers or the workmen care a snap any longer for your war, your plans, your victories, your rule? . . . They don't. They are goaded on by threat of court martial and imprisonment, while you sit back and have all the fun."

Herr Blesch shook his head in negation.

"Oh, yes," cried Heinrich, "it is fun organizing this, that, and the other; creating grandiose schemes, holding the destinies of thousands of human lives in your hands, ordering, disposing . . . the greatest game in the world. You are so preoccupied with schemes that you have no moments for friendship or life . . . everything, everybody is utilized to serve only your ambitions . . . until they are saturated, like those of dad... , then when the brain no longer makes its demands of all the physical resources, you and your kind give themselves to the body, pouring out wealth and expending power in the seduction of anyone whom the whim of the moment commends to the eye and to the senses.

"I'm not blind. I've seen it. I have been brought up among your kind. There may be rare exceptions. You, perhaps, are one . . . but you're having your fun, the greatest game in the world . . . Rosa von Gleiwitz, and I . . . where do we come in? . . . Just pawns in the game . . . Rosa and a spy . . . nonsense . . . Rosa and . . . a lover . . . that's her secret..."

"So," interrupted the countess, "you class yourself with her, Heinrich?"

"What is the worst you can say of her?" stammered the lad. "You imagine she may have been the tool of some plot which might thwart or hinder your own ambitions and schemes. So you set up yourself upon a high pedestal and preach nonsense about morality and the state. What is the truth? As I believe, Rosa has loved, perhaps does love, this man in a way you have never known . . . or have forgotten. She found what life never gave to her before."

"I think we have heard quite enough, Heinrich," said Herr Blesch in heated tones. "Your views might be interesting later. We . . . do not expect a woman of this class to behave . . . ah . . . as a prostitute."

"Let me continue," interrupted the countess, realizing that perhaps Heinrich unwittingly was fighting her own battle.

"Thank you, countess, but I refuse to be silenced..." Heinrich continued breathlessly. "At the lowest estimate, supposing your interpretation can be admitted to be right, Rosa's had her little fun . . . just as you are having yours . . . and, as every girl and every lad, marshalled and dragooned by your kind, snatches it whenever a chance offers, whether in Berlin or Brussels, Elberfeld or Lille. Do you grudge her just that?

"You have yet to disassociate yourself from my father upon the grounds that he has wearied of profits and prefers seduction, Herr Blesch. I warn you . . . you may be a paladin in organization, a master of mechanical technique, the supreme industrial force, but you have lost touch with the people; you fail to understand their emotions, ambitions, fears, anxieties. You may be able to control them with the aid of martial law . . . though personally I doubt it. But the people are the key to the situation, military, social, political, industrial. Keep faith with the people, Herr Blesch . . . or, I warn you, they will break you."

"Young man," said the Kommercienrat, rising, "I have listened to you with patience. Were it not for your wounds, and for my friendship with your father, I should persuade myself to send for the police. I have listened to vituperation of this kind before. For you, I have pity, an overwrought, hysterical lad. Your utterances are treason. Men who have dared to speak in this vein to my workmen have been shot, or are now in jail. You had better go to bed and cool your head . . . I have my duty."

"Herr Blesch, I, too, have my duty. You must help this young woman in her trouble; she, too, is the child of a friend whose life was devoted to the foundation of your fortune. You must help her."

"You dare say 'must' to me?"

"I do. My alternative is clear. I go to the workmen in Elberfeld. I know the secrets, I hold the torch. I will fire the revolt. Then, what of your ambitions, your plans and schemes, Herr Blesch?"

"You threaten me, Heinrich? You are a public danger, a madman!" He placed his hand swiftly within the centre drawer of the desk and drew out a revolver.

"Shoot me like a dog, if you will," jeered Heinrich. "Then telephone to dad, and tell him what you have done! You forget I'm all he's got. He still possesses one absorbing hobby—myself . . . You have not realized that his other ambitions are satiated." Heinrich sank back exhausted by his effort, then said very quietly: "Consider; what I ask is simple. Give Rosa her passport to the frontier . . . and forget."

"Heinrich," said the countess, "leave us for a little while . . . I wish to consult with my husband." With uncommon grace and sympathy she assisted the lieutenant to the door. "You will find wine set in the library. We . . . I will join you later." The Countess von Arenfels closed the door and turned to her husband.

"The boy is mad," said Herr Blesch bluntly.

"Oh, yes, perhaps . . . but there is wisdom in his madness, Karl."

"Wisdom? . . . Where? . . . What?" demanded the Kommercienrat.

Tears dimmed the countess's eyes as she placed her hands upon her husband's broad shoulders. Rosa in all her weakness had fought and won, where the countess, with all her natural gifts, for three years had feared to do battle.

"Karl, what does it matter? . . . Rosa has had her fun . . . you have had yours . . . within a few weeks, it will be finished . . . the W Plan," she whispered . . . "Where do I come in, Karl?"

The countess ran her delicate fingers lightly over the rugged set face, then pressing her body against the massive frame she kissed him. She clung to her husband, weeping quietly. The countess must not lose this fight; as it was her first, so it must be her last. The man held her back from him with strong arms, looking down upon this woman shorn of pride, who was his wife. She felt his figure quiver, and then looked up, an appeal smiling through the tears in her eyes.

"Sophie," he whispered, "you are so true, so good, so perfect, that I had forgotten . . . you are also beautiful." He gathered the woman to him.

The countess and her husband entered the library. Lieutenant Messer rose awkwardly and stiffly as they entered. Herr Blesch poured three glasses of wine, and raised his glass. "Heinrich," he said simply, "I salute you;" then smiling to his wife he touched her glass.

"Within a day or two, Heinrich, I shall ask you to take Rosa to the frontier . . . My wife and I go to her now . . . Good night."

Herr Blesch held the door open for his wife. In the hall stood the butler.

"Shall I put out the lights and lock up now, sir?" he inquired.

"In a minute or two, Joseph, but see Lieutenant Messer to his room."

"Certainly, sir," he added wistfully, "just like the old days with Fraulein von Gleiwitz in the house again."

"Just like old days, Joseph," replied the countess, placing her arm upon that of her husband. "We need the old days over again."

"They say," said the butler, "that history always repeats itself. God be with you both."

The countess softly entered Rosa's apartment. The girl, weary to exhaustion, sat before the empty fireplace, still fully dressed. The thin ashes of what had once been the W Plan lay scattered at her feet. Rosa had, too, offered up as a burnt sacrifice the selfless devotion of her life, the sanctity of her love...

They might think that she had some secret lover who had masqueraded in Barmen, and lied glibly to the stricken widow, while she herself silently applauded, then had satisfied his lust; but the willing sacrifice of her honour had saved the discovery of Duncan's identity. She could do no more. What did it matter now? She might remain in Barmen . . . her work lay there so long as she had strength for the task: possibly she would one day go to her sister...

The vision of the Cross was before her eyes . . . sacrifice was still the science of power . . . Her life was ended . . . Duncan Would remain a memory in her dreams—rippling waters; purple hills and love sublime; little hours in the forest . . . sunset.

The countess sank upon her knees beside the still, wan figure. "Rosa, dear, you will be glad . . . You will go to Switzerland . . . My husband has arranged this for you... I want to ask your forgiveness . . . and to thank you. Through you, I have found Karl. My debt to you is a heavy one . . . Will you forgive me?"

Rosa sighed. "I have nothing to forgive . . . You cannot know all," replied Rosa through her tears. "You have given me hospitality and help; your friendship and affection... Is that not enough? For me, everything is in the past . . . and I am happy. I will go to my sister . . . you, too, are happy, Sophie . . . your sunrise over the hills... I am glad." And so they remained quietly talking for many minutes, until the door gently opened.

"Sophie," whispered Herr Blesch, "I want you."

"Come and join us for a little moment, Karl."

He entered and leant over the chair. "Good night, Rosa." He kissed her tired face . . . "Come, Sophie." . . . The door closed again.

8

IN THE DEPTHS

A shaft of light stole through the iron grille into the cell. Colonel Duncan Grant slept on peacefully, the light playing on his face. A soldier, his heavy boots ringing upon the stone passage-way, came to the door. He fumbled with a bunch of keys which he held in his right hand, finally inserting one in the lock. The noise stirred the sleeper. He opened his eyes but did not move. The soldier set down some bread and a metal cup of water upon the end of the plank bed, glancing furtively at the sleeper. Seeing he was awake, he smiled sheepishly and said: "Your breakfast." Grant needed friends. Even a shy lout of a peasant temporarily imprisoned in a military uniform, with a woeful smile, might colour the misery of the hours ahead.

"Thank you," said Grant, stretching and sitting up. "What happens next?"

"I don't know," said the sentry, "I'll try and find out."

Rye bread, dry and hard—the water helped it upon its course . . . and Grant was hungry. The atmosphere was close. He could hear the sound of voices. He walked across to the grille, and pressed his head hard against the iron bars. He could distinguish nothing of the conversation from the blurred voices: he could see only the walls and floor of the passage, upon which the shadow of the passing sentry from time to time fell. He sat down upon the bed. He would like to wash and shave. The sentry re-appeared. The key turned and he came into the cell.

"Any chance of a wash?" Grant questioned, adding, "and a shave?"

"I'll fetch some soap and water," said the sentry.

"And a towel," added Grant.

The sentry went out, taking the cup with him, returning with a bowl of water, soap and a towel.

"The barber will come later," he said, "if the officer of the guard permits." He turned the key on the inside and stood watching the prisoner wash himself. Grant took off his shirt, throwing the water over his chest and head.

"What's the next move?" said the captive.

The sentry glanced cautiously over his shoulder through the grille. "You'll go before the officer at ten o'clock."

"What's the charge ?" said Grant.

"Desertion and striking superior officer. The evidence isn't all here yet. Court martial case, the sergeant says."

Grant dried himself briskly, then handed the bowl, soap and towel back to the sentry, who left the cell, locking it behind him. Grant sat down again. His watch, papers, money had been taken from him. But he possessed his precious tunic and his mind was alert.

He walked round the cell examining it. There was no means of exit. He had better wait and think. He would for the present play the part of the docile captive . . . events would shape themselves . . . he must first discover the nature of the charge, the attitude of the officer . . . perhaps a cunningly devised excuse would save him from a severe penalty . . . after all, many men had appeared before him as commanding officer charged with desertion, often merely technical offences and with striking a superior officer, perhaps the result of a drunken brawl . . . the men were contrite. England, still less

Germany, could not afford to lose good officers and able men, who expressed willingness . . . he himself had tempered justice with mercy . . . he would plead not guilty to the charge of desertion and the extenuating circumstances of drink . . . no, that would not do . . . of a drug as the excuse for striking . . . but not self-administered . . . he had had a large sum of money in his possession . . . that he could prove . . . he had gone to a brothel . . . they had drugged him in order to secure his money. He had been sufficiently sane to realize that, and had staggered to the railway station . . . after that he could remember nothing until his arrest in the train. It was a slender hope, but he could tell the story with conviction, and plead for mercy.

And if he were not sentenced to death, then he would be sent back to his regiment—the 139th Saxon Regiment, under escort. He was Otto Gedern. But . . . he would then be in a worse plight than he was now . . . he bore no resemblance whatever to Otto . . . where was Otto? . . . Well, no one would ever discover that. He must avoid being sent back to that regiment at all costs. Why did he desert? . . . Perhaps that was the key to the riddle . . . but he had pleaded not guilty to desertion...

Grant considered. Here was a new line of thought . . . he wasn't a Saxon . . . They had made life Hell for him . . . for he was a Bavarian. That was why he had had the idea of going south to Bavaria. He wanted to fight, but in the ranks of his own mother blood... It had become an obsession with him. The excuse was very thin. Why! he himself could riddle it with objections. But it would do for want of any other at the moment. He would wait until he had been charged, and would demonstrate a soldier's best behaviour.

The sound of footsteps came along the corridor. They halted before the door of his cell. He stood up. A voice called him to attention. He sprang to the alert facing the door, his body rigid, head thrown back. The key turned and the door opened. An officer, one sleeve empty and pinned across his breast, closely followed by a sergeant, an elderly man of the reserve, and the friendly sentry entered the cell.

"What's the man charged with?" said the officer.

"Desertion and striking his superior officer in the execution of his duty."

"These are very grave charges," said the officer. "You have, of course, your defence?"

"Yes, sir," said Grant.

"The commandant will see you at ten o'clock. Meanwhile, anything you want?"

"I would like to clean myself up a bit, sir," said Grant with humility. "A shave, sir, and clean my boots."

"A very serious charge, sir," said the sergeant. "Most irregular to allow privileges in such cases. The sergeant of the police told me he is a most violent man."

"I'm sorry, sir," Grant sighed.

"I'm afraid you'll have to go without the shave, but you can clean your boots," said the officer, not unkindly. "Please see to that, sergeant."

The door clanged to, and Grant was left in silence. Later the sergeant returned with an escort of two men, to one of whom Grant was again handcuffed. They left the cell, and marched across the wide barrack square, upon which youths, almost children, in small squads were being drilled. They glanced in his direction, their eyes frightened at the dishevelled figure. Grant held his head high, a gaiety in his pace. The file was halted, and he fell in at the tail of a line with other defaulters. Duty sergeants and corporals strolled along to look at the curiosity. Some laughed, others whispered anxiously among themselves.

The defaulters went within the charge-room one by one. Most came out unescorted; two with escort were marched to the guardroom from whence Grant had come. He was the last of the line. A call to the alert . . . and he was pushed through the door of the charge-room . . . confronting the commandant. For a moment the light coming full from the window dazed his vision, then a figure, regarding him intently, loomed before his eyes.

A man with a blotched face, and puffy eyes, brushed grey mustachios and bald head sat behind a table, supported by two officers who stood beside him. He bent his head to examine the charge sheet, then again looked Grant over carefully.

His lips sneered sarcastically: "Sergeant, who is this dirty creature disgracing my barracks?" Grant felt the rage of bitterness overtake him. He set his teeth.

"Otto Gedern of the 139th Saxon Regiment," replied the sergeant quickly.

The commandant evidently had had a disagreeable morning. His complex was to be cruel; he was soured with disappointment by the loss of a higher command; and, fretting in this senile backwater, when a chance chivvied the malice of his mind, savage passion possessed him.

"You dirty *schweinhund!*" he jeered. "You are charged with desertion and with striking your superior officer. What is the evidence, sergeant?"

"The leave pass of this man was granted from the sixth to the sixteenth of June, from his regiment in the line. The leave was granted to Dresden. The ticket had been used as far as Dusseldorf. He was found in possession of two hundred and fifty-one marks, whereas his pay book shows recent withdrawals of only forty marks . . . that was on the fifth. He was seen at Mainz Station by a corporal of the military police . . . you have, sir, his telegraphed statement before you . . . posing as a wounded soldier. He struck the corporal of police. He boarded a train and was arrested by Sergeant Ulms of the military police at Karlsruhe. His papers and effects are on the table, sir."

"Send in Sergeant Ulms..."

"What do you know about this case, sergeant?"

"Received a message from the military police post at Mainz that a man answering to the description of the prisoner was travelling in the main line train due at Karlsruhe at twelve-thirty after midnight. I went to the station, caused the train to be stopped at the signal halt and boarded it. The conductor who had this man already under suspicion took me to the compartment. As I was about to interrogate him he attempted to jump through the doorway. I arrested him and handed him over to the sergeant of the main guard. He was charged with desertion and with striking. I questioned him. He stated that he was not a deserter and that he struck the corporal of police," he paused and glanced towards the prisoner, "because he didn't like the look of him."

The commandant half rose, fixing a monocle; a look of wonder, followed by one of intense satisfaction, entered his gleaming eyes. He sat back again deep in his chair, rubbing his hands together.

"*Mein Gott!*" he swore quietly. "You . . . you dirty lout . . . Otto Gedern . . . you dare to say that you struck one of the military police . . . because . . . you did not like his face?" He uttered a foul blasphemy.

"Not at that moment, sir," interjected Grant briskly. A subaltern tittered. The commandant glared at him.

"What do you mean, 'not at that moment' ?"

"I was not quite myself," said Grant. The comic truth of his statement suddenly struck him. He smiled broadly. The sergeant, sensing the situation, and hoping for approval, struck him on the back, saying: "Take that grin off your face."

"Any further evidence?" demanded the commandant.

"None, sir," replied the adjutant beside him. "The corporal of police from Mainz is on his way. I would ask for a remand, unless you wish to proceed with the case."

"Are you guilty, Otto Gedern?"

"Not guilty of the first charge, technically guilty, I regret, sir, to the second. I was ill, sir."

"You are remanded . . . Get out," the commandant screamed. The file marched.

Grant returned to the cell. The key turned and he was left alone. He dreaded another appearance before the commandant. He was familiar with the type. Here was a popinjay turned vulture . . . a failure in war, he had been deprived of his command, and his services relegated to the trivial duties of a barrack commandant . . . here, his wings clipped of authority, performing the routine of a clerk, the repression from which he suffered had discovered an outlet in tyranny.

He was a bully, the last resort of incompetent authority . . . His disappointed, degraded spirit wreaked a daily revenge upon his distracted lieutenants, most of whom had been severely wounded in the early days of the campaign . . . he delighted to torture young recruits with the whip lash of sarcastic blasphemy and obscenities, while enjoying the protection of his rank and uniform. He was hated and despised, and he knew it. The debased mind gloried in victimization, revelled at the sight of men squirming under his tyranny. Grant had observed such types at home, fortunately very few. But he could not hope for help or mercy from the commandant, nor was it probable from the subordinate officers whose reputations were in his hands.

Grant lay upon his bed in reflection. The sun had moved round to another side of the building and no longer lighted the cell. The air was heavy. The exhaustion and anxiety of the past days were playing havoc with mind and body. He felt physically sick. Food was brought: he ignored it.

Fantastic thoughts crowded in upon his mind. He was a beaten man . . . he could not escape . . . he would be shot as a deserter . . . and his soul in just retribution, sent to join that of Otto Gedern . . . no, never that! He would defy this commandant . . . declare himself a British officer, a colonel of the Inverness Regiment . . . they would shoot him like a dog . . . and . . . one day his regiment would know. That would be a better way out. But probably at home they would sneer at him . . . no one would know that he had secured the W Plan... It would die with him . . . and . . . Britain would be overwhelmed.

The works were going steadily forward, men tunnelling day after day, completing the galleries . . . and Scots, too . . . they were willing workers! God curse it. He would rather be with his regiment, enemy in front and rear. The idea fired his imagination . . . How they would have fought, his regiment, his men! Surrounded, no surrender, to the last round of ammunition, a battalion eclipsed in imperishable glory . . . years hence his name would be writ large in the annals of his regiment: a glorious tragedy like those at Darghai, Magersfontein, Le Cateau . . . What an end!

But this . . . the vile uniform of a besotted enemy . . . and . . . God damn it! why had he bragged to the Commander-in-chief? He was dishonoured, had achieved nothing . . . nothing . . . nothing! . . . Yes, yes, he had . . . he possessed the W Plan . . . the general had been right . . . Duncan Grant had done his best. "Oh, God, help me," the spirit cried. But reason quickly undermined the hope of the spirit . . . God wasn't on his side . . . there wasn't a God at all, and . . . even if God did exist, He didn't care a damn about the British. The Germans were just as good . . . no God had stepped in at Loos, why should He now?

The W Plan was inspired, it was a *coup d'état*, a master plan . . . God had made it . . . Curse God! The W Plan . . . Yes, of course . . . Rosa had it . . . Rosa hadn't seen him for years . . . she had run away and left him . . . of course she had an excuse, a good one . . . then they had again met by chance . . . Rosa recognized him . . . he was a spy . . . she had pierced his armour . . . then she had made love to him . . . Christ! what a fool he had been. Rosa was no different from any other woman . . . she was a German . . . she had wrung his secrets from him . . . she possessed the W Plan . . . Rosa was just like the harlot in Barmen!

Grant sprang up, kicked the planks savagely, and smote his head with clenched fists. Rosa like . . . my God! . . . No . . . His brain was reeling . . . Rosa! He had doubted her . . . he was only fit to die. Rosa . . . my God! The tears welled into his eyes, great sobs shook him. Rosa was going to Switzerland . . . She would reach the British Legation . . . No matter about him . . . his work was finished.

He would be tried and condemned to death . . . as they led him out he would declare himself—Colonel Duncan Grant of the Inverness Regiment . . . a spy. He had failed . . . but Rosa would succeed—God speed her! . . . Rosa would succeed . . . through her his work would be completed . . . in death he would triumph . . . again doubt, bitter doubt gnawed into his reason . . . if she failed?

He strode up and down the cell. He beat the walls with his hands and wept, then collapsed in exhaustion upon the bed, where he lay for many minutes. He looked up, with scared eyes. Someone was watching him through the grille . . . a helmeted head . . . it was the commandant. A chuckle escaped from the officer's lips, as he called with an oath for the key. He would like to interrogate the prisoner. The sergeant of the guard, a newcomer, with a file of men came to the cell door. It was opened.

Grant stood up. His frame was quivering with rage and terror. The commandant leaned against the wall folding his arms, and delicately fingered his moustache.

"So you do not care for our hospitality, Otto Gedern," he said with a sneer. "The commandant comes to comfort you. Your wife... I presume the photograph in the pay-book is your wife . . . will be anxious. We shall, of course, acquaint her with your burial . . . the dung heap of our barracks is well kept, is it not, sergeant?" He roared with laughter. "Your body in due course will grace our Bavarian fields. Thus will you give back to the Fatherland what you sought to steal away."

His voice was rising in a thin crescendo. "You damn swine! dirty rat! You sit and snivel in my barracks." His glance fell upon the untasted food. "You despise our food. You're a cur, a coward, a traitor." The commandant was squealing in uncontrolled passion . . . "I'll teach you to strike a superior officer. You bastard! . . . you don't like the look of our police... I'll beautify your own bloody face!" and snatching a riding switch which dangled at his side, he struck Grant savagely across the face. A deep red line ran from the chin across the forehead as the switch had bent itself round his head. Blood began to ooze from the cut.

The immobility of the man enraged the commandant . . . the sight of the blood had only whetted his appetite . . . he was living in a mental El Dorado; such a rare opportunity seldom presented itself. Grant reeled under the blow, but braced himself to meet the storm.

The commandant panted heavily, the physical exertion of his passion extracting heavy toll from his overwrought nerves. He advanced a pace. "You deserve to bleed "—the soldiers of the escort blanched with terror, anticipating a further outrage—" You damned pig, posing as a wounded soldier."

"Sergeant," he bellowed, "have the swine stripped and see if there is a wound on his body and report to me tomorrow morning."

He advanced near to the prisoner, "I know your regiment, you dirty renegade—Saxons," he jeered, "you slunk away even from that white-livered mob of skunks!"

Grant's tottering reason gripped one fact . . . the very accusation of the infuriated commandant was a part of his plea against the charge of desertion . . . he would use it.

The commandant gibbered with excitement. He had ceased to control the rush of words. Such sanity as he possessed deserted him. He was a devil. He advanced a step nearer, and struck at Grant with his fist . . . he longed to feel the hot blood of his victim wetting the palms of his hand . . . he lusted for blood. Grant warded off the blow with his arm. His reason was going . . . he would strike this foul creature to the ground. Seeing the light in his eye, the commandant, like every bully, a coward at heart, recoiled, and struck fiercely with his riding whip in self-protection at the white-angered, blood-smeared face. The sergeant intervened as the prisoner fell as if lifeless upon the bed. Grant's mind was stunned, his consciousness deserted him.

The commandant chuckled with sensuous joy as if leaving the bull ring after a private rehearsal. What a day! . . . He would dine with relish upon pork . . . pouring red wine down his throat.

The sergeant watched the dreaded figure swagger across to the commandant's house . . . then he turned swiftly. His soldier's honour had been besmirched by the commandant's cruel, cowardly attack . . . This wretched man had done nothing to deserve this . . . nothing . . . he had stood immovable before the storm, inflexible under the first savage blow. The prisoner was no coward—deserter perhaps . . . but not prompted by any craven spirit.

The soldier returned to the guard-room in which the men were whispering together in fright. "Bring water and towels. Give me the key, quick."

He ran to the cell and entered. The prisoner was lying huddled upon the bed, his arms drooping limply to the floor upon which blood was dripping from a gash in his head and two hideous wounds upon his face. The sergeant raised the senseless body. The guards bathed the blood from the head and face and cleansed the wounds, removing the stained shirt.

"Fetch blankets and a palliasse," said the sergeant. They laid him in comfort, spread a blanket and raised the head upon a pillow. The prisoner opened his eyes. He looked round with terror, breaking to rage.

"It's all right, my lad," said the sergeant. "He's . . . gone." Grant sank back. The sergeant left the cell, returning with lint, bandages, rum and water and a portion of his own rations. He bound the head, reviving the prisoner with the spirit.

Grant sat up . . . "That's better," he said.

"Now eat; you need it." Grant ate slowly. Life was coming back at the hands of kindness.

"Thank you. . . comrades."

"That's all right, lad," said the sergeant gruffly, and withdrew, leaving one man in the cell with the prisoner. Grant lay back and closed his eyes. His head throbbed: he drew the blanket closer round him. On a summer evening he was shivering. The sentry passed him more rum. Then the weary, stricken man slept. The sentries were relieved every two hours in the cell.

As the night passed, the sleeper grew restless. He called aloud from the profound unconsciousness of sleep. Words came in torrents, bitter and sweet, rage and infinite pity, in the German and in the English tongue. The young sentry called for the sergeant. He came bustling into the cell.

"He speaks English," said the sergeant. Grant awoke and sat They changed the bandages. The bleeding had been checked.

"Now take some more rum and have another sleep." Grant lay down again and slept. It was almost nine before he opened his eyes. The shock had passed. His head was clear. They brought him an ample breakfast with hot coffee.

The sergeant looked in. "The commandant will want to see you at ten o'clock. We'll take off the bandages and make you look as spruce as possible." The guard helped him . . . clean boots . . . a comb and brush. He was handcuffed again to the sentry and marched across the square.

The story of the commandant's foul assault had echoed round the barrack rooms. Now came his victim. Curious glances were thrown in his direction, heads craned from barrack windows. He walked resolutely. The duty non-commissioned officers outside the charge-room regarded him with sympathy. He was marched in before the commandant, and avoiding the man's eyes looked straight before him above the man's head.

The commandant surveyed him with curiosity. He spoke to the sergeant.

"You have carried out my orders, sergeant?"

"Which, sir?"

"Fool . . . you had him stripped?"

"Yes, sir!"

"Well?"

The sergeant spoke deliberately and slowly. "He . . . had . . . no wounds, sir."

"He has something to go on with now," said the commandant with a sneer, turning to his adjutant beside him. "When I visited the cell, the man tried to strike me, and I taught him a lesson."

Grant caught the adjutant's eye and saw it flicker.

The commandant pursued his theme. "You were a witness of the assault, sergeant." The clock ticked off the passing seconds of silence.

"You heard me, you damned idiot, didn't you? You saw the assault?" he screamed.

Again, deliberately, the sergeant replied: "I did, sir."

"Is there any further evidence, *Herr* Adjutant?"

"Yes, sir, the corporal of military police from Mainz."

"Send him in then."

The corporal, with some heat, told the story of the assault, and of the subsequent chase at Mainz Station.

"Have you any questions to ask the witness?" snapped the commandant.

"Yes, sir," said Grant speaking for the first time; and, turning his head towards the big man, his mouth quivered in a smile. "I'm sorry, corporal. I hope I didn't hurt you."

The policeman's face wreathed itself in smiles. Otto Gedern was evidently a sportsman, and he had heard how he had stood under the commandant's whip.

"That's all right, my man," said the corporal, addressing the prisoner.

"Hold your blasted tongue," screamed the commandant. "Get out, all of you! Remanded for court martial."

Grant was back in his cell. The sergeant came to him after a short while. "The court is convened for tomorrow morning.

You are entitled to the advice of an officer as your counsel. Is it your wish to see an officer before the court assembles?"

Grant considered . . . hope was creeping back . . . sympathy was with him . . . the flimsy defence which he had concocted in his despair had gained immeasurably from the commandant's assault . . . but what was it that the commandant had said which had impressed his reeling mind? He pressed his head with his hands . . . "Cowardly Saxons, dirty pigs." That statement linked itself with his line of defence. He was not a Saxon, but a Bavarian, and he wanted to fight beside his own kinsmen . . . so he had run south . . . he had overstayed his leave, but only by two days, but he had surely shown an endeavour . . . the drug story weakened that part of the case: perhaps he had better plead that he struck the corporal in temper—the man was a good fellow, he would not overstate his evidence after the incident of that morning in the charge-room.—Otto's plan, almost complete, was being foiled by the policeman at Mainz. He had shown that he had pluck . . . the court, even if the fact did not come out in evidence, as it would not, would have heard of the outrage committed. Grant was calm now, and resigned . . . almost happy.

He knelt by his bed and prayed : his prayers gave him confidence and contributed strength. Then he called to the guard and requested a pencil and paper, and noted down the points of the case which he proposed to present. Later a voice in the corridor asked : "Where is soldier Otto Gedern?" The sergeant of the guard brought an officer and escort to the cell.

"I have seen you before, Otto Gedern," said the officer, whom Grant recognized as the lieutenant with the armless sleeve who had visited him previously in the cell. "I have orders to act as your counsel. The court assembles tomorrow. Since this little affair occurred," and he smiled, looking down upon his empty sleeve, "I have resumed my study as a barrister. I may be able to help you, but you must first tell me frankly the whole story, and I will see what I can make of it. You are no coward, Otto; you may be a fool . . . and I have heard also that you can speak English. Is that true?" Grant nodded. "That is a qualification which is valuable and our army cannot afford readily to lose." He turned to the sergeant. "You may withdraw with the escort. If I want you, I will call."

"You are advised not to plead guilty," the barrister continued. "Now tell me your story."

Grant placed the notes before the officer. His paybook would reveal three years' faithful and regular service in the field. He had committed no previous offence of any seriousness. He was unpopular with the Saxons and could not achieve promotion, his ambition . . . he was a Bavarian. He had taken advantage of his leave to try and join his Bavarian comrades . . . the journey south proved that. He had overstayed his leave by two days. And . . . had not the commandant cursed him for a Saxon ?

"What was that?" interjected the officer . . . "That is important... I must use that." His zeal as a barrister was being fired. Soldiering days would be over one day, perhaps soon. He was a lawyer today. "Who are the witnesses? Who heard him say that?"

"The sergeant of the guard and the escort of two men."

"Perhaps I shall be obliged to call the commandant," he smiled. "Now as to striking your superior officer. Were you drunk?" Grant wavered for a moment. The officer eyed him keenly. "I want the truth."

"No, sir," said Grant.

"Well, why did you do it?"

Grant considered a moment. "The truth," reminded the officer

"He was going to interfere with my plans," replied Grant.

"Perfect," commented the barrister, rubbing his one hand upon his cheek, a little mannerism. "Quite enough . . . quite reasonable. Now I want a little more in support of my case. Tell me about yesterday evening . . . this mess," and he indicated the cuts upon Grant's head and face. "Tell me the story."

Grant narrated the events simply. "What a devil!" whispered the officer below his breath. "And what did you do ?"

"I stood quite still, sir," said Grant.

"Have you evidence of that?"

"The sergeant and the escort saw it."

'Very well, Otto Gedern, don't worry over much: and, by the way, I want you to look your best. As orderly officer I refused you the barber : as your counsel, I will now order him. My client," he smiled, "is going to win the sympathy of the court. Those cuts will show themselves when you have had a shave. The commandant is your best friend . . . and don't forget it. Now remember, tell your story before the court, as you have told it to me . . . exactly as you have just told it . . . The truth... I do not wish you to refer to the commandant or to any events which have taken place since your arrest. Leave all that to me. I can best judge the temper of the court. I must take my cue from the prosecutor."

"Thank you, indeed, sir," said Grant, standing up.

"I will see you before the court sits, and the barber will come tomorrow morning."

"Thank you again, sir."

Grant was left in the cell with his own reflections. He was happy. His mind wandered back to happy days upon the heathered moors of his own home, fishing in the swift water . . . a sand grouse shoot upon the sand flats of the Blue Nile . . . stalking gooral in the Indian foothills . . . and his thoughts were much with Rosa . . . He wished some at home could peep and observe the gruff kindness of the sergeant, the tenderness of rough-handed peasants turned soldiers. Even the commandant had his prototype in British base camps. His mind was elevated . . . Englishmen in their tens of thousands, Germans, too, had gone forth in their millions, aided by their women, each one with a vision—intangible, ethereal, divine, love of family and pride of race . . . their thoughts were of boyhood days, when youth stepped forth from his cities to find his god in all the wonders of nature.

Civilization had culminated in the most furious output of man's created works that ever disgraced the history of human progress—guns, munitions, tanks, machine-guns, bombs, poisonous gases, mines, and every conceivable device for the wholesale slaughter of mankind, the destruction of his works and of the beauty of God. . . what a monument indeed to civilization!

The poet and philosopher in the man swept him . . . even as a burbling brook tumbles headlong from the snow-capped peaks of the mountains, stretching white fingers to Heaven, and rolls onwards in a great stream, carrying upon its troubled waters the obstacles which would impede its progress; and, ever swelling into a mighty river, belches forth into the ocean . . . so is the stream of human progress . . . it sprang from Heaven on high: it has tumbled and cascaded through the dim ages; it has swelled in the stream of medievalism, and has driven on, dashing its sure course through barriers of repression; it has passed through the maelstrom of conflicting civilizations and now is surely rolling on into the open sea of the boundless brotherhood of man. Nothing shall stay its torrent . . . its destiny is sure . . . for the destiny of man is in God.

And Rosa, his sweet love, she was with him... He pulled the blanket over him. He was tired and happy. He slept. A sentry peered through the grille and returned to the guard-room. "He's asleep, sergeant."

"Leave the poor devil, then. I see the commandant has added a further charge of striking . . . He's got enough trouble now. Let him sleep."

9

JUSTICE

Grant awoke early and lay meditating on his presentation of the case until the barrack barber came. The inflammation and swelling of his face and head had gone, but there remained two accusing red weals across his face which the removal of a four days' beard made only the more apparent. Grant carefully dressed and brushed himself. Breakfast was brought, and shortly before nine the officer acting as counsel looked in through the grille.

"Ah, that's better," he said. "Keep your courage up; you'll need all of it. I should tell you that the commandant has preferred an additional charge against you, that of striking, or alternatively of attempting to strike, him in the execution of his duty when he visited you in the guard-room."

Grant stood back, aghast. Observing his consternation, the officer added : "Don't you worry about that. You can leave it to me."

An hour later he was conducted across the barrack square under escort of a sergeant and three men. The court was to sit in the library and its members with the witnesses were already assembling. Grant noted them carefully in turn. The two military policemen were standing together in conversation with their backs turned towards him. Two officers of artillery in field-service dress carrying sheathed swords, obviously members of the court, were smoking. They glanced in his direction. The sergeant of the guard and two soldiers who had witnessed the commandant's assault were drawn up in line with other formal witnesses of arrest, among them the conductor of the train, who appeared ill at ease. The party was called to attention as the adjutant crossed from the charge-room, and entered the library. A moment later an officer of field rank, limping slightly, and who aided his progress with a stick, approached in company with two other officers, one of whom Grant noted as having been present in the charge-room upon his last appearance there.

He studied the face of the field officer, certainly the president of the court. He was a man of slight build and small in stature, dark hair and moustache edged with grey, his face lined and pale, aesthetic rather than that of the typical soldier. The two officers with him, one of whom carried a folio of papers, looked hurriedly in the direction of the prisoner. Grant placed the latter as the prosecutor.

After a few minutes' delay, all those attending the proceedings were summoned to the court room where its members, Major von Oppeln, the president, Captain Reichman, Lieutenants Meichner and Deusel, were duly sworn. The prosecutor, Captain Brauen, and the defender, Lieutenant Mettelinck, were formally introduced and sworn. The court took their seats, the prosecutor his place at the end of the table, the officer acting in defence beside the prisoner.

The proceedings were formally opened by the president.'

"Soldier Otto Gedern of the 139th Saxon Regiment is charged—Firstly—with desertion upon active service . . . Secondly—with striking his superior officer in the execution of his duty . . . Thirdly—with striking his superior officer in the execution of his duty." He looked up for a moment. "You are Otto Gedern?"

Grant replied : "Yes, sir."

"There are three charges. Do you desire the charges to be proceeded with separately or together?" he said, addressing Captain Brauen.

The prosecutor rose. "Separately, sir."

"And you?" he said, looking towards the defending officer.

"All together," said the latter.

"We seem to have some conflict of opinion in regard to procedure. What reasons have you, Captain Brauen?" said the president.

"Each of the charges against the prisoner is very grave. The court must weigh each one separately," replied the prosecutor.

"And you, Lieutenant Mettelinck ?"

"It is clear, as the president must know from the precis of the case, that the first two charges are closely identified the one with the other. The second arises from the first. That is the defence. The prisoner was only acquainted as to the third charge this morning. I have, of course, read the summary of evidence. I would also prefer this charge to be related to the first."

"I must require the court to be cleared," said the president, "while we consider the question of procedure."

With the exception of the officers composing the court, all present withdrew from the library. A sergeant, acting as usher, after a few minutes recalled the prosecutor, defender and the prisoner with escort.

Major von Oppeln then addressed the court. "We have decided," he said quietly, "to hear the three charges concurrently. The summary of evidence suggests that they are closely correlated and it will suit our convenience in determining the guilt, or otherwise, of the accused, to hear the whole matter." Then, turning to the prosecutor, he said: "Will you open your case, please?"

The prosecution first produced the field service books of Otto Gedern and his other effects in proof of the fact of determined desertion.

The evidence then of the police corporal from Mainz was heard.

"Do you wish to cross-examine this witness?" said the president.

Lieutenant Mettelinck rose. "Had you ever seen the prisoner or spoken to him before you demanded his pass?"

"No, sir."

"What precisely was he doing when you spoke to him?"

"He was standing on the platform smoking a cigar."

"Did any words of anger pass between you before he struck you?"

"No, sir."

"Will you show the court exactly what he did ?"

"He raised both hands unbuttoning his tunic pocket . . . so," the corporal demonstrated. "Then he made as if to remove his warrant and . . . well . . . he struck me."

"From the prisoner's demeanour at the time would you say that he was angered or intoxicated?"

"Certainly not, sir . . . He answered me civilly. I was never so surprised in my life as when he struck me."

"Thank you. That is all."

There followed the other witnesses with formal evidence as to arrest.

The president, looking towards the prosecutor, said : "That disposes of your case in respect of the first two charges. Do you now desire to proceed with the further charge? In determining our verdict we shall, of course, as I have indicated, have regard to this last, but I think it may be confusing to the issue to introduce it at the present time."

"That was my wish, sir," said the prosecutor, adding: "Since the court has ruled that the three charges be taken concurrently, a course with which I respectfully disagree, I do not think it will be necessary for me to proceed with the further charge. The facts as to the first two will doubtless be sufficient."

"That," said the president, "I must remind you is a matter for the court. The case for the prosecution is so far closed, is it not?"

"So far, yes, sir," said Captain Brauen.

"The court will now hear the defence."

Lieutenant Mettelinck rose again. "The defence of the accused is a simple one," he said. "This man, Otto Gedern, as the court will observe from his field service books, has served with his regiment in the field for two years and seven months. He has not been subject to stoppages of pay, his character has been good."

Captain Brauen rose quickly from his seat, thumping the table. "I object to evidence as to character at the present stage."

"Please sit down, Captain Brauen. I have assumed from the depositions that the case of the defence is that the charge of desertion bears only a technical interpretation. Is that so, Herr Lieutenant?"

"Thank you, sir, that is part of my case. Have I your permission to proceed?" The president nodded. "The accused has served without promotion, nor has he been wounded. He has the appearance and demeanour, as the court will note, of a good soldier. He is a Bavarian and in consequence he found himself out of sympathy with his comrades. Desiring to serve with his own kith and kin he took the opportunity of leave to try to come south. The evidence for the prosecution substantiates this. He was well on his way, when he found his plan being foiled by the well-meaning interrogation of a corporal of military police at the Mainz railway station. The court has heard that no angry words passed: the prisoner was standing on the platform smoking. He did not realize that he was striking a superior officer: his case is that there was someone obstructing a well-intentioned and, I suggest, honourable project, and he struck to remove the obstruction. He has expressed his sorrow..."

"I object," interjected the prosecutor, raising his arm.

"I think," said the president to the defender, "that every accused person on trial for his life, where the facts are not disputed, expresses sorrow. We can leave that till later." The prosecutor sat down, a sardonic smile of satisfaction on his face.

"Very well, sir. That concludes the case for the defence. The papers of the accused and the evidence before you amply substantiate his case."

Major von Oppeln fixed his regard upon the prisoner. "We have now heard both sides of this case, Otto Gedern—that is, so far as the first two charges are concerned. Do you desire to give evidence on oath?"

Grant winced as if he had been struck. A still silence fell upon the library. Captain Brauen leaned forward across the table keenly watching the prisoner, whose eyes were closed, his lips slightly moving. Grant must perjure his soul . . . for England.

Lieutenant Mettelinck was beside him. "You heard the president's question, did you not?"

Grant re-opened his eyes. "I ask your pardon, sir. I should like to give evidence on oath." He was sworn. Categorically, clearly, and in detail he reiterated upon oath the case as outlined by his defender.

"Have you any questions to ask the accused?" asked the president of the prosecutor, who immediately rose to cross-examine.

"Your leave commenced on the sixth of June, did it not?"

"Yes, sir."

"Upon what date did this brilliant idea of deserting from the 139th Saxon Regiment and joining some Bavarian formation first strike you?"

"I had been thinking about it for a long time."

"Why, then, didn't you proceed at once on the sixth or seventh of June?"

"I was trying to make up my mind."

"Where did you spend the days between the sixth of June and the sixteenth?"

"In Brussels."

"What were you doing in Brussels?"

"Nothing in particular, sir."

"Is this court to believe that you were eight or ten days in Brussels doing . . . nothing in particular. You know, as well as I do, how soldiers who expend their leave in Brussels spin out the days and hours . . . creeping from one wine house to another, from the brothel to every low haunt of vice..."

"I," interjected the prisoner quietly, "I . . . have no experience."

"Then this was a last-minute idea, was it?"

"Yes, sir."

"How came you in possession of so large a sum of money?"

"I have saved it."

"With what object?"

"Getting down to Bavaria."

"And yet when the opportunity legitimately came for you to proceed on leave and make the proper inquiry in Bavaria, you remained as a coward in Brussels, as you state, trying to make up your mind?"

"Not as a coward, sir."

The prosecutor shrugged his shoulders with a sneer upon his face, and threw his papers down upon the table.

"My cross-examination," he paused for dramatic effect, "is finished."

"Please clear the court for a few minutes," said the president, and when its members were alone he turned to his colleagues. "The case so far is quite clear, I think. It will be for you, gentlemen, to consider your verdict. But we are agreed to hear the third charge before we proceed to such consideration. Are there any further questions which any of you would like to ask of the witnesses, including the accused ?"

The president turned to each officer in turn. None desired further evidence. "Then we will proceed," he said. The sergeant-usher reassembled the court.

"Now, Captain Brauen," said the president, "there is a further charge preferred against the accused, arising as the court has determined from the first two which we have heard."

"I do not propose to call any evidence. The facts as to the first two charges, and what the court has heard are sufficient."

Captain Brauen had heard the facts concerning the commandant's assault. His case was a good one. He had considered that the mere fact of preferring a third charge, and then of dismissing it after hearing the earlier evidence would be sufficiently damning and would definitely establish the superiority of the prosecution over the minds of the court.

"You will call no evidence, then? Is the court to dismiss the third charge?"

"Yes, sir. You have ruled that the charge shall not be taken separately. It is only additional evidence as to the base character of the accused..."

"Captain Brauen," said the president sharply. "The court has not asked the prosecution for evidence as to character. You have determined not to proceed with this charge. You have no right, therefore, to refer to evidence which has not been contributed. Sit down. I shall now call upon Lieutenant Mettelinck to make his pleading upon behalf of the accused."

The defender rose briskly.

"If I may speak personally, I regard myself as being happy in being able to advise and defend the accused, Otto Gedern. The facts before the court clearly establish that this man is a good soldier. The prosecution has been anxious to demonstrate that the fact of Gedern's tarrying in Brussels is proof of his cowardice, and intention to desert.

"I submit that here was a man with a fixed idea, but an imbued sense of discipline prevented him from giving effect to his project, until the moment came—near the end of his leave. He was at the parting of the ways.

"He chose a hazardous course of which his present position is sufficient proof; but may I be permitted to remind this court of the writing of the great authority, von Clausewitz, who in a treatise upon the virtues of leadership and courage said : 'Even foolhardiness . . . that is not to be despised.'

"He carried through his project with enterprise and resource. The fact of his striking the corporal, and the instant decision for which the act called, are in a sense—a strictly military one—not discreditable. The procedure of the accused admittedly was foolish. I suggest, however, very seriously that the intention was noble, even praiseworthy.

"I propose now to prove to the court that this man is worthy of its sympathy and respect. I am not pleading in mitigation of any severe sentence but that he may be permitted to go forward with a project, which I have already suggested may be praiseworthy. The prosecution has elected not to proceed with the third charge, nor to call evidence. The defence has a right to refer to this charge, which I feel sure the court will admit."

The president bowed his head.

"This man, Otto Gedern, has shown exemplary behaviour since his arrest. He is no coward." Lieutenant Mettelinck was speaking not with the voice of the perfunctory advocate but with conviction, a sense of fervent duty, and from the heart.

He waved his hand towards the accused. "The wounds upon this man's head were inflicted with a riding-whip. He stood unflinching under the first blow. A field officer," he paused, "struck him, piling contempt upon abuse. Part of the accusation made against him was that his regiment is a mob of white-livered skunks!

"It is no part of the defence of the accused that his regiment consists of men unworthy. The defence is that due to misunderstanding upon a territorial, I might even be permitted to say, upon a racial basis, he desired rather to serve, not with this fine regiment, but with a Bavarian unit.

"But it is, on the contrary, a part of the case for the prosecution, arising from the third charge with which process has not been taken, that because this man is Saxon, as the prosecution supposed, he, a prisoner and an innocent man, is therefore an object of contempt and fitted to be vilified, struck and wounded, while he suffered such insult and assault in silence and without defence.

"This man is no coward! My whole case is that he is a Bavarian, and a man of singular bravery. The court elected to consider the three charges concurrently. The prosecution has repudiated its right to call evidence in support of the third charge. I ask for my right to call such evidence in defence of this brave man. The wounds which he bears alone fully substantiate what I have said. If this man has erred technically, his bearing and the evidence clearly demonstrate that he is not guilty of the grave charges preferred." The defender ceased, and quietly folded together his notes.

The president looked up and addressing the prisoner and escort said : "You may sit down." The sergeant drew up a bench. "I will now hear the prosecution."

"The court has just heard the speech for the defence," said Captain Brauen with a sneer. "Not a single plea in substantiation of the prisoner's case has been adumbrated. The defence has introduced matter quite irrelevant."

"I gave my sanction," interjected the president quickly.

"The facts which I would clarify are that this man deserted his regiment in the line. Presumably, then, he sought various ways of escape. Hiding first in the purlieus and alleys of Brussels, he finally, with an artful cunning, stowed himself away in a goods train, reaching Mainz. Here he posed as a wounded soldier; and as such stole sympathy, and, but for the vigilance of the military police, would perhaps have escaped. As it was, he violently assaulted the police, but due to the excellence of our system of detection was arrested.

"His whole story I submit is a tissue of lies. The court will have observed how this man, realizing the sentence which will shortly be passed upon him, hesitated in taking the oath."

"Captain Brauen," said the president dryly, "you must not attempt to anticipate the verdict of this court."

"I apologize, sir. But the facts..." His voice trailed. The president was watching him keenly. He hesitated : then recommenced. "I shall not refer to matters raised by the defence in regard to the third charge."

"You may not," the voice of the president rose in staccato tones.

The prosecutor continued: "The charges I submit are amply proven. Even supposing, which I cannot, that there is any truth whatever in the ridiculous plea of the accused, I suggest that rather than such serving in mitigation of the offence, this plea is in itself an aggravation. The cohesion of the army depends upon loyalty. Chaos would result if every soldier with a grievance elected to impose his will upon that of the state. But, I suggest, it is sufficiently obvious that the prisoner's plea has no validity whatever. I submit that this man is guilty of cowardice, of desertion; and when he found himself in a corner, he struck his superior officer, as a fox driven to earth would snap at a terrier."

Grant's hopes sank. The prosecutor in his final words had seized upon the weakness of his case.

The president spoke. "We do not desire to hear any further evidence. The court is closed while we consider our verdict." The prisoner and escort were ushered outside. Captain Brauen and Lieutenant Mettelinck withdrew, saluting the president.

Major von Oppeln addressed the court. "In determining our verdict it is no part of our duty to be guided by consideration as to whether this man is brave or a craven. The law is quite clear. We are here, in the first instance, to decide whether the charges are proven. With any other matter we may deal when we consider what sentence shall be imposed."

He turned to each member of the court and asked for a verdict. Each member without hesitation in respect of both charges quickly gave his reply—" Guilty."

"My own judgment confirms your opinions."

The president called out: "Sergeant, open the court."

All those who had attended the trial crowded into the library.

"The court," said the president, speaking deliberately, "finds the prisoner 'Guilty' upon both charges."

A pause followed... "Lieutenant Mettelinck, on behalf of the accused, do you desire to submit any evidence, or to make a statement in mitigation of sentence?"

"Sir, I have already stated—and I suggest it is also proven—that this man is no coward. He is willing and anxious to serve. He is a man of good education also. He speaks English fluently. This is an asset with which the army cannot lightly afford to dispense. I appeal to the clemency of the court."

"The court will now be closed while the sentence is considered."

Men rose . . . feet shuffled . . . a general sigh of relief from the tense atmosphere . . . the court was cleared.

The president again addressed himself to his colleagues. "It is now our duty to consider the sentence which will be imposed. The law, as you know, gentlemen, prescribes the death penalty in respect of both the two charges which have been submitted and proven. It is within our competence, however, to mete out a less sentence if in our opinion, after careful consideration, there is anything which can properly be urged in extenuation on behalf of this man.

"I am inclined myself to think that there is something behind this case which has not appeared in the evidence either for the prosecution or the defence. Human nature is a curious complex, subject, especially under war conditions, to strange hallucinations, obsessions, and passions. In my judgment Otto Gedern is obviously a man of courage, resource and initiative. His plea upon oath was made with conviction, which was not shaken after cross-examination. The fact that the third charge was not proceeded with is entirely in the prisoner's favour. We must pay due regard to this.

"Nevertheless, a point or first importance was urged by the prosecution, namely, that if any man with a grievance takes the law into his own hands and seeks to impose his will upon that of the state, the result would be chaos. For disciplinary reasons, therefore, you may consider, gentlemen, that the extreme penalty should be imposed. First, I would like to have your views, Lieutenant Deusel?"

"Well, sir, I think it certainly is a point in favour of the accused that no evidence was produced to disprove his own story. Everything that he has stated was supported by the facts as produced by the prosecutor, and, sir, I think he's a brave man. I would not impose the death penalty."

"And you, Lieutenant Meichner."

"I agree with Lieutenant Deusel, sir. He's a fine type of man, and his offence is largely technical."

"Captain Reichman, what is your view?"

"This man has been proved guilty. The facts as to the case are generally known in the barracks; the sentence which the court imposes will have its influence upon the recruits in training. Since many are drawn from the ranks of industrial workers, now being rigorously combed, we are experiencing difficulty. A severe disciplinary example will be of value at the present time, not alone in respect of recruits, but upon the civil population, who will doubtless learn quickly about this case. This man has been proved guilty. In my view the death penalty should be exacted."

The president spoke. "I am obliged to you, Captain Reichman. The points to which you have drawn the court's notice are important. Before this court assembled I was handed an envelope containing an army order. It is marked 'Secret and confidential.' It is unnecessary to remind you that you are upon oath not to disclose matters arising from process in this court. The order which I have here is an instruction to presidents of courts martial. It gives powers to such courts to exercise clemency in cases where, in the court's judgment, the accused may have acted upon impulse, and especially where, if other factors stand to his credit, he possesses any expert military qualifications.

"In such cases, the order instructs the court to impose the death penalty, but, without awaiting any further directions from higher authority, to inform the accused of the extenuating circumstances which its members have in mind, and to commute the sentence to one of service with the 15th Reichswehr Composite Division, in disciplinary charge of whom is the 3rd Guard Grenadier Regiment. Such men will be sent under escort to the base depot of the Guard Grenadier Regiment in the Lille command."

The president continued : "I concur with the view advanced by Captain Reichman. The order of the court will be that sentence of death has been duly imposed. This I think will have the effect which you desire, Captain Reichman. But, in my view, there are circumstances in this case, some of which we can only surmise, since evidence has not been offered, which declare it to be our plain duty to commute the irrevocable sentence of death. I understand, Lieutenants Deusel and Meichner, that this, too, broadly is your view. Now that I have read this army order, I should like, also, to carry you with me, Captain Reichman."

"I agree, sir. And, in fact, were it not for the reasons which I advanced, I should greatly regret the exaction of the extreme penalty."

"Very well, then, we are agreed," said the president. "I will cause the court to be reassembled."

This was the end of the drama. Grant was pale, but he stepped briskly into the court-room beside his escort. Prosecutor, defender and witnesses ranged themselves behind the accused. When the court was duly assembled, and after a short space of silence, the president rose.

Addressing himself to the prisoner, he spoke quietly. "We have, with meticulous care, considered this case. Having due regard also to your character and service, our verdict was unanimous. The sentence, also, which the court will impose is our unanimous decision.

"Soldier Otto Gedern, you have been found guilty upon the charge of desertion upon active service, and upon that also of striking your superior officer in the execution of his duty. The sentence of this court is death."

Tense silence prevailed. So it was all over, reflected Grant. Days of futility . . . everything lost . . . a failure. Rosa . . . lost to him for ever . . . his Rosa, alone, now and forever . . . And the plan . . . the W Plan.

A wry, mirthless smile fleeted across his lined face . . . God! What a failure! His mind was numbed.

The president was speaking again: to the condemned man the voice seemed to come from very far away. "The court has, however, as I have indicated, had in mind your previous service and qualifications, and acting with the powers conferred upon us, the sentence of death, which we have imposed, is commuted, again unanimously, to that of service under rigorous discipline with the 15th Reichswehr Composite Division." A sigh of relief escaped the lips of the police corporal from Mainz. "You will proceed under escort as soon as arrangements are made." In compliance with the army order to the court, the president ordered the sergeant-usher to remove Grant's shoulder straps upon which were woven the regimental numerals.

"Have you anything to say, Otto Gedern?"

Grant did not answer at once. Indeed, the full meaning of the president's words had not yet filtered through the blanket of black, hopeless fog which shrouded the nerve centres of his brain. What was it that the president was saying? God! Couldn't they leave him alone? ". . . the sentence of death, which we have imposed, is commuted"? What was this? And then suddenly light filtered through the gloom . . . his mind struggled from its hell.

"May I say, sir, that . . ." He hesitated, "I thank you."

The president bowed while the faintest smile passed across his face as he said: "Germany will look to you to repay the clemency of this court."

He then handed the documents to the adjutant, and the court closed. The prisoner returned to the cell. The handcuffs were removed, and his property, with the exception of his pay book and official papers, was restored.

A few minutes later Lieutenant Mettelinck entered the cell. Grant sprang up. "Thank you, sir, from the bottom of my heart." Then slowly he added : "Perhaps one day, sir, I may be able to be of some service to you . . . I shall hope so."

"There's something curious about you, Gedern. I believe there to be more behind this case than I know, or than you have told the court. But never mind that, you have my very sincere good wish . . . Farewell."

"Thank you again, sir," said Grant, with emotion.

Late in the afternoon the corporal of police from Mainz, accompanied by an escort of two men, visited him. "You are to come with me now to the railway station. And . . . no more tricks, Otto Gedern."

Grant, remembering the sigh in court, put out his hand. It was generously gripped by the big corporal, who then, with that curious paternal affection which often characterizes men whose duty calls them to disciplinary service, took kindly charge of the prisoner. After his deficiencies in kit had been made good, Grant was marched to the railway station. The prisoner and escort were provided with accommodation in the guard's van; and Grant, sleeping soundly, was awakened to find the train slowly entering Koln Railway Station.

The party changed at Koln and after some hours' delay joined a leave train proceeding to Lille.

Recovered from the shock of the past few days, although his face bore the wounds of the commandant's whip, and a pallor had replaced the warmer glow of his skin, the mind of the prisoner began again to engage itself with that part of his life which had been so dramatically interrupted. A decade of time seemed to have elapsed since he parted from Rosa.

Some queer, psychological change appeared to have wrought itself in him: his ego seemed to be altered. It was almost impossible to realize that he and Colonel Duncan Grant were the same personality . . . his feelings more readily adjusted themselves to a conception of an emancipated Otto . . . for his gratitude to the court and to the defender were genuine and sincere, but such an expression came from himself as Otto Gedern, reprieved deserter, not from Colonel Duncan Grant, the spy.

This introspection was extraordinarily confusing. He could scarcely realize his position nor had he yet capacity to analyse his attitude towards the two conflicting duties which displayed themselves before his mind—the W Plan, the Commander-in-chief, England; and the new lease of life generously granted to Otto Gedern, soldier. It was all overwhelmingly difficult. Of course there was Rosa.

Telegrams began to flash through his mind . . . Where was Rosa? . . . Going to Switzerland. Why? The W Plan . . . Were they not united? . . . More so than ever through the W Plan... His duty must be clear . . . The W Plan. What was the date? . . . Of course it must be the twenty-first of June . . . where was he going? . . . he had scarcely heard what the president had said. At any rate to his stunned mind it had meant nothing, but life instead of the grave.

"Corporal," he said, "where are we going?"

"To Lille."

"What regiment . . . didn't the president of the court say something about a disciplinary corps . . . I didn't hear."

"Yes, you're to be posted to the 15th Reichswehr Division with the Guard Grenadier Regiment."

The mind's wireless operator began again to send out messages. Guard Grenadiers . . . seen from a barley field . . . convoys of lorries . . . prisoners of war . . . Scots, willing workers . . . condemned German prisoners working with them . . . interpreters . . . men like moles . . . the destruction of the British Army . . . the W Plan.

He began again to reflect—so this was then his fate. Colonel Grant's life had been spared in order that, as Soldier Otto Gedern, he might participate actively in the work of destruction . . . a Scot . . . a willing worker . . . the just retribution of fate. But he would see what he had not seen—the W Plan in being . . . how amazingly interesting!

He was neither Duncan Grant nor Otto Gedern. He was living in a new dimension . . . almost a resurrection from the dead . . . he had been so near to the commandant's dung heap . . . he was a new man, reborn. But where was Rosa . . . she had a claim, nay more she was of him, Duncan of her—inseparable—" Till death us do part..." Death had been foiled . . . he must be Duncan Grant!

The train dragged into Lille. The party marched to the military police headquarters and reported for instructions. They washed, shaved, and ate a hearty meal. A little later orders were received to march to the 2nd Motor Convoy column. A lorry would be proceeding during the night to the Guards' depot, where the prisoner would be handed over and the escort relieved of further duty. As night fell the escort was placed in a ration and supply lorry forming part of a column. They arrived at the sentry post. How well Grant recollected its stern discipline. The lorries drew into the park behind the barbed wire enclosure. The escort and their prisoner climbed down.

"Report at the guard-room over there," said a sergeant, pointing to gleams of light coming from a muffled window.

The sergeant of the guard took over the papers with quick decision. "Name?" he queried, addressing Grant.

"Otto Gedern."

"Spell it." He was entering information upon a foolscap form. "Your number is 60719. 15th Reichswehr Composite Division. Read this order," He passed a typewritten order pasted upon a board. "Prisoners are forbidden to converse under penalty of instant death. You understand?"

"Yes, sergeant"

"Corporal, march your escort back to the lorry. Here is the receipt for Otto Gedern. Look sharp now."

* * * * *

Grant found himself in a large encampment of wooden huts. Immediately upon arrival he was conducted before an officer, who examined the papers relating to the court martial, handed to him by the sergeant in charge of the escort. The officer studied the papers and then addressed himself to the prisoner.

"You are under sentence of death, Otto Gedern. You will find in this command that you will enjoy complete liberty within the confines of the camp. You will have every opportunity to be happy. The work upon which you will be employed is of a special character. It is hard and demands the best of which you are capable. We allow no shirkers here : no second chances. The penalty imposed for noncompliance with any order of whatsoever nature is instant death at the sole discretion of the officer responsible for the issue of that order. You have been fortunate so far that the court martial has dealt leniently with your offence. In this command there is no appeal to the clemency of a court, no extenuating circumstance for offence which can be permissible. Orders must be immediately, energetically executed. That is the spirit of this command. The penalty for failure, I repeat, is instant death. Do you understand?"

"I do, sir," said Grant.

"I observe," said the officer, "that a qualification noted is that you can speak English. Is that so?"

The officer rang a bell and upon the entry of an orderly, said: "Send the interpreter from C. Battalion to me at once," and then addressed himself again to Grant. "The interpreter of C. Battalion, consisting of Englishmen, will examine your proficiency. If the test is satisfactory you will be posted for duty to that battalion."

Every doubt was swept from Grant's mind. The events and revelations of the twelve days, prior to his arrest, sketched themselves vividly in his mind . . . he was back again in the barley field . . . a convoy of men whose black silhouettes stood out against the night. Englishmen, French, Italian, Russian, Poles and Scots, were passing . . . men going to and from the underground galleries which formed the W Plan. Now he was to be a cog in the wheel of this vast machine designed literally to undermine the whole strength of Britain—a mechanical Samson, willing Scots, figuratively shorn of their hair, to bring down the temple of an empire in ruins. He was a free man now, a new man, living in a new world hedged in by iron discipline and barbed-wire entanglements.

But he was different from any of the inhabitants of that new world for he alone knew the W Plan, at least in its entirety. Even if the Commander-in-chief had failed him, within the confined limits of his new world he could still serve his general and England. He would wait for events to develop. Perhaps his chances of success today were greater than ever previously.

A knock was heard upon the door, which immediately opened to admit a short, brusque little figure, somewhat grotesque in military uniform. He saluted clumsily.

"Good evening, Herr Hauptmann. You sent for me?" he queried.

"I want you to test this man as an interpreter in English. He claims facility in the language."

Some five minutes of conversation between the two men, the one a gentleman of culture, who carefully feigned a little hesitancy, the other a German whose business habits prior to the war had brought him daily in touch with those of wealth and culture in London, made it plain to the examiner that Grant possessed a rare fluency in the English tongue.

"I am satisfied," he said, turning to the officer. "This man possesses a satisfactory knowledge of English."

"Then he will be posted for duty to C. Battalion." He wrote out an order. "Take this to the adjutant, and you, soldier Gedern, accompany the battalion interpreter."

10

A GAME OF CARDS

Grant was posted to the 3rd Company of the battalion, and found himself in a narrow, dimly lighted hut, on either side of which were two tiers of bunks in which were men sleeping. At regular intervals equipment, but no arms, were hung at the foot of the bunks. An armed sentry stood at the door. Grant passed in.

"You will be for duty at three o'clock tomorrow morning," said the grenadier, and he pointed to a vacant place in the row of bunks. Grant hung up his equipment, and climbed up to a straw palliasse, suspended upon tightly-stretched fencing wire. Lulled by the warm atmosphere and the rhythmic sound of the deep breathing of many men, sleep took him to herself.

He was rudely awakened. Voices, familiar as from some other age, urged him to show a leg. He was one of a company of some sixty men, speaking what passes for English in a dozen different dialects, cursing, tumbling against each other in the dim light, pulling on short field boots, adjusting equipment. He was unnoticed. A sharp order was called out and the men filed outside, Grant among them. Their names were called, familiar English names, with a few of German origin as it were to give leaven to the list. His own was the last to be called by the company interpreter.

"Otto Gedern, take your place with the second squad." A gap was made in the ranks for the new recruit, and the party marched to the canteen at which coffee and bread were served and every man issued with a haversack ration. They were then packed, squad by squad, into a convoy of waiting motor wagons. Through the gloom Grant could observe other groups of men filing from out of the huts and canteen towards the waiting convoy. Not one single word had been spoken by anyone with the exception of the short, sharp orders of the guards. The men sat huddled together upon the floors of the wagons which rumbled steadily towards the forward zone. It was still dark when the column came to a halt.

The men clambered out, and were formed into parties of fifties, each accompanied by two grenadiers and an interpreter, a German soldier, with the rank of corporal. They marched in file towards the mount of Kemmel which loomed in the near distance. An occasional star shell illumined the ragged outline of the hill, the sharp sound of musketry, the heavier report of shrapnel told of that timidity and nervousness which heralds dawn in the battle area. As they reached the hillside, the way led through huge mounds of tumbled earth banked upon either side of the narrow path. The figures of men, dimly defined, could be observed high upon the slopes of the deepening channel, throwing aside the tons of new earth and debris which poured upon the hillside from the wide mouths of enormous tubes which thrust themselves from the hillside. "The Messer excavator," was Grant's mental comment.

The party entered a large tunnel, opening out to a great subterranean hall, the roof of which was supported by concrete pillars and which was brilliantly illuminated. Grant could discern the sound of smooth-running machinery, as of a great power station : at regular intervals heavier vibrations as of some distant explosion could be heard, followed immediately by the tumult of huge chains locking swiftly in the cogs of giant wheels, and then the muffled noise of loose earth falling.

This sepulchral orchestra was accompanied by yet another sound, entirely distinctive, as if of a torrent of water swiftly intaken to the mouth of some phantom mammoth of the depths. Here was the Messer excavator and endless winding gear in motion, accompanied by the Speyer drainage system by absorption. A continuous stream of men swathed in clay came from the mouths of two tunnels leading from the main galleries to the great hall, upon either side of which were stationed begrimed engineers in charge of the intricate controls governing the complex machinery.

Above each of the tunnel entrances was fixed a large letter of the alphabet. Grant noted them carefully. These entrances indicated the commencement of the long galleries leading to the heads of the mined shafts. A large party of men was now drawn up upon one side of the great hall, while an officer, megaphone in hand, standing before a chart, detailed the parties and numbers of men required for each section of the work. As the instructions were given, the parties left the hall and disappeared through the mouths of the tunnels, while the noise of machinery continued without interruption.

Orders came to the squad to which Grant was attached. They were marched away in file, passing into B gallery. In its wide mouth an electrically driven light-railway train was waiting. First the train was loaded to capacity with heavy shells: the working party was then crowded into empty trucks, and the train proceeded along the wide, lighted gallery. The sound of machinery within the enclosed space became almost deafening; it was difficult to separate from each other the variations of sound which Grant had noted while in the main hall, but insistent always was that of the mammoth suction of water.

At regular intervals the gallery opened to right and left of the track and gave way to galleries sloping downwards running at right angles to the main track. These were the shafts connecting the upper series, upon which Grant's party was travelling, with the lower trellis of the W system.

Where these communication galleries met the main shaft, the track opened out to admit sidings upon which were trucks heavily laden with all the munitions of war, rations and fodder. Large parties of men were at work unloading the wagons, and reloading them into hand-operated trucks to be taken for store to the more remote parts of the shafts, or for immediate service to the farther ends of the lower system galleries. Everything was organized and the work proceeding as with mathematical precision.

As the train passed these points Grant noted above the clamour of machinery a sharp order in French and again in some unfamiliar language which he thought to be Polish or Russian. The train drew on, moving rapidly for about half an hour, at the end of which it drew into one of many sidings at the foot of a gradual slope upwards, about one hundred yards long. The letter G was posted at the foot of this gangway, and Grant realized that in the course of his journey he had penetrated some five miles beneath the British entrenched positions and that now he was standing almost directly beneath the village of Flètre.

It was almost impossible to give credence to such an extravagant conception . . . of the W Plan in being, being driven forward with increasing energy and faultless organization . . . and, of the ignorance of the armies of the Allies, with all their elaborate systems of espionage and intelligence, aided by every device known to the usages of modern warfare . . . and of the fact that outside those closely-guarded ranks of workers, over whose head the penalty of death hung always, he alone knew the details of the plan, he alone, a workman unloading the heavy shells which would complete the downfall of Britain, and change a world's history and geography . . . he alone appreciated the significance of the gigantic scheme which his hands were helping to complete.

The party worked steadily for some hours, and was then moved back along the railway track, as Grant judged it, by some four miles. The wagons were placed upon a siding and the party disembarked. A truck was waiting to be unloaded, piled high with cases of explosives. The interpreter in charge of the group called the men around him.

"Be careful of that stuff. It's dynamite. Load it in these trucks."

The explosives were carefully handled and disposed in hand-operated trolleys. The interpreter leading the party carried a plan of this section of the galleries in his hand, while the two Guard Grenadiers posted themselves respectively at the head and tail of the column. They marched forward diagonally from the direction of the shaft which they had left, but on the same level. This gallery, Grant realized, would be one of the short arms connecting the main galleries. At the apex of the two short arms the party was halted. The dynamite was carefully stored against the wall of the shaft, obviously preparatory to being moved forward to the end of a main shaft, when the works were completed ready for the blowing of the mines.

The party returned to the trucks when a rest of half an hour was ordered and the men brought out their rations, and were permitted to converse. Grant found himself in conversation with a corporal of Royal Engineers. The men talked listlessly of the last game of cards, or of the simple matters of home life. Grant noted that all reference to the work in hand or to the life of war was studiously avoided. He made an effort to engage the interest of the corporal, who prior to the war had lived in a Berkshire village. Grant had hunted around Newbury and knew the Thames reaches by Pang-bourne intimately : as a boy he had swum a lake to find swans' eggs, and had tickled trout in the Pang.

The corporal was friendly. They would have a yarn when they were back again in camp. Grant had penetrated the stoic reserve of the southern county estate carpenter, which had previously been the man's familiar occupation.

A plan, desperate though it might be, was beginning to sketch itself in Grant's mind . . . even if he could not deliver the W Plan . . . could never reach headquarters . . . even if Rosa, now so far away, heaven knew where, separated from his life, might not reach Geneva . . . would it not, perhaps, be possible prematurely to blow up one section of the galleries and at least give some warning of the approaching danger ?

He reflected upon such a project . . . a small explosion would be useless for his purpose . . . the detonation would perhaps do little more than suggest that probably one of the larger dumps of shells or other explosives had gone off behind the lines . . . but surely it would indicate something most unusual. He dared not examine again the map still secreted in the collar of his jacket. An explosion of the tons of dynamite which they had just handled would, so far as he could judge it, erupt somewhere in the forward zone if indeed it succeeded in accomplishing anything beyond temporarily wrecking some of the subterranean galleries . . . if it were possible correctly to tamp the charges and lay a mine, without doubt a surface explosion could be caused . . . then again if the dynamite could be moved to the far end of one of the long arms of the galleries and fired from such a point, a vast explosion could be occasioned behind the British lines, for example at Flètre or Poperinghe . . . supposing such a thing did happen, there would, of course, be an inquiry . . . engineers would be summoned who would investigate the cause and this labyrinth of devilment would then be exposed.

But what could he do in order to achieve such a project? . . . he knew nothing of mine laying, of the technique of charges, or tamping explosives. Moreover, it would be impossible to move the loads of dynamite from their present position, and, in any case, to explode them meant certain death for himself and for any others whom he might persuade to assist him.

Death held no terrors for him: but, for those deadened, hopeless souls with whom he toiled amid the din and in the fetid atmosphere of this living tomb, death might still hold out the fear of the unknown, a sting so far untried. The very silence of these men, their mute obedience to orders, a minute breach of which would cause the certain fall of the sword hanging always over their heads, was a token of their fearfulness . . . and they still possessed their compensations within the camp—drink, tobacco, good food, hectic music and the deep sleep of exhaustion and forgetfulness . . . The sun still shone in the sky; perhaps one day even the prison gates would open.

Grant might take one man into his confidence, two or three, but of more he doubted. The company was filtered with informers, English-speaking Germans, and he must first convince one or two men of his true identity in order to break down the barriers of reserve and fear with which each individual was hedged.

The long hours passed in toil, disposing of munitions, penetrating in and out of the long galleries, with which in this section of the works the party seemed to be familiar. This part of the stage was being set finally for the great drama. In the lower galleries Grant had a glimpse of long lines of armoured cars and guns of heavy calibre; in the upper a whole treasury of all the most modern appliances relating to mobile warfare. At one time the party crossed a new gallery in the course of construction—the Messer machine was at work, blasting, breaking, hauling, swallowing tons of new soil, carried by the endless winding gear to great tubes which took them in and threw them miles away upon the slopes of Mont Kemmel.

Twenty-four hours of continuous work, with short intervals for rest, had passed. A relieving squad mechanically took over the task. The men composing the working party were pallid with physical exhaustion, stifled with the damp heat of the atmosphere, numbed by the roar of machinery. They now tumbled into the waiting wagons which took them back through the long gallery to the main hall, filled with lines of fresh men from the encampment, relieving groups in other parts of the workings.

As they left the shaft head and passed into the cool night a great sigh involuntarily escaped from each man as he greeted the fresh air, and drank it deeply into his lungs. The sound of machinery receded and was blanketed by the growing walls of the long avenue through which the files of men shuffled to the waiting motor convoy. The men sprawled in the bottoms of the wagons, some in deep slumber, others sleeping fitfully as they were jolted against each other by the swinging wagons. Within the encampment the men, after being provided with hot coffee and rum, went back to the long low hut to sleep...

* * * * *

Grant woke, refreshed. Some men were cleaning uniforms and equipment, others sitting about conversing, while others still slept heavily. Grant joined a little group who were stripping the mud from their equipment and laughing over some ancient jest, the corporal of engineers, Waller by name, among them. They strolled together towards the canteen already filled with men, some leaning against the counter, others playing a variety of games—cards, billiards, darts.

The men were separated by instinct into their varied national groups, though, against each little coterie, inquisitive spectators stood idly watching the varied recreations of a new and strange race. Through an aperture Grant could see the bound and rebound of a football, and heard the cries of Englishmen, though many of various races were participating in the rough and tumble, ruleless game.

Grant and Waller seated themselves at a little table, smoking, with cups of steaming coffee before them, and resumed the discourse upon trout. Waller confessed to having been an accomplished poacher; and, when the spirit moved him, still had given a Sunday to this pastime. He found that the excitement of lawlessness stimulated the blood of his veins, and by its adventure provided spice to an otherwise monotonous existence.

Grant encouraged him with enthusiasm, commenting: "It would be grand to have a little adventure again. This life must get on your nerves a bit."

Waller regarded him suspiciously, and added in an unfriendly tone: "It is forbidden to criticize . . . here."

"Of course," said Grant..." Let's go out and sit in the sun."

Grant led the way and deliberately chose a clear space of ground, removed from the sound of English voices and beside a group of Russians noisily playing together. They lay down. Grant must win this man's confidence. He sketched the configuration of the English countryside by heaping the dust with his fingers until the three ridges between Reading and Newbury, and flanking the course of the Thames to Wallingrord, with the intervening Hog's Back running high through Bradfield and Bucklebury, lay planned upon the ground, the contours roughly conforming to the letter W. Then he filled in the villages by placing pebbles and stuck pieces of dried grass into the ground to denote the woods.

"You know this ground very well . . . for a German soldier," commented the corporal.

"I remember as a boy, my father was staying at Englefield for the shooting."

"Your father . . . shooting?" questioned the corporal slowly.

"Yes; he was with friends. I remember that I stole away from the house down to a stream haunted by trout which runs through Bradfield. I lay so still beside a tiny foot-bridge, bare arm dangling in the water. The trout came snuffling to my finger-tips like a favourite hunter for lumps of sugar. There was a big sleek fellow I had spied under the bridge. My finger felt his fat belly as he snuggled to the invitation of my gentle tickling. Then my fingers closed and I hurled him over my shoulder into the green meadow . . . Great fun that! . . . Better than sniping at some poor devil's head, corporal?"

"You talk like an English gent, but you aren't an interpreter with this lot"—he jerked his thumb over his shoulder—" are you?

That seems a waste to me. You know our interpreter—well, you've heard him, anyway—some bloated waiter. If it wasn't for . . ." He checked himself deliberately and smiled wryly.

"Can you keep a secret?" said Grant in a lowered voice, looking the man straight in the eyes.

"We have to, here," said the corporal quietly. "Why, I daren't even think for fear of talking in my sleep."

"Well, don't worry about your sleep," laughed Grant, and added very seriously: "You must believe me..." He paused without taking his eyes from those of the corporal. "I am a British officer . . . my name is Colonel Duncan Grant, Inverness Highlanders."

Corporal Waller gasped, frowned and then shook his head, saying : "You're kidding me."

Grant thrust his face nearer to that of the corporal. "You've got to believe me," he said, and then pointing to the map which they had drawn in the dust, whispered : "We worked in galleries shaped like that"—he traced his finger along the course of the hills—" last night . . . think it out."

The corporal pondered. "What are you doing here ? What are you getting at, anyway?" he said with hesitation.

Grant parried him. "Do you want to break this damned monotony? . . . If I'm a German I'm pretty well off as things go in wartime . . . well fed and safe . . . that's true, isn't it?" The corporal nodded . . . "But I am British . . . this plan," he clapped his hand emphatically upon the little heaps before him, so that tiny springs of dust squirted up through his fingers, "will destroy England . . . you must have thought about it . . . it undermines the whole of the British lines . . . The dynamite we shifted yesterday, one day soon will be exploded . . . just like those little puffs of dust . . . Thousands of men . . . Englishmen . . . will be destroyed. Do you believe me ?"

"Yes," said Waller reluctantly, "I believe that . . . I've figured it out . . . we all know that . . . but we dare not discuss it . . .

Even if you are a British officer, what can you do? We go on with the work, driven to it. It's no business of ours, anyway."

"Corporal Waller," said Grant, "you have my life in your hands . . . I have delivered it to you... I, too, have yours . . . so far as any man knows here, I am soldier Otto Gedern, qualified as an interpreter . . . but I need you . . . I'm here to defeat this plan . . . think, man, of those Berkshire hills and vales . . . compare that sweet countryside with this foul business . . . you, an Englishman, will help me, Waller? . . . and keep my secret."

The man glanced up at Grant suddenly. Then his eyes lighted; the heavy bearded jaw thrust itself forward. "By Christ, I will," he said between his teeth. Grant placed his hand in that of the big, characteristic yeoman and gripped it tightly.

"But it's you must give the orders," Waller added; "I'll do what you tell me."

"How many of the others in our group understand what we're working upon ?" asked Grant.

"I can't rightly say," said Waller, pausing. "Generally speaking, I suppose most of the lads have some idea, but they daren't talk about it. It's only occasionally that a chance word in the course of the work, or when we're alone together, gives me the impression that most of them have figured it the same as me."

"Do you understand mining, corporal?"

"No, I'm a carpenter by trade, but I've had some experience in the 'Brickstacks' 'way back in nineteen-fifteen . . . I've got a pal here, McTavish, of the Borderers . . . he's been a miner all his life and was taken prisoner with me on the La Bassee Canal . . . he was a sergeant in the mining company."

"Do you trust him, Waller?"

"Yes; he thinks much the same as me . . . he'd had a bit too much to drink one day . . . I had a hell of a job with him . . . he turned savage . . . said he'd like to blow up the whole bloody business and go west in the mess.

"Thank God! no one heard him, but I got the wind up properly. Every other man is a spy, at least, one begins to think so with everyone dressed the same, and these interpreters hanging round every odd corner . . . the guards don't matter to us: they just stand around like statues unless there's any shooting to be done and even that doesn't happen now."

He paused, and then said with weariness in his voice : "We just go backwards and forwards."

"Now, Waller, listen to me. I am determined to blow up these galleries. It's our job . . . mine . . . yours. We're British . . . we're going to have one gigantic adventure together . . . better than poaching, Waller . . . blow the whole business sky high. There's enough dynamite down there to bust up Europe . . . Are you game, corporal?"

"I'll do what you tell me," the man said slowly.

"Well, go and find friend McTavish and bring a pack of cards with you. We'll find some more volunteers for this job before we're through with it; and then they can join our card party as a bit of camouflage."

Corporal Waller slouched away, hands thrust deep in his pockets, shoulders hunched, his shaggy head gazing gloomily upon the ground. Grant rolled over on to his back and lit a cigarette. The plan, a final throw of the dice, was taking shape in his brain as he watched the thin smoke eddying up to be lost in the deeper blue of the sky. He was lying thus when Waller returned with McTavish, a bow-legged, rugged little man, with a shock of red hair. They squatted beside him.

"Waller and I," said Grant, "have been talking over old days together. He pleads guilty to being a poacher . . . so do I."

"He's a gent," interjected Waller . . ."one of the landed gentry." The three men laughed. "He was a poacher just for a kid's bit of devilment . . . I'm a craftsman at the game."

Grant laughed merrily and said: "As a matter of fact . . . I'm a Scot."

McTavish had opened his wizened eyes a little wider. "So you're a gentleman, are ye?" and he was gazing at Grant with increasing astonishment... "Then, what the hell are ye doing here?"

"I was just going to tell you, McTavish, when . . . you've dealt the cards." Grant continued: "Waller trusts me; he's under my orders. Is that right, corporal ?"

The man expressed an affirmative by a poise of the head and a deep-throated "Aye."

"Don't get excited, McTavish . . . you're coming in with us . . . my name's Grant, Colonel..." The man sat back on his heels in bewilderment. "Yes . . . Colonel of the Inverness Regiment." Then speaking deliberately and pausing between each sentence he said: "I know . . . Waller knows . . . you, too, McTavish, know, the nature of the work upon which we are engaged. You're a miner . . . Could you blow up the dynamite we were shifting yesterday?"

"I certainly could, sir."

"Could you wreck the galleries, McTavish?"

The man considered, "With some preparation I could do that, sir," he said slowly. "At least, in part."

"Not entirely, then."

"No, sir, that would mean . . . well, I don't know; but what's the idea, anyway?"

"Waller and I have agreed to blow that dynamite sky high . . . you understand how to do it . . . we need your help . . . we're going to have it, aren't we, McTavish ?"

The man's eyes narrowed until their bright blue irises were lost in wrinkles of reddened skin, the mouth spread with a broad grin exposing an interrupted row of teeth, yellowed with tobacco chewing.

"Help you?" he queried. "If it hadn't been for Waller, I'd have blown the lot up long ago. Help you?" his voice was rising. Grant hit him playfully, saying: "Your deal, McTavish."

Grant then outlined the plan in his mind. It was to allow eight or ten trusted men into the secret of the project. The party would be sent to work upon this portion of the gallery on the morrow. As the forepart of the column turned the apex connecting the two communicating galleries, the men at the head and tail of the column would turn upon the guards and interpreter and overpower them; quickly the fuses would be laid and the dynamite exploded. That might be the end, but what matter? . . . one glorious adventure. The plan they considered was feasible if sufficient men could be pledged to the scheme. They agreed to meet again together for a game of cards during the afternoon. Meanwhile, each of the three would try quietly to win recruits for their enterprise among his friends.

* * * * *

The interpreter to the group had long nursed the desire to obtain employment in the canteen in which his experience and proficiency in European languages would render him valuable; and moreover, the prospect of such ease and plenty cried loudly day by day from the temple of his being—a fat stomach, the symmetry of whose curves was in danger by reason of the arduous nature of the toil to which the body was exposed. He discovered Grant in the canteen, and bringing two tankards of lager seated himself beside him.

The interpreter purred his flattery. Otto Gedern was obviously a fine soldier; he had noted the zeal with which he applied himself to his work, while he himself—he waved his hand in deprecation—was scarcely fitted for such tasks. Herr Gedern, too, spoke the English language with perfection. The interpreter would recommend him for control of the group, while he himself would ask to be relieved and relegated to a more humble office, that was, of course, if Otto Gedern desired the post which self-effacement could create. His beady eyes twinkled with eagerness as he gazed over the brim of the tankard into which he had plunged to hide his excitement.

Grant, the player of many parts, took his cue. He was flattered at the suggestion and would desire such an opportunity better to serve the Fatherland, but requested the interpreter to tell him how such an appointment could be arranged.

The plump little man would see the adjutant: he would go at once and, so saying, he rose from the table, hurrying busily from the canteen, in whose atmosphere, as he threaded his way quickly by long practice through the tables, he already felt the reincarnation of his former cosmopolitan life.

Grant sat in meditation . . . in sole charge of a group working in a comparatively isolated part of the workings, issuing orders in a language not understood by the armed guards, he would be master of the situation. The guards could be overpowered, and then in the secrecy of the workings the explosives could be disposed by experts, the fuses laid, and a great mine blown which would vomit forth somewhere near the British front and support lines, and would, whatever other result was achieved, certainly wreck a part of the galleries, delay the progress of the plan, and probably provoke suspicion within the British lines. He had already won over two good men to the project, and before the party set out to the workings on the morrow he felt sure that the adherence of three or four other men would be secured. He would be able to deal with the rest of the party within the workings when the time came.

The interpreter came hurrying through the crowded canteen, making his way swiftly, his face wreathed in smiles. Obviously, his project had succeeded.

"The adjutant would like to see you at once," he said. "I am promoted," he gushed, "to the office of second corporal in the canteen; you will be elevated to that of interpreter."

"I am very much obliged to you," Grant said. "Come along; we will return to the canteen in celebration." They left the canteen, the fat little figure pirouetting across the floor with the air of the *maître d'hôtel* disposing an honoured guest.

"The interpreter tells me that you are a zealous soldier and very fluent in the English language. He recommends you for promotion to the office of interpreter, not I think," he said dryly, "without some less obvious motive that his own services might better be employed in the canteen. With this latter view I happen to concur," and he smiled as he viewed the fat figure now bent in humility. "I have looked through your papers, Otto Gedern, and am satisfied that you possess the qualities necessary. I am glad to have this confirmed," he laughed a little, "by our ambitious friend here. You will take over his duties at once." And turning to the orders of the day, he added, "And will be in charge of your group tomorrow. You understand?"

In the afternoon Grant met Waller and McTavish in the hut. His appointment as interpreter had already been posted in the daily orders. Five other men were seated at a table conversing, and looked up quickly as Grant entered the room.

"What about a game of cards?" said Grant.

"Come on, boys," Waller called out over his shoulder.

The eight men formed one of many little groups resting and playing in the sun. With legs stretched out in a circle and heads together they began playing. Waller introduced the five men, Clarkson, Davis, Hughes, Partington, Maulkin—adding: "We're all in the game . . . the other one . . . with you."

Between the throw of the cards, as they fell almost automatically, Grant outlined his plan. McTavish, Clarkson, Davis, and himself would lead the column; Waller, Partington, Maulkin and Hughes would bring up the rear. As the first part of the column turned the bend and the apex of the two connecting galleries where the explosives were stored, upon an order from Grant, they would turn on the guards, disarm and destroy them. Clarkson and Hughes at the end of the column would take over the arms of the guards, and prevent entry or exit from the gallery, while McTavish with other skilled miners laid the charges. Events would then shape themselves. Grant informed the men that he possessed plans of the whole system secreted in his collar. It had been his project to deliver them to the British lines. They were to understand that this was the W Plan.

McTavish suggested the possibility, after the mine had been blown of being able to force an exit through the crater, if the miners were not destroyed by the force of the explosion itself. That would depend upon what could be arranged to prevent a blow-back down both the galleries intersecting at this point.

The party broke up and strolled across to the canteen where, in twos and threes, they joined the main body of the men of their own group, who were making merry in one corner. Grant set himself out to cultivate friendship with the men, to which advances, in place of those of the alternately ingratiating and hectoring little fellow whom he had replaced, they readily responded. At eight o'clock they had orders to be within the hut, and the roll was called; the sentries took post while the men climbed into their bunks. Grant was in a state of high excitement and slept but fitfully.

At three o'clock on the following morning the hut was astir, and, throwing on their equipment, the men stumbled through the darkness to the waiting lorries. After a jolting journey to the shaft head, they reached the great hall. An officer came across to Grant, and handed him a plan of a part of the workings with a detail of instructions for the working day . . . the dynamite was first to be shifted clear of the gangway, and a recess cut and strutted in the wall, to be constructed to contain it . . . thereafter, the group was to report at the head of G shaft for digging operations. They were given picks and shovels, and entrained for the cross gallery halt.

Having detrained, Grant assembled his party within the gallery and addressed them.

"We have important and dangerous work to do today. My orders will be obeyed . . . immediately and absolutely. I want you to understand that."

He then marshalled the column with his chosen men at its front and rear, himself leading the way, walking beside the armed sentry. He judged the gallery to be about two miles in length, along which the party was moving briskly in step. Thirty to forty minutes had passed before he saw in the distance the wall facing the end of the gallery, which denoted its abrupt change in direction. He glanced backwards to McTavish and his confederates, and, in a moment, had turned the corner.

He cried to the party to halt, at the same time wresting the rifle from the hands of the sentry beside him. The three men behind sprang upon the astonished man, stifling his cries and throwing him upon the ground, while Clarkson, rifle in hand, took post closing the gallery. Grant ran round the bend and discovered that Waller with his comrades had as effectively dispatched the rear guard. The working party stood huddled in amazement and fear against the wall of the gallery.

Grant called them to attention and spoke.

"I am a British officer : there are men here who know the fact."

"That's right, sir," cried voices from the end of the gallery.

"Men skilled in mine laying will report to Sergeant McTavish in front; the others will remain with Corporal Waller here under my orders. Anyone who attempts to leave the gallery will be shot. Get to your posts."

A dozen men joined McTavish, the other thirty odd remaining with Waller. A conference then took place between the miners and Grant as to the best means of blowing up the gallery. After a quick discussion it was decided to move the dynamite some twenty yards from the apex down one arm of the gallery, which at the turn would be blocked with soil dug from the sides of the shaft, so as to afford some protection for the mining party from the force of the explosion. The men set to work with fury to dig out a cave in the wall, piling the soil as they did so. Within a short space of time a wall with a small aperture to be filled later had been made. The miners, with the assistance of a carrying party, then stacked the charges of dynamite in the recess, while the main body of the party withdrew through the aperture to within the other gallery, where they used every effort to strengthen the wall to give them all the protection possible.

McTavish carefully laid the fuse, which Grant then lit. Enthusiasm and excitement had given added strength to the working party, who toiled without respite. Grant and the miners returned to the main body of men in the adjoining gallery and the aperture was hastily filled. There lay now between the working party and the mine not only the thick triangular wall, but another built around the end of the gallery some ten feet thick, and every moment growing stronger in its resistance.

11

NO MAN'S LAND

Grant stood, watch in hand . . . two minutes to go . . . He called upon the men to cease work. "Thank you lads," he cried. "Splendid. This . . . is for England." Then glancing at his watch he said: "We have just over one minute to go," adding with a laugh : "Better sport than tickling trout, Corporal Waller."

The second ticked loudly from his watch; his heart thumped in his throat . . . in a moment a tremendous roar engulfed his ears and senses. The men, who had withdrawn some thirty yards down the gallery, were thrown from their feet and hurled against the walls. The soil rocked beneath their feet; the roof, balks of timber, pit props and tons of earth descended upon prostrate bodies. Mountains of soil from the barrier were thrown violently down the gallery and were carried by a tempest of wind. The lights had gone out; the air was heavy with dust.

Grant recovered consciousness to discover one leg pinned beneath a considerable weight, otherwise he was a free man in the blackness of the devastated pit. He struggled with the loose soil and timbers, freeing the imprisoned leg; then thrust out his hand which met the soft warm body of a man. He moved his fingers over it and shook it. The faculty of hearing was creeping back. He heard sounds—a man shouting hysterically, low moans as of someone in pain; the man beside him stirred.

Grant shouted through the darkness: "Call out your names, one by one." He counted sixteen, among them McTavish, Hughes and Partington. He could detect their muffled groans from the depths of the gallery. He then cried: "Are you free to move?" Three men answered that they were imprisoned by the fallen roof. To the remainder Grant called to come over to him if they could. He waited, and could hear them laboriously working their way over and through the debris towards him. He still possessed the matches with which the fuse had been lit. He must carefully conserve these, though their light could be spun out considerably by lighting torches of splintered timber. But he feared also to illuminate the devastation, for fear that the urgent call of humanity might delay the party from extricating themselves from the shaft, while seeking for buried comrades. The possibility, sketched by McTavish, of emerging from the galleries somewhere within the British lines, possessed him. The men were now gathered round him.

McTavish stretched out his hand : it met Grant's shoulder. He shifted it clumsily upwards, patting Grant on the cheek. "Good for you, sir," he half sobbed.

Grant had made a rapid mental appreciation of the situation. They must make their way past the barricade and try to find an exit upwards. They crept forward slowly over mountains of debris which seemed at times as if it would entirely block further progress. At one time Grant felt his back touch the roof, but the gallery had been constructed securely. Later, as they groped forward the surface of the wreckage inclined downwards. The air was fresher, distinctly so.

"Where do you reckon we are now, McTavish?"

The man considered. "Weel," he said in his high-pitched voice, "I should say aboot th' bend." Grant struck his first match and they gazed around. Someone laughed : then for a moment all were convulsed with mirth.

They were in a part of the gallery not very severely damaged. Behind them were vast piles of earth and timber in grotesque disorder. The undamaged gallery wall curved slightly. McTavish suggested a line of progress to the left. He and some of the men still gripped their shovels. The match flickered out. Grant lit another and sought for pieces of timber from which strips were taken of which to make a continuous torch. The men with shovels, under the direction of McTavish, commenced digging, propping the roof of the new gallery with loose timbering from amid the wreckage. The earth was piled loosely, and, as they worked, heavy falls from above continually choked the mouth of the tunnel.

McTavish inspected with his keen understanding. "We're no so far frae fresh air," he said, sniffing deeply. The workers in short reliefs continued cutting and then, having cleared a wide area at the foot of the incline, began to proceed at a steeper angle. Avalanches of soil necessitated extreme caution, but they were skilled in such a task, which hour after hour, almost in silence, went forward. At last a cry came from the new tunnel. A shaft of light filtered through the loosened earth some twelve feet above the foremost workers.

"It goes against me leaving th' other lads behind," said McTavish wistfully, resting for a moment on his shovel.

Grant pondered the unspoken question. "We may be able to bring relief later. Our first duty is to go forward."

The Scot sighed and continued his work, until the intervening earth suddenly collapsed, rolling pell-mell down the shaft, revealing the clear blue of the sky above.

A new sound met their ears, that of the continuous burst of shells and of rifle fire. A black curl of smoke for a moment blotted out the sky. The mine had burst in one or other of the opposing lines, perhaps even in no man's land between them. Grant moved cautiously towards the lip of the crater and listened. He could detect the sharp crack of machine-gun and rifle fire upon either side—the crater then was somewhere in between the lines. The hour he judged from the sun, was between one and two in the afternoon, eight or nine hours since the mine had exploded. Clearly, whatever result had been achieved in the underground galleries, and that could only be a matter for conjecture, the springing of the mine had made a considerable impression upon the battle area. The intensity of defensive firing clearly indicated that both sides were in a state of high nervous tension.

He ordered the men to go a little way back into the tunnel, where a conference was held. It was agreed that after nightfall each should make an attempt to reach the British lines. He divided the paper which he had been given into thirteen pieces, and with charcoal traced upon the back of each piece the words : "W Plan." These were placed in the breast pockets of the men, to whom also Grant clearly outlined the main features and intentions of the Plan itself. They were instructed that anyone successful in reaching the British lines, should ask immediately for a message to be sent to General Headquarters, referring definitely to the W Plan.

If Grant himself failed to reach the lines, the full detailed W Plan was sewn into the collar of his tunic, and the ground could be searched by patrols for his body. This could be readily identified by the two white armlets which he tied round them by tearing off the arms from his shirt.

As the afternoon drew on the noise of firing diminished. Grant sent a man forward to the crater lip to observe. Twenty minutes later the man returned to report that so far as could be judged, they were encircled. The sound of fitful firing came from three sides at a distance of not more than one hundred yards, while from the back, similar sounds appeared to be some distance farther away.

Grant judged that the explosion must have undermined, at least, the front British line, and that the latter had been redisposed to meet a threatened attack. As dusk fell the rattle of machine-guns and rifle fire increased from the British lines, while a barrage of shrapnel fell across no man's land and upon the crater itself. Grant withdrew his men into the safety of the tunnel . . . they would wait until the night life outside became calmer. As the moon rose fully, casting a beam into the crater mouth, the firing gradually ceased.

The night became silent—broken only by an occasional burst of fire and a stray shell: while light rockets soared into the air. Then Grant, with McTavish, leading the party, crept up the tunnel to the top of the crater. Grant found himself in a turmoil of broken trenches, barbed-wire entanglements, deep shell craters and shattered trees. The force of the explosion had thrown aloft limbs, clothing and fragments of flesh. Battered bodies, piled themselves beside abandoned stretchers. The stench of blood and of gas pervaded the hot night air: it sickened the palate and caught the throat tightly.

Now, as Grant crept forward, wriggling upon his stomach, he felt the touch of broken bodies, portions of which protruded hideously from the debris of a wrecked trench : ammunition boxes, splintered rifles, coils of wire, trench stores of all kinds, impeded him at every move and turn. Rats, the four-footed vultures of the Western battlefields, scurried across his path. The mine had devastated the front and support lines—Heaven alone knew at what a cost of British lives. Death had cut swiftly with his scythe, and now, his foul breath fanned the nostrils with the nauseating smell of blood: he winked his eye from aloft with each burst of shrapnel; and his dry laugh chattered from the mouths of a score of machine-guns.

The W Plan was coming home very . . . very . . . slowly.

Grant was near the line now, not more than seventy yards, McTavish beside him, their bodies cleaving to the ground. A sudden burst of rifle fire commencing at one point and spreading itself up the line caused Grant to sink low into the depths of a shell-hole. Star-shells illumined the sky and lighted the ragged landscape.

McTavish thrust his head cautiously above the edge of the hole. He whispered to Grant. "I can see some men moving. They may be our boys trying to get in." A loud cry was heard above the musketry. "Some poor devil's hit," commented the observer. The rifle fire and illuminations ceased abruptly.

After a few minutes Grant crept on from shell-hole to shell-hole. When within fifty yards of the line he could dimly discern the moving silhouette of heads above the trench parapet. A little to their left a small patrol was leaving the front line. It passed through the wire carefully, crouched low as a star-shell from the German line faintly lit the panorama, then bore away to the left, either searching for wounded or investigating the cause of the latest alarm. It was agreed then between Grant and McTavish that one alone should first attempt to penetrate the line, while the other waited in a shell-hole. If one was detected, the other would raise cries to attract attention and allay alarm. In this project McTavish insisted upon leading.

Grant watched the wizened active body writhe its way across the ruins of a trench system, nearer, always nearer, to the head which bobbed above the trench. Then he heard McTavish shout: "Hey, Jock!" and rise to his feet. The startled sentry fired. McTavish, still crying aloud, ran towards the trench. Panic had seized the men who now thickly manned the line.

A flash momentarily blinded Grant, bullets whistled past his ears, and then he saw the body of McTavish hanging limp, jerking upon a strand of wire. From his position in the shell-hole Grant cried desperately in English . . . "Cease fire!" The troops, their nerves tried to exhaustion with the events of the past twenty-four hours, every moment expecting a fresh catastrophe or attack, renewed their furious indiscriminate fire in his direction. Bombs falling short of his position, added to the chaos and din, while trench mortars searching the ground, shrieked spitefully beside his retreat.

Placing his hands before his mouth in fury he shouted : "Cease fire, you bloody fools . . . Cease fire! . . . Cease fire!" A whistle was blown from the line: the firing, now desultory, ceased. Men climbed out over the parapet towards the body of McTavish.

Grant started to run, staggering through twisted barbed wire which clutched at the cloth of his trousers and lacerated his flesh . . . he shouted continuously . . . "Don't shoot". . . Someone threw a bomb in his direction which burst beside him, cutting his forehead and face . . . he heard the patrol upon the parapet cursing . . . he plunged forward, eyes blinded by blood and perspiration, deafened with the panic of rifle fire and a babel of sound, his limbs weary almost to exhaustion . . . there was a blinding flash . . . a roar! Grant collapsed in a heap just short of the riddled body of his friend and compatriot.

The panic-stricken patrol gathered the two bodies roughly into the trench. A young officer commanding the company in the line came forward and inquired if the men were dead. He flashed an electric torch upon their faces and uniforms.

"Bloody Huns," he commented . . ." this devil's still breathing . . . take them down to the aid post . . . I'll report at battalion headquarters."

He passed through the communication trench, which the troops were feverishly reconstructing, to a concrete, dome-shaped, stronghold and passed through the blanket shielding the door, revealing the officer-commanding seated before a rough table.

"We've got two Huns, sir. One dead, the other is still breathing. I've sent them down to the aid post."

"Have you got their papers, or any identifications?"

"No, sir," he stammered, "I forgot."

"Go and get them quick." Then turning to the adjutant, the colonel said : "Go with him, Mason."

When they reached the post they found one body, that of McTavish, laid outside the dug-out upon a stretcher. "Dead," commented the adjutant as he entered. Grant was seated limply upon the skeleton of a chair. The blood had been washed from his head and the skin wounds bandaged. He was unconscious. The orderlies had cut away the rags of trousers, exposing legs hideously torn by wire, and one, the right, broken below the knee.

The tunic had been thrown upon one side. Mason took it up and searched the pockets. He extracted a small piece of paper bearing the words in English : "W Plan." There was nothing else. He examined the pockets of the dead man, and discovered a similar slip. The orderlies sponged Grant's leg, while the medical officer pressed rum and water to his lips.

"What's the matter with this man?" questioned the adjutant sharply. "Anything serious?"

"Nothing much . . . to you," acidly replied the doctor, a civilian drawn from a comfortable country practice, weary of military imperiousness.

"Can't you make him talk?" snapped Mason.

"I'm trying first to bring him to life," said the doctor dryly.

Dismissing the company commander with the two slips of paper and the tunics of the men to report to the colonel, Mason stood impatiently beside the wounded man.

Grant opened his eyes, stared vacantly before him, and mumbled a few words in German. Several minutes passed: he shivered as a deep draught of rum coursed down his throat.

Then he sat erect, suddenly, crying: "Don't shoot, don't shoot, you bloody fools!" The effort caused him to sink back with a groan.

"Take it easy," said the doctor, sponging his head.

"What's your name?" interjected the adjutant.

Grant blinked and paused, then said mechanically: "Otto Gedern." . . . Where was he? back in the cell . . . his face was bandaged . . . what had become of the commandant? . . . his mind was drifting . . . the sentence of the court . . . death . . .

commuted . . . the pot-bellied interpreter—he chuckled—the galleries . . . the mine . . . Waller, little McTavish . . . where was McTavish . . . hanging on the wire...

Duncan Grant, propped by two stretcher-bearers in his chair, his tortured mind assailed by rage and despair, alternately shouted hoarsely and wept.

Convulsions shook the battered body . . . the soul in its no man's land struggled to reach the mocking light of sanity. Suddenly he raised his hands to his neck. The fingers felt for his collar. "Where's my tunic?" he shrieked, ". . . the W Plan."

"That's better," said the adjutant. "What's this W Plan?" Grant gazed at him for a full minute, then lurched forward in his chair. "Are you a British officer?" he groaned. Mason nodded.

"Good God! then why the Hell . . ." The voice trailed away.

"Are you English?" snarled Mason. "What's this blasted uniform?"

Grant attempted to rise, his eyes blazing. "I . . . must . . . telephone . . . to the Commander . . . in . . . chief," he jerked, the words coming in staccato.

Mason laughed. "That's rich—Otto talks to the Commander-in-chief—wouldn't the correspondents love it?"

"If you don't want to drive this poor devil off his head—he's pretty near it, Captain Mason—" said the doctor, "you'd better leave him alone for a bit. I'll patch him up and when he's got over the shock I'll send him to battalion headquarters."

The elder man sternly faced the younger, who turned and left the dug-out.

The doctor loved all humanity . . . his profession, for himself, was the highest calling to service for mankind. He knew village life unknown to the vicar . . . he had carried an ever-growing family from birth, through childish complaints, the maids through their first birth pangs, the men through secret foolishnesses—some he had buried. He hated war . . . the shattered bodies . . . the futility of it all . . . this weary, broken figure, except for some uncontrollable chance might be some lad from his own Dorset Downs. Carefully he smoothed the brow and waited. A sigh escaped from the drowsing figure. The doctor bent over him, holding his two hands firmly between his own. Grant looked up into the doctor's eyes. The master of healing had drawn the patient under the spell of his skill.

Quite calmly and very slowly Grant spoke. "They shouldn't have shot McTavish . . . I called out, 'Don't shoot' . . . but they went on. I . . . I'm Duncan Grant, no . . . not Otto Gedern . . . I've got the W Plan . . . my tunic . . . Tell . . . tell. . . ." the voice was fading away, "the Commander . . . in . . . chief."

Fatigue, wounds, rum and morphia had had their effect. Grant was asleep, his reason saved by that constant, wonderful, unerring skill, love and knowledge of a country doctor.

The medical officer not only disdained the restriction and regulations of military life, but himself possessed initiative and a will of his own. Placing the wounded in charge of stretcher-bearers, he left the aid post, and avoiding the battalion headquarters, walked through the communication trench to the signallers' dug-out.

"Hullo, sergeant! good evening," he said cheerily. "No trouble here I hope. I want to talk to someone of the staff. Against regulations, maybe, but I'll stand the wigging for this."

With some reluctance the sergeant cleared the line, and when communication was established the doctor asked to speak with the chief of staff. There was some delay; then he was informed that he could speak, but only for a moment, with the military secretary.

He opened the conversation at once. "I'm a doctor. I've got a man in my aid post, wounded. German uniform . . . says he's Duncan Grant . . . W Plan . . . he has something to report to the Commander-in-chief."

"What's that?" shouted Colonel Jervois. "Grant . . . W Plan . . . with you . . . he must be brought here to me at once."

"He's asleep," said the doctor, "but I'll pack him into an ambulance as soon as I can... Be careful of him . . . he's wounded and it may be touch and go with his brain-box... I'll send him to No. 7 General Hospital."

The doctor hung up the receiver, and standing in the trench he stroked his greying moustache thoughtfully. "I'll get his tunic from the colonel . . . it seems to be important . . . Duncan Grant . . . poor devil . . . W Plan . . . wonder what it's all about . . ." He slipped through the blanket into battalion headquarters.

"Well, how's your pet patient?" sneered the adjutant.

"He's a little chilly," parried the doctor, "and I've come for his tunic."

"Dear old nurse," laughed the colonel. "Well, we don't need that any more. By the way, has he said anything? I can't make head or tail of this W Plan business . . . seems odd written in English . . . and he speaks English, too, doesn't he, Mason?"

"Yes, fluently; probably a deserter."

"I must report the matter to the brigadier," said the colonel.

"I," said the doctor, "must take the responsibility for having already informed the chief-of-staff direct . . . the patient is asleep . . . he will wake up in No. 7 General Hospital... I must get him off in the ambulance . . . Good night, colonel."

* * * * *

A fresh breeze was blowing off the sea through the wide-flung windows and gently fanned a face upon the white pillow. A man was sunk in deep slumber; and so, for many hours, motionless, except tor the rise and fall of the white linen to his regular breathing, he had rested in the quiet peacefulness of this room overlooking the sea.

A nurse, keeping her patient vigil, sat beside the bed reading, sometimes glancing through the window across the white-flecked, blue waters as some great ship, following the curve of the coastline, slowly entered the harbour, or steamed out, accompanied by a busy escort, to that homeland whose white cliffs lay just beyond the horizon.

After long hours the patient stirred a little; his lips moved murmuring—" Rosa." His eyes opened for a moment. Then he slept again, the mouth parted in a faint smile.

The door opened quietly to admit Colonel Jervois, who quietly beckoned the nurse to him.

"Has he yet waked?" he whispered.

"Not yet, but he has moved. I do not think he will sleep much longer."

"I will remain, then."

For a full hour he sat upon the window ledge in the bright sun, wrapt in thought . . . eleven men, eight of them wounded, had been brought in during the night . . . patrols had brought in two dead bodies . . . they were in German uniform . . . the men were English, and, one, Hughes, unwounded, a former Welsh miner, had been sent to headquarters . . . the man was dazed and had told a wild, incoherent, incredible story interlaced always with the name of a Colonel Grant, with the white armlets, who had the W Plan . . . and here was Grant back again, haggard, torn and dishevelled beyond belief, twenty-two days after he had flown away upon his mission.

The patient stirred again, opened his eyes, then tried to move while the nurse gently held him, and smilingly inquired if he was ready for breakfast. As she moved to raise the pillows, Grant recognized Jervois, seated behind her, framed in the window.

The staff officer rose, and, crossing to the bed, took one hand in his, pressing it.

"You're home again, Grant . . . home . . . thank God."

"Home..." Grant's brow puckered... "Yes... I suppose so . . . where's McTavish . . . and the others?"

"Eleven came in during the night," answered Jervois, who had been warned against agitating the patient in a too eager quest for information. There was silence for many minutes.

Grant considered, his fingers nervously plucking at the sheets, then spoke slowly. "There are still many, about thirty men, down the shaft . . . McTavish wanted to dig them out before we left . . . and there were thirteen men with me... I tried to stop the shooting..."

"We'll find these men," said Jervois, pressing his hand. "Don't worry about that... I've already had a talk with one of your men—Hughes by name."

"What did he say?"

A nurse entered carrying a steaming tray which was placed upon a table astride the bed, while pillows were packed behind the patient's back. Jervois poured out the coffee and Grant smiled happily. This was comfort indeed. He sipped it.

"What did Hughes say?" asked Grant after a while.

Slowly and deliberately Jervois spoke. "That you had the W Plan."

"Yes, yes, of course, in my tunic . . . where's my tunic?"

The nurse, rising swiftly, glided to the door. She reappeared after a few moments. Grant was talking rapidly, Jervois seated at the foot of the bed wrapt in attention.

"Get on with your breakfast," mocked the nurse. "Here's your tunic." Grant took the mudstained, grey-green garment in his hands, and asked for scissors—Rosa's stitches—he reflected and paused.

"Have you any . . . other news, colonel?"

Jervois shook his head.

"Not from Switzerland . . . our Legation . . . a lady?"

"None whatever," said Jervois.

Grant quickly slit the collar. Two envelopes, one from either side, soiled and damp, were exposed. "These are the W Plans . . . Everything you want is here."

Grant's brow puckered. "Colonel," he asked, "what happened to little Mayne . . . I waited for him."

"Ah, a brave lad, Mayne . . . he did not return. We have heard since that he was detected and shot down over Tourcoing. He brought down two enemy machines with him."

"Poor little Mayne," said Grant quietly. "I knew he would come . . . if he could."

Jervois rose from the bed. "I must go at once to the Commander-in-chief. Grant..." he said, the voice broken with emotion, "you've saved the army."

A wan smile crossed the wounded man's face.

Jervois was leaving the room but turned again to meet Grant's voice. "Don't forget my men . . . Hughes will tell you."

The wounds and fracture had been dressed and set, and Grant was lying back upon his pillow, his gaze turned towards the sea. He watched the afternoon leave-boat steaming out from the harbour, the whirling seagulls in its wake. He was deep in meditation . . . purple hills . . . a sea melting into the crimson of an evening sky . . . a face framed in gold . . . Rosa.

The door opened softly. The Commander-in-chief, the man who could win a battle in the morning and in the evening help Belgian farmers to stack their corn, stood watching, his eyes filled with that devotion which three years of cruel war and its fierce necessities had failed to dim.

Grant turned his head—"General!" he exclaimed.

The general swiftly sank upon one knee beside the bed: and, as he had done on parting, so now his strong hands affectionately gathered the young man to him, as he studied the face beneath the bandages. Tears dimmed his eyes.

"I cannot thank you," he stammered, and remained, his head bowed, dumb with emotion: then rising he stood before the open window, his broad back to the patient.

The general drew a chair beside the bed. "Grant," he said, "will you tell me the story . . . not about the plans. I have already issued my orders," adding firmly : "The W Plan will never be put into operation. It is dead . . . You, thank God, have killed it . . . for ever."

"There is nothing to add, general. I left a letter with you, sir; it is a request that no one will ever know that I have been concerned with this, that no . . . I don't know how to put it . . . reward shall be given if I am successful."

"My dear boy," exclaimed the general, "that is absurd. Of course..."

I have your word, sir. Can't we leave it at that?"

"If that is your wish, Grant," said the general quietly, "I can say nothing else . . . I'm sorry; but is there nothing I can do?"

"Yes, sir, yes," the wounded man's voice was rising with emotion. "I hate this war . . . It's Hell! . . . I'm degraded, foul, I can't escape; I am haunted . . . Let me go, sir . . . Let me go." The general gripped his hands.

"Steady, lad, steady... I know what you feel. Don't I feel it, too? But, I am sure now . . . quite sure, that we are near the end. I am going to send you to England among your friends."

"No, sir, I beg of you, let me stay here until I can walk . . . then . . . let me go away. I wish to hide in some quiet place in Switzerland . . . Is that possible?"

"That I will arrange," said the general. "I will come to see you again, Grant . . . now I must go to the conference which waits for me. God bless you . . . Duncan Grant . . . and from the bottom of my heart, I thank you." The door closed gently behind him.

12

THE GARDENER

It was now late in the afternoon. The garden so brilliant with colour in the sunlight, its fountains and miniature streams twinkling like a myriad gems, was now bathed in soft reflected light from the mountain tops, while the firs, pines and larches, which at midday provided pleasant shade, were stretching long shadows over the green lawns.

High up on either side grand forest-covered hills arose, culminating in majestic peaks, some formed in fantastic shapes, great rocky pinnacles, others festooned with glaciers, tipped with snow.

The gardener still toiled, his work at once his leisure, and his whole life. Duncan Grant had seen him in the early morning when the dew sparkled on the ground. Again, at midday, he was standing in a fairy pond stripped to the waist removing every stray leaf which might mar the mirror of its loveliness, or break the perfect reflection of the surrounding flowers and shrubs.

A fountain sprayed his bronzed body glistening in the sunlight: it was sculptured to perfection, the torso beautiful to see as he twisted and bent, the body straight as a larch, the arms like the roots of some giant conifer, the fingers, despite the nature of their work, long and delicate as its fibres.

Duncan, leaning upon a stick, stood beside Rosa, the pale delicacy of whose features contrasted vividly with the transcendent loveliness of her golden hair. He spoke to the gardener, making some comment of approval. The gardener's face, swarthy in colour, rugged of feature, broke into a happy smile. He showed some of the rarest jewels, miniature alpines, gentians, primulas, violas, soldanella, collected from the high passes and last green patches which cling to the snowline.

As they moved about this part of the garden he found one gem, perhaps the choicest, snapped and sapped of its vitality. Hard by a slug, swollen and obscene, spread its grossness upon a stone. A new light came into the eyes of the gardener; swiftly he squeezed out its life between his strong thumb and forefinger. He shrugged his shoulders, looked at Rosa as if with a question; then added simply that it was because of the slugs that he must work to protect his defenceless flowers.

The garden, with its long borders of bright antirrhinums backed by tall dahlias and delphiniums, its cool lawns, pools and fountains, winding paths which at every turn presented a new vista of beauty or of grandeur, lay high over the tempestuous waters of the Inn in the Lower Engadine.

Many people, from many lands, had come thither to find rest, leisure, recreation and new health in this wonderful fairy valley. Some were older men from the cities, weary with the irritations and pressure of industrial life and finding freedom again after more than three years of blockade and uninterrupted industry: some, women, exhausted with the pleasures and dissipations of European capitals: others, just tourists retreading long forbidden paths, passing through, yet often remaining in a scene so wholly captivating; while here and there were men broken, maimed and shattered, who in the stillness of the mountains sought to gather the fleeting fragments of a youth snatched by the rude hands of war.

Thus through his work was the gardener himself, the healer and evangelist. Often he would pluck some fragrant, perfect bloom and lay it beside a dreamer as he slept. Many weeks after the last sound of battle had been stilled in silence, Duncan Grant and Rosa had been reunited in Geneva, where they had been quietly married. Now in the peace of Vulpera, amid the rugged grandeur and sublime beauty of jagged peaks and soft valleys, they stood hand-in-hand in contemplation of the ever-changing landscape in its evening kaleidoscope of colour.

Duncan pointed to the majestic medieval castle of Tarasp, perched high upon a rocky eminence dominating the valley, and idly told Rosa of the tyrannies which in the name of God, religion, and civilization had in past ages spread misery, rapine, and death throughout the villages, which, some high on the mountain side, some beside the rushing river, give life to the valley.

Their reflections were broken by the sound of a heavy footstep. Half turning, Grant observed a gross person approaching. He was heavy eyed with dissipation, a vast belly protruded itself in front of the body, rolls of flesh piled themselves above his collar, fat fingers decked with diamonds thrust themselves from the starched linen of his sleeve ends: a great cigar lay between the bulging lips.

It was Herr Adolf Messer.

The creature shuffled up the pathway, pausing before the fairy pond; and, flicking cigar ash upon its placid waters, broke the mirror, making an ugly stain upon the picture.

The gardener was watching.

The man, who had so richly profited from his country's ruin, and whose very presence constituted a living memorial to his shame, leaned heavily against a young spruce, which bent itself as if recoiling from his touch. He raised one foot heavily among the graceful flowers. As earlier, so now, the stem of a choice flower snapped, and was ground under foot.

The gardener was watching. The light in his eyes changed to fierce hatred. He moved forward swiftly, the muscles in his arms tightening so that the bone of his fingers showed white under the bronzed skin, until he faced the human slug.

Duncan held Rosa's frail hand tight in his own. He whispered to her—"Tyranny . . . in the twentieth century."

The human slug, its bloodshot, glittering eyes beneath languid lids, observed the gardener. He discerned the hatred in the eyes, the threat in demeanour. Savagely he pushed his foot among the alpine gems; then, again flicking his ash into the pool, he sneered . . . as long ago a Pharisee regarded a publican. He spat and shuffled back along the path, while the gardener cleansed his garden.

The gardener looked up from his toil at the lovers and smiled . . . "Another slug,"he said...

The evening passed into sublime afterglow. Duncan drew Rosa to him. Their voices were soft, so that the sigh of a gentle wind in the pine tops formed an accompaniment to the matchless refrain of love.

"You remember the boy, Heinrich, old Messer's son. He had lost everything, but his ideal . . . a love for all humanity . . . for that, and unknown to him, for us, he fought . . . and won."

"Our love, too, is symbolic," murmured Grant, "something greater, more profound than we know. We are the embodiment of a great human principle . . . some new force growing out of all the misery of mankind, against a world whose motive has been sheer force . . . The gardener is the living symbol of our new world; that other . . . of the old."

A fan of Sherlock Holmes?
Then meet Solar Pons

The original fan fiction from the great August Derleth—the Sherlock Holmes of Praed Street.

"the best substitutes for Sherlock Holmes known." – Vincent Starrett

"an excellent series of adventures in detection in their own right." – *The Chicago Tribune*

For more details and a full list of titles:
visit https://www.hachetteindia.com/home/yellowbacks

Yellowback range available...

1. The Old Man in the Corner by Orczy, Baroness Emma
2. The Complete Max Carrados Vol 1 by Bramah, Ernest
3. The Complete Max Carrados Vol 2 by Bramah, Ernest

THE ARSÈNE LUPIN SERIES BY LEBLANC, MAURICE:

4. Arsène Lupin 1: The Extraordinary Adventures of Arsène Lupin - Gentleman Burglar
5. Arsène Lupin 2: Arsène Lupin vs. Herlock Sholmes
6. Arsène Lupin 3. The Hollow Needle
7. Arsène Lupin 4: 813
8. Arsène Lupin 5: The Crystal Stopper
9. Arsène Lupin 6: The Confessions of Arsène Lupin
10. Arsène Lupin 7: The Teeth of the Tiger
11. Arsène Lupin 8: The Shell Shard (aka The Woman of Mystery)
12. Arsène Lupin 9: The Return of Arsène Lupin (aka The Golden Triangle)
13. Arsène Lupin 10: The secret of Sarek (aka Island of Thirty Coffins)
14. Arsène Lupin 11: The Eight Strokes of the Clock
15. Arsène Lupin 12: The Secret Tomb
16. Arsène Lupin 13: The Countess of Cagliostro (aka Memoirs of Arsène Lupin)
17. Arsène Lupin (bonus book): Arsène Lupin (novelised by Edgar Jepson from LeBlanc's original play)

18. The Complete Raffles by Hornung, E. W.
19. The Mysterious Mickey Finn by Paul, Eliott
20. You Play the Black and the Red Comes Up by Hallas, Richard
21. The Mr. Moto Omnibus Vol 1 by Marquand, John P.
22. The Mr. Moto Omnibus Vol 2 by Marquand, John P.
23. The Complete Father Brown Vol 1 (with original illustrations) by Chesterton, G. K.
24. The Complete Father Brown Vol 2 (with original illustrations) by Chesterton, G. K.
25. A Peter Wimsey omnibus: Murder Must Advertise & The Nine Tailors by Sayers, Dorothy L.
26. Was it Murder? by Hilton, James
27. The Complete Just Men Volume 1 by Wallace, Edgar
28. The Complete Just Men Volume 2 by Wallace, Edgar
29. Carnacki by Hodgson, William Hope
30. Grey Mask by Wentworth, Patricia
31. The Case With Nine Solutions by Connington, J. J.
32. Murder by Matchlight by Lorac, E. C. R.
33. The Crossword Mystery by Punshon, E. R.
34. The Cask by Crofts, Freeman Wills
35. The Bells of Old Bailey by Bowers, Dorothy
36. Crime Unlimited by Hume, David
37. The A. A. Milne Mystery Omnibus (contains: The Red house and Four days' wonder) by Milne, A. A.
38. She Faded into Air by White, Ethel Lina
39. The Wheel Spins by White, Ethel Lina
40. The Spiral Staircase by White, Ethel Lina
41. Murder of a Lady by Wynne, Anthony
42. Thirteen Guests by Farjeon, J. Jefferson
43. The Daughter of Time by Tey, Josephine
44. The Man in the Queue by Tey, Josephine
45. A Shilling for Candles by Tey, Josephine
46. The Franchise Affair by Tey, Josephine
47. Tragedy at Law by Hare, Cyril
48. The Moonstone by Collins, Wilkie
49. The Woman in White by Collins, Wilkie
50. The Circular Staircase by Rinehart, Mary Roberts
51. The Benson Murder Case by Van Dine, S. S.
52. The Philip Marlowe Omnibus by Chandler, Raymond
53. Monsieur Lecoq by Gaboriau, Emile
54. Aurora Floyd by Braddon, Mary Elizabeth
55. The Big Bow Mystery by Zangwill, Israel
56. Dossier 113 (aka The Blackmailers) by Gaboriau, Emile
57. The Mystery of a Hansom Cab by Hume, Fergus
58. The W Plan by Seton, Graham
59. Inspector French's Greatest Case by Crofts, Freeman Wills

60. Mr Bowling Buys a Newspaper by Henderson, Donald
61. A Voice Like Velvet by Henderson, Donald
62. The Deductions of Colonel Gore by Brock, Lynn
63. The Rogue's Syndicate by Froest, Frank
64. The Middle Temple Murder by Fletcher, J. S.
65. The Millionaire Mystery by Hume, Fergus
66. Below the Clock by Turner, J. V.
67. The Rouletabille Omnibus: The Mystery of the Yellow Room and The Perfume of the Lady in Black by Leroux, Gaston
68. The Complete Dupin by Poe, Edgar Allan
69. The Complete Thinking Machine Vol 1 by Futrelle, Jacques
70. The Complete Thinking Machine Vol 2 by Futrelle, Jacques
71. The Complete Thinking Machine Vol 3 by Futrelle, Jacques
72. The Complete Montague Egg by Sayers, Dorothy L.
73. The Complete J. G. Reeder by Wallace, Edgar
74. The Complete Charlie Chan Vol 1 by Biggers, Earl der
75. The Complete Charlie Chan Vol 2 by Biggers, Earl der
76. The Dr Nikola Omnibus Vol 1 by Boothby, Guy
77. The Dr Nikola Omnibus Vol 2 by Boothby, Guy
78. A Prince of Swindlers: The Simon Carne collection by Boothby, Guy
79. The Slim Callaghan Omnibus by Cheyney, Peter
80. The Fu Manchu Omnibus by Rohmer, Sax
81. The Bulldog Drummond Omnibus: The Complete Peterson Rounds by Sapper
82. The Avenging Ray by Seamark
83. The Richard Chandos Omnibus by Yates, Dornford
84. The Alan Quatermain Omnibus: King Solomon's Mines & Allan Quatermain by Haggard, H. Rider
85. The 39 steps by Buchan, John
86. At The Villa Rose by Mason, A.E.W.
87. The Eye of Osiris by Freeman, R. Austin
88. The Weapons of Mystery by Hocking, Joseph
89. The House of Dr. Edwardes by Beeding, Francis
90. The Seven Secrets by Le Queux, William
91. Call Mr Fortune by Bailey, H. C.
92. The Three Taps by Knox, Ronald
93. The Girl at Central by Bonner, Geraldine
94. The Experiences of Loveday Brooke, Lady Detective by Pirkis, Catherine Louisa
95. Mary Louise by Baum, L. Frank
96. That Affair Next Door by Green, Anna Katherine
97. Dead Letter by Regester, Seeley
98. The Tragedy of Pudd'nhead Wilson by Twain, Mark
99. The Big Clock by Fearing, Kenneth
100. The Woman in the Window by Wallis, J. H.
101. The Sexton Blake Collection Vol 1 by Hal Meredeth (or many?)
102. The Complete Simon Iff Stories by Crowley, Aleister
103. The Castle of Otranto by Walpole, Horace
104. The Adventures of the Infallible Godahl by Anderson, Frederick Irving

THE COMPLETE SHERLOCK HOLMES

105. A Study In Scarlet
106. The Sign Of Four
107. The Adventures Of Sherlock Holmes
108. The Memoirs Of Sherlock Holmes
109. The Hound Of The Baskervilles
110. The Return Of Sherlock Holmes
111. His Last Bow
112. The Valley Of Fear
113. The Case-Book Of Sherlock Holmes

114. Graustark: The Story of a Love Behind a Throne by George Barr McCutcheon
115. Beverly of Graustark by George Barr McCutcheon
116. Truxton King: A Story of Graustark by George Barr McCutcheon
117. The Prince of Graustark by George Barr McCutcheon
118. The Complete Zenda Omnibus by Anthony Hope
119. The Mad king by Burroughs, Edgar Rice
120. The Fantomas Omnibus by Souvestre, Pierre

121. The Problemist by Clinton H. Stagg
122. The Dorrington Deed-Box by Morrison, Arthur
123. The Lone Wolf by Vance, L. J.
124. The Complete Martin Hewitt Collection Vol 1: Martin Hewitt, Investigator & Chronicles of Martin Hewitt by Morrison, Arthur
125. The Complete Martin Hewitt Collection Vol 2: Adventures of Martin Hewitt & The Red Triangle: Further Chronicles of Martin Hewitt by Morrison, Arthur
126. Seven Keys to Baldpate by Earl Derr Biggers
127. No Pockets in a Shroud by McCoy, Horace
128. The John Silence Collection by Blackwood, Algernon
129. Lady Molly Of Scotland Yard by Orczy, Baroness Emma
130. Skin O' My Tooth by Orczy, Baroness Emma
131. The Wrong Box by Stevenson, R. L. and Lloyd Osbourne
132. Tutt and Mr Tutt by Train, Arthur C.
133. The Clue by Wells, Carolyn
134. The Complete Trent Case Book by Bentley, E. C.
135. The Luck of the Vails by Benson, E. F.
136. The Rome Express by Griffiths, Arthur
137. The Complete Curious Mr Tarrant by C. Daly King
138. Rope and Gaslight (2-in-1 text) by Hamilton, Patrick
139. Prince Zaleski and Cumming's King Monk by Shiel, M. P.
140. The Assassination Bureau Ltd. by London, Jack
141. Introducing Clubfoot by Williams, Valentine
142. Master of Mysteries: The complete Uncle Abner collection by Post, Melville Davisson
143. The Red Redmaynes by Phillpotts, Eden
144. Thrilling Stories of the Railway by Whitechurch, Victor L.
145. The Grey Wig: Stories and Novelettes by Zangwill, Israel
146. The Lodger by Lowndes, Marie Belloc
147. The Man from Manchester by Donovan, Dick (Joyce Emerson Preston Muddock)
148. Mr. Meeson's Will by H. Rider Haggard by Haggard, H. Rider
149. Devlin the Barber by Farjeon, B. L.
150. Checkmate by Joseph Sheridan Le Fanu
151. Recollections of a Detective Police-Officer by Waters
152. The Widow Lerouge by Gaboriau, Emile
153. The Expressman and the Detective by Pinkerton, Allan
154. Zadig and Vathek by Voltaire
155. The Stillwater Tragedy by Aldrich, Thomas Bailey
156. The Memoirs of Constantine Dix by Pain, Barry
157. Ashes to Ashes by Ostrander, Isabel
158. The Jewel of Seven Stars by Stoker, Bram
159. The Thomas Love Peacock Collection by Peacock, Thomas Love

THE COMPLETE DERLETH SOLAR PONS

160. In Re: Sherlock Holmes - The Adventures of Solar Pons
161. The Memoirs of Solar Pons
162. The Return of Solar Pons
163. The Reminiscences of Solar Pons
164. The Casebook of Solar Pons
165. The Novels of Solar Pons: Terror over London and Mr. Fairlie's Final Journey
166. The Chronicles of Solar Pons
167. The Apocrypha of Solar Pons

168. The Triumphs of Eugene Valmont
169. The Female Detective by Forrester, Andrew
170. Cain's Jawbone by Torquemada
171. The Great Impersonation by Oppenheim, E. Phillips

THE DASHIELL HAMMETT COLLECTION

172. The Complete Sam Spade
173. The Complete Thin Man
174. The Complete Continental Op Vol 1
175. The Complete Continental Op Vol 2